I knew I should knock it off, tell her I loved her, but I wasn't in control. "Drunken" Trent was and he was ruining my life...

I paused for a moment. Wiping the dripping water from my nose, I stared at her before I looked away and continued with my thought. "Well, maybe it would be better for you to leave now," I said, taking a towel from the counter to dry my face and hands before I wrapped them tightly around my cuts. "You know, you should be there for John when he wakes up," I said, turning around to face her.

"Why are you doing this?" she asked, shaking her head in disgust.

She should be disgusted, running after a man who used her and treated her like shit! Drunken Trent was pissed.

"I'm not doing anything. You're the one who's leaving. I'm simply suggesting that you do it sooner rather than drawing it out for later," I snapped back. I wanted to kick Drunken Trent in the fucking balls for saying that.

"You don't mean that," she said, shaking her head once more. "You're drunk and you're going to feel like a fucking asshole in the morning for saying that to me."

"Am I? You see, I don't think I am. You knew I was an ass coming into this, and I knew you were a pain in mine. Did we really think this could work? I mean it might have, had you not still been in love with your fucking stepbrother!" I roared, the veins in my neck popping out with rage.

"Shut up! Shut—up!" she yelled, covering her ears. "You know what? Fine! You want me gone, I'm gone," she screamed, getting in my face.

She pushed my chest and, because I was so drunk and she was a fucking Amazon, I fell back onto the sink, my back hitting the mirror, sending a crack down the middle of it. "Good, get your sexy, fat ass out of here, baby, because clearly you never gave a fuck about me," I yelled as she left the bathroom in a hurry.

I pushed myself off the counter and slipped on the tile floor, falling on my ass and hitting my head against the back of the sink. I sat up and, finally, Drunken Trent was taken down, leaving me to pick up the fucking mess he left behind.

"Lexi!" I yelled, holding my head as I fought off Drunken Trent one last time. I pushed myself away from the sink and stumbled towards the door frame. "Lexi, stop," I called to her.

She was by the dresser, shoving her things into her bag and grabbing anything else that she might need from mine.

"Save it, asshole," she spat over her shoulder.

Lexi:

I live on a farm—scratch that, I lived on a farm. I was on my way to LA to live amongst the rich and famous, to work for the rich and famous. I did not leave a farm, and a seriously complicated relationship, just to dive back into another one. Yet, there I was, falling for a rock star who was *so* not my type of man, it was scary. Could I ever truly leave the farm and the man I left behind and start over? Was this new relationship just a rebound from the last?

Trent:

I had one type of woman all my life. I had this image of her from as young as a boy. She'd be petite, beautiful, long blonde hair, quiet, someone who would stand behind me as I rose to fame with my band mates. I did not see myself with a Southern, loudmouth Amazon of a woman who drove me up the wall. I didn't have time to be chasing a woman. They usually came to me. But here I am, trying to win over a woman who wasn't even my type.

KUDOS for *Not My Type*

In *Not My Type* by M. E. Gordon, Lexi is leaving the farm behind, along with her abusive ex-boyfriend, and heading off to California to work for the rich and famous—she hopes. Actually, she's going to LA to live with her brother to look for a job. She doesn't really care as long as it gets her away from home, and John. But the last thing she expects is to run into Trent from the rock band One Night Stand, who tells her right up front that she's not his type. So why is he chasing her all over, trying to get to know her? As with the first book in the series, this one is filled with fun, frolicking, and some spicy sex scenes, along with a few bite-your-nails moments, a perfect companion to curl up with on a cold winter day. ~ *Taylor Jones, The Review Team of Taylor Jones & Regan Murphy*

Not My Type by M. E. Gordon is the second book in her One Night Stand series. One Night Stand is a rock band just on the verge of stardom, and the last thing our spunky heroine, Lexi, wants is to get involved with a member of the band. In fact, the first time she meets Trent from One Night Stand on the plane to LA, he lets her know in no uncertain terms that she is not his type. That's fine with Lexi, she just wants him out of her hair so she can get on with finding a job working for the rich and famous in Hollywood. But wouldn't you know it, the first day on her new job as a waitress (she doesn't have the experience to work for the rich and famous yet, but you have to start somewhere), she runs into Trent and the band again. She refuses to wait on them and switches tables with another waitress, but that doesn't stop Trent from pursuing her, even though she's not his type, no, not at all. *Not My Type* is a cute, fun, and clever story, filled with wonderful characters, a dash of humor, a pinch of suspense, and a generous helping of steamy sex scenes— the perfect recipe for a really great read. *Regan Murphy, The Review Team of Taylor Jones & Regan Murphy*

ACKNOWLEDGMENTS

When I write these books about the men of One Night Stand, it's hard not to get attached to them and somehow feel like they are "my boys"—my handsome sometimes difficult to handle, but always entertaining, boys. I hope that as you read each one of their stories you too can come to love them and care for them the way I do.

I'd like to take a moment to thank everyone who has made this book possible. To my publisher and editor, thank you for fixing my almost-always-incorrect grammar. I'd like to thank my cover designer over at The Illustrated Author, you've made another beautiful cover for the boys of One Night Stand, and I can't wait to work with you on the next one.

To my kids, thank you for being awesome and excited with me when my new books come out. I promise one day you can read them, if you're into sappy romance novels, of course. To all the friends and family who have helped bring this story to life, whether that be proof reading or bouncing ideas off of, I couldn't do it without you.

My amazing husband, you are everything I've ever wished for, and I would not be able to do this whole author thing without you. Having you by my side, along with all the love you have for our children, makes the stories I have locked away seem possible, because my story with you came true. I know we joke about it, but with each man that I bring to life on paper, there's a little of you in there, and maybe that's why I love these characters so much. Thank you for being you, from the "Megan, dammits" all the way to the "I love yous" and everything else in-between.

Not

My

Type

M.E. Gordon

A Black Opal Books Publication

GENRE: ROMANTIC SUSPENSE/STEAMY ROMANCE

NOT MY TYPE
Copyright © 2017 by M. E. Gordon
Cover Design by Melissa Stevens
All cover art copyright © 2017
All Rights Reserved
Print ISBN: 978-1-626947-81-8

First Publication: OCTOBER 2017

Published by Black Opal Books **http://www.blackopalbooks.com**

DEDICATION

To everyone who told me to keep going

Chapter 1

Lexi

"Mom, I'm gonna be fine," I reassured her for the millionth time.

She practically sobbed as she held me tightly around the neck. "I know, I know. You're just going to be so far away. It's not like when you went away to college. You were only an hour away. This is across the country!"

"Come on, Mom, I'm livin' with Ben, it's not like I'm goin' there not knowin' anyone." My brother had moved out west as soon as he had enough money. He was a dancer, an aspiring actor. He had it rough in our small town, but he was thriving in LA. And soon I was going to be thriving right along with him.

"Your brother better watch out for ya. If he doesn't, I'm comin' all the way to California and bringin' ya back home with me," she scolded in my ear.

I rolled my eyes. Southern women could be way too dramatic, and unfortunately that also included me.

"I'll be fine, Mom. Okay one last hug and I gotta

run, don't wanna miss my flight," I said hugging tightly onto my tear-stricken mother.

"Call me when you land. If you don't, I'm gonna suspect you've been kidnapped. Then I'll have to call the police and come find ya myself," she said, holding my cheeks between her hands.

"Got it! I'll call ya as soon as the plane touches down." I heaved my pack onto my shoulder and reached down to my carry-on bag. Dragging it behind me, I proceeded to my gate. I'd admit I was a little sad to be leaving. Virginia was my home and the farthest I had ever gone from there was one state away, when I attended West Virginia University, and that was a cultural shock from the small farming town I grew up in.

I was moving to California to become someone else. I had this dream to work with movie stars and attend red carpets. Sure I had a backup plan, which involved a boring accountant degree that I spent four years getting. I was gonna give myself one year to live the way that I had dreamed. I didn't want to be famous. I just wanted to work for them. I wanted to be an assistant to the stars. *Oh crap, where'd I put my ticket?* I searched my pockets frantically. *Oh lord!*

I finally found my ticket after turning my bag inside out. I wasn't the most organized person in the world. *Now where did I put my phone? Found it!* Anyway, I was determined to make it out there, as long as I could keep calm. I knew it was going to be fine. *Which way am I going again?*

"Now boarding group A," the older woman at the entrance to the terminal said.

I sat there in the uncomfortable chair weighing my options and wiggling back and forth. I was boarding group C, and I had to piss like a sailor. *Do I get up and run to the bathroom now or wait till I'm stuck on the plane and use the tinny weenie bathrooms they have.* Glancing around, I weighed my options. *Decision made, I'm running for it.*

That's better.

I stood at the mirror in the bathroom and checked my hair, *flat. My mother would be so disappointed.* My mother had tried to get me to tease my hair from the moment I came out of the womb, but there was no use in it. It was dark brown, long, straight, and had absolutely no body to it.

I fixed my tank top and unbuttoned, light, flannel shirt. Turning to the side, I checked my fine ass and attempted to tussle my flat hair. *Looking good, Lexi.*

"This is the last call for boarding group C flight Six-Twenty to California. Once again, this is last call for boarding group C, Flight Six-Twenty to California."

Oh, shit!

I ran out of the bathroom, practically knocking an old lady over, and booked it to the terminal. *How the hell did everyone board so fast?*

"Wait, please wait, I've got a ticket!" I yelled from about twenty feet away as the woman was closing the door to the gate.

Breathing heavily, I handed her my ticket.

"Cutting it close there, darling."

"The important thing is that I made it, right?"

"Sure is, you have a nice flight. It's a full one," the lady said, winking at me.

I was really wishing I would've remembered to check-in to my flight the night before. I made sure to take a mental note for the next time I had to fly. *Don't wait till the last minute to check in, or pee!*

I was the very last person to board. It wouldn't have been so bad if it wasn't a five-and-a-half-hour—with my luck, six-hour—flight across the US, and it also wouldn't have been so bad if every loving seat wasn't filled. *Yes, I found one!*

"Excuse me, is anyone sitting there?" I asked, crossing my fingers and praying to the Lord Almighty that the little old lady said no.

"Oh, I'm sorry, dear. My husband is just using the restroom. He'll be right back," the sweet lady said, holding her purse in her lap like I was going to steal it.

"Okay, thanks," I grumbled sadly.

"I think they're all taken back here. You should go back up to the front," the flight attendant who managed the back of the plane said while gesturing in the other direction.

I knew exactly which seat she was talking about. The one with the two men in the front row, the middle seat between them was empty and apparently waiting for my ass to fill it.

Oh, how I wanted any other seat on that plane to be open. I glanced down at the man sitting next to the window in the third seat of the first row. He was a red mohawked, tattooed, character, who was tapping his fingers on the book that lay across his lap. I eyed him up and, for the life of me, I had no clue how he was sitting in the skinny, tight-ass jeans that he had on. I was pretty sure they wouldn't even fit over my calves, *and I have nice defined calves.* He smiled up at me from under his sunglasses, letting them fall down the bridge of his nose. *Who wears sunglasses on a plane, at night? Good grief, he just winked at me.* I had decided then and there that that flight was going to test all of my patience, another thing to add to the list along with my dramatic flair, a very short fuse. Not all Southern women were demure, patient, and proper. I happened to be a part of the loud, ornery, and short-fused breed of Southern women, or so I'd been told.

After cringing at the clown near the window, I took notice of the man sitting in the first of the three seats. The best way to describe him would be ex-con, biker gang member, and possible steroid user. He was huge. His long legs almost touched the cockpit wall his broad shoulders completely covered the back of his chair and at least a few inches of the chair that I was being forced to sit in. He had a beanie hat on so I couldn't see his hair, but my guess? He was bald. He had a five o'clock shadow, just the right amount of scruff to make a girl swoon. I couldn't tell what color his eyes were because he refused to look up at me, or acknowledge I was standing right next to him. His large fingers were intertwined and resting on his lap. His dark gray shirt hugged his large muscles perfectly. I was going to need to be splashed with a bucket of cold water to keep from staring. Lucky for me, I was distracted.

"Excuse me, ma'am, we need you to take a seat," the flight attendant said through a fake-ass smile.

"I'm workin' on it. There wouldn't happen to be any other available seats…anywhere?" I asked, pointing to the back of the plane.

"No, I'm sorry it's a full flight and this is the very last seat. You should be happy it's a front row seat, there's more leg room," she said, gesturing to the larger amount of space between the seats and the wall in front.

"Lovely." I smiled back, tossed my pack in the seat, and went to grab my carry-on bag so I could toss it into the above cargo slip. You would have thought that maybe one of the men would have offered to help. "Oh, don't worry, darlings, I'll get it myself." *Damn Yankee assholes, no manners!*

The clown near the window pushed his sunglasses up his nose and settled into his seat. *Patience, Lexi, patience.* Of course the only open space available in the cargo was right above the steroid-using heap of muscles. Now I wasn't no frail, whiny woman. I grew up on a farm. I knew how to lift hay barrels, move a cow. I had my own version of muscles, farm muscles I called them. I also wasn't no skinny super model, but I was tall, almost six feet, one inch—okay, fine, in heels I was definitely six-foot-one. I was proud of the way I looked, but that sure as hell didn't mean I wasn't a little self-conscious in front of sexy, biker, muscle man or the somewhat dashing clown.

"Looks like you've got it just fine without our help, Zena," the heap of muscles said from below me.

I had just lifted my bag up and was trying to stuff it in so the flight attendant could close the hatch when I heard his smart little comment. *Oops.*

"What the *hell*?" he roared, standing from his seat.

My carry-on fell off his lap and onto the floor.

"Oh my! I'm so sorry. It must have just slipped from my Zena grasp," I said, drawing on my Southern accent and placing my hands on the curves of my hips.

Chapter 2

Trent

A nice relaxing five-hour flight was what I had imagined. Then I found out I was taking the second flight that left seven hours after the first one. Then it was brought to my attention that I was going to be stuck on the flight with Reece. Since my lap piece Kitty was traveling with us now and she just had to bring her friend Piper, I so valiantly volunteered to take the second flight with Reece.

At the least, I got a kiss out of it, which pissed Kane off. For some reason that girl, his girl, his wife, loved me. She would always sit on my lap and snuggle up on me. I didn't mind really, but I longed to have her—someone like her—be mine. I longed to have what she and Kane had.

Not only did I want someone to sit with me like she did, I wanted someone to fight with and make up with. So, because I loved my Kitty so much, I gave up *my* seat so she could be with her man and friend. Reece, not so much. They kind of kicked him off the flight, and I got stuck with him.

While we waited to board the plane, I sat reading a *Rolling Stone* while Reece people watched next to me, gawking at every woman who walked by.

"Trent, Trent! Look at that one!" Reece said, hitting my arm. "Oh man, why can't girls like that be at our shows?" he asked. Shaking his head, he watched the girl in question walk by.

I looked up and immediately looked back down. There was a time when I would have watched her walk by. Hell, I might have even tried to get her number. *What the hell is wrong with me?* I needed to get back on my game. I just wasn't in the mood to gawk at women with Reece. He always had a way of taking it too far—you know, crossing the creepy line.

While Reece repelled women with his tight ass pants and wild, red Mohawk, I had a tendency to scare them. Moms would clutch at their children, old ladies would hold their purses tighter, and if it was late at night, most women moved to the opposite side of the street. I had a don't-mess-with-me look and, for the most part, it worked. The tattoos, beanie hat, big muscles, and shades helped out too.

"Trent, did you see her?" Reece asked again.

"Yes, I saw her."

"And...should I try to infiltrate?"

I looked up from the *Rolling Stone Magazine* that I was trying to read and stared at him. "I don't give a fuck what you do, little man, have at it," I said, before returning to my reading.

"Dude, little man? What the fuck, Trent?" he said loudly, gaining the attention of everyone around us.

"Keep your loud-ass voice down. I'm not trying to get kicked out of here."

"Don't call me little man, and I won't have to get loud," he said through his teeth.

"Whatever, Reece—jus—"

The fine piece of ass that Reece kept drooling over stood in front of me. Licking my lips, I sat back in the uncomfortable chair and looked up at her. Tight-ass jeans, thin lacy tank top, long blonde hair, and a beautiful face stared down at me. Reece hit my arm encouragingly.

"I know this is going to sound crazy but—" She froze in front of me, twisting her hands then shoving them into her back pockets while pushing her moderate-sized tits in my face.

"What can I do for you, sugar?" I asked, folding the magazine over my lap to cover my ever-growing friend.

"Are you—I mean—oh wow, I'm so nervous," she said, taking a breath and fiddling with her hands again. "Are you Trent Walker from ONS?"

"No, he's not," Reece said, standing from next to me and taking her hands before I could get a word out. He turned her toward him as she looked him over. "He's not in ONS, but I am. Reece McAndrews, at you very sexy service."

"But if you're Reece and he's not Trent—"

"He's my bodyguard, I'm sure you can imagine how some fans get out of control. They're not all like you, my love," he said, suavely kissing the top of her hand.

"Oh, I'm sorry…well, I'm not totally sorry," she said, giggling. *Typical Reece.*

"Would you like to get a drink?" he asked.

"Yeah, I'd love that!" She smiled before turning back to me. "Again, I'm sorry, I could have sworn you were Trent," she said, looking down at me.

"He gets that all the time, no worries," Reece said, responding for me.

When they turned to leave, Reece flashed me the

finger and mouthed, "That's what you get, little man."

Opening my magazine back up, I settled back in the hard-ass chair and prayed the plane was going to take off without him.

No such luck. We were on the plane, sitting in the front row, waiting for everyone else to board. After hearing about his escapades in full detail, I was beyond pissed. Not only did he screw me out of that piece of ass, he was going to sit next to me for five hours and rub it in my face. *Thank god, there was an empty seat between the two of us*. If I was forced to sit next to him, I might have made his face match the color of his hair.

"In just a moment, we will be getting ready to head over to the tarmac. Thank you again for flying with us today," the woman over the intercom said from the back of the plane.

Finally. We had been sitting for what felt like forever. In a rush of bags and hair, a woman walked onto the plane completely out of breath. From my seat, I glanced up at her as she fixed the bag on her shoulder and searched for a seat behind us. She walked past me—jeans and cowboy boots. *Right out of the country, she's never going to make it in LA.*

I had a thing for petite blonds, so she did nothing for me. I sat back in my seat, folded my arms in my lap, and closed my eyes. When I sensed someone standing next to me, I glanced up, and cowgirl was standing next to me arguing with the flight attendant about finding any other seat on the plane. *See? My bad boy persona came in handy.*

"No, I'm sorry it's a full flight and this is the very last seat. You should be happy it's a front row seat, more leg room," the flight attendant said to her.

"Lovely," the cowgirl said. She threw her bag next to me and then leaned down to grab her other bag. Her hair fell like a veil over her face. It was so long it almost touched the floor. "Oh, don't worry darlings, I'll get it myself," she said, after neither one of us—or anyone else, for that matter— helped her with her bag. The smell of her shampoo drifted under my nose. *Fuck, she smells good!* As I said before, it was going to be long flight. She might smell like a dream, but she wasn't the one in mine. She was tall and looked like she could bench press Reece.

"Looks like you've got it just fine without our help, Zena," I said under my breath. I assumed that she hadn't heard me, that is, until her bag fell right on my head, then in my lap. "What the hell?" I roared, standing up and tossing her bag on the floor.

"Oh my! I'm so sorry. It must have just slipped from my Zena grasp," she said, drawing on a Southern accent that I found very annoying. She placed her hands on the curves of her hips. My eyes followed the move of them and then ran up her body to her large tits and cute round face. Like I said before, she was tall. I didn't have to look down too much from my six-foot-five stature, to see into her honey silver eyes. They were the most unique eyes I had ever seen. They looked dangerous but beautiful. *Maybe she's a Southern witch?*

She stared back at me, her hands on her hips and her mouth in a thin hard line. *I do not need this for five hours.* "Sit your Southern ass down, I'll put it up there," I said, gesturing her to the middle seat, while I grabbed her bag.

"Excuse me?" she seethed.

I turned back to her, confused and, frankly, just tired. Her bag in my hand, I waited for her to move.

"Give it to me, I can do it myself," she said, reaching for the bag.

"I don't have any doubt that you can't, but I'd feel safer if I just put it up there."

"Give me my bag," she demanded.

I did my best to put on my angry face. "No, sit down and I'll do it."

"You don't scare me, so you can un-scrunch your eyes and loose the tense muscles. The whole roid-rage, ex-con thing you got going on isn't as terrifying as you think it is. Not to me at least. Now give me my bag," she said calmly and casually while she moved her long hair from her neck, and, fuck, I was stunned, unable to come up with anything witty.

"Excuse me, we are trying to keep the flight on time, so if you could just put the bag up and take a seat we can get on our way," the flight attendant said next to us.

"I would, but muscles over here won't give me my bag," Cowgirl said sweetly, pulling the accent again.

Funny, I didn't hear it when she was yelling at me. "Fine!" I shoved the bag into her chest, making her take a step back to keep her balance. "Drop it on my head again, and you're going to wish I was a roid-rage, ex-con," I said, getting in her face before I sat back down in my seat.

"What a charmer!" she said, while shoving the bag above me.

She slammed the cargo hatch shut and plopped down next to me. The damn plane seats were so narrow, my shoulders had a tendency to hang over the chair next me, and my legs did the same. When she tried settling into her seat, she hit my shoulder with her own in an attempt to move me. I turned and looked down at her, shaking my head, a little more than amused.

"Would ya mind movin' onto your side, please?"

"Yeah, I would mind. I'm rather comfy where I'm at."

"Oh ma God! You are insufferable!" she said, hitting the back of her head on the seat behind her. "Can't ya just...I don't know...tilt the tree trunk a little so I can at least get my seat belt on?" she asked through a fake-ass smile.

"Sorry, tree trunks don't really bend. Looks like you're going to have to go digging."

"Ugh!" she huffed, turning as much as she could to find the belt and click it.

The plane taxied down the runway and rose into the air. As soon as the seat beat sign went off, she took out a laptop and started typing.

Talk about an awkward flight. I was next to Zena and, if she wasn't bothering me with her incessant clicking of her keyboard, Reece kept shoving pictures of the blonde from before in my face. I was in my very own hell. I flipped open my tablet and started going through old pictures to kill time.

"Cute kids, how old are they?" Zena asked from around my shoulder. I moved the tablet from her view and stared down at her. "Calm down, Papa Bear," she said, sitting back and sighing dramatically.

"They're seven and four."

"Well, you and you're baby momma are extremely lucky to have such cute kids. I've seen some pretty…well ugly ones," she said, shuffling and going through the papers in her hand for the millionth time.

"Jokes aside, they're not my kids, and I don't and won't ever have a baby mamma." I glanced back down at her and counted at least twenty papers shoved between her legs, under her arms, under her legs, under the laptop, on top of the laptop. She was a hot fucking mess. "What are you doing? Ah, you have papers shoved everywhere."

"Not that it's any of your business but I'm getting things in line to go job hunting."

"Right, well good luck with all that. I'm sure your future employer will really appreciate all the peanut grease," I said, chuckling. I couldn't help myself.

"Whatever. Why don't you just try to stay on your side of *my* chair and mind your own business, okay?"

"Done and done." And with that I didn't say another word to her.

Four and a half hours into the flight I had fallen asleep, maybe it was the pounding of the keys next to me or the five beers I let myself have, but I was knocked out. When I woke back up, my shoulder was stiff. When I tried to move it, it wouldn't budge. I was perplexed for a moment, before I looked over at my shoulder.

There, sleeping very soundly on it, was my annoying neighbor. Her arms were wrapped around my bicep, holding onto it like a cherished stuffed animal. Her dark brown hair was pulled back. A few strands fell around her face. One particular piece was caught in her eyelash. I wanted to brush it away, like I did when Mackenzie would fall asleep in my arms. But this wasn't the four-year-old niece that I loved. This was a stranger, an annoying, snoring stranger who, for some unseen reason, thought I was her personal pillow. As I looked down at her, I remembered that beneath her closed eyelids and long black lashes, beautiful eyes—like I'd never seen before—rested. *I shouldn't want to see them. I shouldn't want to touch her. She's not even my type.*

The plane hit some turbulence, startling not only me but the head that rested on my shoulder. I kept watching her. I watched as her hand unclasped my arm and moved the hair that was stuck in her lashes. Her eyes opened slowly and, before I knew it, she was staring up at me. Honey colored eyes, with rings of silver and black were fixed on mine in a dreamy haze.

Chapter 3

Lexi

I opened my eyes, and, for a moment, I thought that I was dreaming. My head rested on a warm shoulder, my hands were also warm and cozily entwined around soft skin. I wiped at the hair that was tickling my eye and tucked it behind my ear. When I was able to focus, I stared up into a face that was somewhat familiar but still very much a mystery to me.

I blinked a few times, expecting the image to wash away, but it didn't, and he didn't. *Why is he looking at me like that?*

"Comfy?" he asked.

His right eye squinted as he spoke and his lips curled up in a creepy, I'm-going-to-get-you kind of way. It clicked then.

I moved my head from his shoulder, quickly undid my arms from his, and sat back in my seat.

"I hope you slept well. It's going to cost you. This shoulder isn't free," he said, adjusting in his seat.

"I didn't mean to—I mean—" *Oh god, why am I stuttering in front of this oaf?*

"I get it. You couldn't keep your hands to yourself. Most women can't," he said, turning his head to me but leaving it glued to the back of his seat.

"Trust me. You want me to keep my hands to myself right now." I sat on them so I wouldn't be tempted to slap him. "What do you expect me to do? You're taking up half my seat. If it's on my side, it's fair game," I said, rolling my eyes and glancing out the small window to see the night sky before looking back at him.

"Don't lie to yourself, sweetheart," he said, leaning over and getting in my face. "I'm irresistible."

The way he made each syllable form around his lips had me watching them and wanting to slap him and kiss him all at once. *What an arrogant ass!*

"I don't think so, muscles. I'd rather jump out of this plane. Don't flatter yourself. You're not my type," I said, leaning over to grab my bag from under my seat. I was trying to keep myself busy so I wouldn't be tempted to stare at him. *Is it possible for someone to get hotter? His scruff was longer, his voice was deeper—Jesus, what the hell am I thinking?*

No more men, especially men that resembled a certain someone from my past. I might have said that he wasn't my type, but the heap of muscles sitting next to me was my kryptonite. Tall, strong, badass, and sexy. *Did it get really hot in here or is it just me?* I reached up to the vent and turned mine on, making if blast cool air on my face. I sat back and took a deep breath.

"You all right there, Zena?" he asked, looking over at me.

I narrowed my eyes on him and shook my head. "Why do you keep calling me that? It's really annoying. What? Are you intimated that a girl might be able to beat ya up or somethin'?" My accent pulled in my anger. I had been working really hard at trying to hide it when I spoke, but when I was pissed, it had a tendency to slip out.

"Whatever, Zena. For the record, you're not my type either," he said leaning over again and getting in my face before he stood up from his seat.

"I'm so relieved. And here I thought I'd just met my soulmate. Whatever is a poor girl to do? Oh, I know! I don't give two shits that I'm not your type!" I said, also standing from my seat.

I tossed my bag back in my seat before I got in his face, his tall stature only a few inches taller than mine. Again, I narrowed my eyes in on him. I went to walk around him and head to the restrooms at the back of the plane when his hand held my upper arm, turning me back to him.

"What are you doin'? Get off of me," I said through clenched teeth, because I didn't want to make a scene. I tried to move my arm from his grasp but I couldn't. A memory flashed to the forefront of my mind and panic set in. When he pulled me closer, I lost it, I didn't care if I made a scene or not, I didn't care if the freaking marshal on the plane tackled me and put me in jail. I tried ripping my arm from his with all my might.

"What are you doing? Calm down," he said, still holding my arm.

"Get off of me, now!"

"Calm down, wait a minute," he said, struggling to keep me in front of him.

"Excuse me, is there a problem here?" the flight attended asked.

The whole plane was awake and whispering and staring at us. Over a dozen lights had turned on, making the plane bright for everyone to see.

"Yes, there's a problem. This bull of a man won't let me go!" I spat at the woman while still trying to get my arm free.

"Sir, I'm going to need you to let her go and take a seat," the flight attendant said.

"Fine, whatever," he said, releasing my arm and shaking his head.

"You are...oh, I can't even think straight right now!" I seethed.

"Don't be so dramatic, I was trying to help you," he said, shoving me aside and sitting in his seat.

"Helping, is that what they call manhandling these days?"

"Miss, if you're not using the facilities, we're going to need you to take a seat," the lady said, touching my shoulder.

I jumped in the aisle and turned to her, my back to the whole plane. "I'm going—"

The sound of laughter filled the cabin. *Why is everyone laughing?* I turned and shot muscles a death glare.

"I tried to help you," was all he said before snickering up at me.

"Why is everyone laughing at me?" I asked him through my teeth.

"Your shirt is up your back, and you have about three papers stuck to it with sweat—oh, and your underwear is showing," he said, smiling up at me.

I stood there, my jaw slack, as I stared down at him. Quickly reaching behind me, I felt the damp papers on my back. I ripped them off and pulled my jeans up before hastily sitting back down.

"You could have just said something instead of tugging on me!" I snapped at muscles.

"I tried, you didn't listen," he said, resting his head on the seat and closing his eyes.

I covered my face with the papers, leaning over my legs, I wanted to continue to curl up in a ball and disappear. Not only was I humiliated, I'd freaked out. I freaked out when he held my arm. I thought that I was over that part of it, past the fear and panic of men like the one next to me. *Guess I'm not.*

I felt him nudge my arm, once then twice.

"What?" I yelled, sitting up and looking at him. *Dammit, why does he have to be so damn good looking?*

"Are you all right?" he asked. "I didn't mean to freak you out, by grabbing you."

"Oh, now you're going to be all chivalrous? Men like you are all the same. You use your size and stature to intimidate women into doing whatever your will is at that particular moment. I'm over it, just leave me alone, please," I said, turning from him to look out the window and at the sleeping red headed Mohawk, who had been passed out pretty much the entire flight.

"You got me all wrong, Zena."

I didn't turn back to him. I didn't look at him for the rest of the flight. It didn't matter what he said, or if I believed him or not. As soon as we got off that flight, I was never going to see him again. So what did it matter?

"We are beginning our descent. Please fasten your seatbelts if they aren't already. We will have you safely at LAX in thirty minutes or less," I heard from the captain over the intercom half an hour later.

Sitting straight in my seat, I went to reach for my seat belt. This time muscles moved so I could find the other side of the seat belt. Once I had it in my grasp, he moved back.

Our eyes met for a moment, and I thought I saw something as I stared up at him. I don't know what it was that I thought I saw, but clearly the altitude and lack of sleep was messing with my better judgment. Hell, I didn't even know his name, plus I had sworn off men like him, and he flat out told me I wasn't his type. Not to mention he was a jerk the whole flight.

When the plane touched down and finally pulled into the gate, everyone stood and went in search of their bags from the overhead compartments.

"Do you want me to get yours down?" muscles asked.

He was standing with his hands resting on the overhead compartment. I was momentarily abducted by aliens, or maybe I was staring at his crotch? Does it really matter?

"Yo, Zena, your bag. Do you want me to pull it down?" he asked again.

I was returned to my body, *crazy body snitching aliens.* His eyes were wide and he was clearly getting annoyed waiting for my answer.

"Ah, so you do answer to Zena. Let's try this again. Zena, do you want me to pull your bag down?"

That's it I'm pissed! I stood and moved toward him. "No, don't touch it, I'll get it myself."

And, with that, I squeezed between him and the seat and reached up to get my bag. He couldn't move back without knocking over an older couple, so he grabbed on to the back of his seat and pinned me tightly between the two.

I could feel his hot breath as it moved through my hair. It was tickling my skin and whirling around my ear. His body was flush up against mine and I swear I felt more than just a belt buckle against my bottom. I paused and turned my head, surprised to find his, so close to mine.

"Not your type? This is a bit desperate, you know?" I whispered to him.

What happened next took me by such a surprise I

nearly went weak in the knees. His hand left the back of the chair and rested on the curve of my jean-clad hip. He pulled my hip closer to his, if that was even possible, and spoke softly in my ear.

"Trust me, if I was trying, you'd know. Why don't you sit all of *this* down so I can get your bag?" He moved his hand from my hip to squeeze my ass as he spoke.

"Did you just insinuate that I have a fat ass?" I said, flipping around so we were face to face.

He smirked down at me. "You said it, but I won't disagree."

"So I'm not your type because I have junk in the trunk and curves that you can hold on to, and you were holding on, I might add. You know, I really enjoy being called fat by guys, it just makes my day!"

He stared at me and then backed up as much as he could, putting enough room between us for me to turn around and pull my bag down without us touching again. When I had my bag in my hand, he reached up and placed his hand on the above storage.

"See? I did it all by myself, no assholes needed," I sneered up at him.

I held my bag and went under his arm to get back around to my seat. He grabbed his bag and the guy's next to me. When he tossed the bag to his friend, the mohawk finally woke up and then flicked off muscles. *I think I like this redheaded freak.*

"We are going to ask that everyone have a seat. It's going to be another minute or so. The airport is doing a drill, so we can't attach the gate just yet."

The moans that followed the announcement were loud and dramatic, mine included.

"I didn't call you fat," muscles said, flopping down into his seat and half of mine.

I turned to him, totally discombobulated. "I honestly

don't have the energy to argue with you anymore." I smiled at him then turned to face anything but him. I didn't consider myself fat, but that didn't mean men like him, or men in general, didn't. So I wasn't a size two beanpole, not many women were. But when you were raised on rich Southern cooking and working on a farm your whole life, chances were, you weren't going to be a size two.

"Tough luck, you're going to have to," he said.

"Listen, I don't even know you, you don't know me. We shared an interesting five-hour flight that I am sure to forget as soon as I'm off of it, so let's just end this in silence."

"Nope, I can't do that. I'm not the guy you think I am, and I need you to understand that before we get off."

I laughed in his face when he said that. "Ha, you're funny, but I think you're exactly the guy I thought you were. The nail in the coffin was when you called me fat."

"I did not say that! I said you had a fat ass, there is a big difference."

"You got that right, a big *fat* difference," I said.

"All right, ladies and gentlemen, we have clearance. Please make sure you take all your belongings, and thank you for flying with us," the flight attendant said over the intercom.

I went to stand up, but he grabbed my wrist and pulled me back down.

"What do I have to do to prove I'm not an asshole?" he asked seriously.

I scrunched my brows at him, confused and taken aback. "You can't, now let my hand go so I can get off the plane, please," I said sweetly. He released my hand and I grabbed my bags "Have nice life, muscles," I said before I walked off the plane and left him sitting there.

I walked out of the tunnel and toward baggage claim

in a daze. I *had* shared an interesting five hours with a man that I was never going to see again, and dang it, I *was* going to remember it.

"Lexi!"

I looked up from the ground and saw my brother walking toward me. "Ben!" I screeched, while I was being engulfed in his strong dancer arms. My brother was tall and built to be a dancer, actor, model, and…well everything that you could be in LA. He had amazing blue eyes and dark brown hair like mine. He was so handsome, he was breaking girl's hearts before he even knew he was. Too bad for them, he was gay. All the good-looking ones were, or so I'd been told.

Chapter 4

Trent

Lexi. I should have guessed she have a name like that. A sexy, short, sassy-ass name. *Damn, I hate when I like a girl's name*. I was standing on the other side of the baggage claim, watching her, as if I was some kind of pervert. Reece had run off to get some food, so I headed toward the baggage claim to get our shit.

This so-called Lexi had put me flat on my ass. I loved the fact that my outward appearance gave off a keep back, bad guy vibe. It kept the crazies away, but I absolutely hated when someone felt that way about me after meeting me. I didn't know what it was about her that made me act the way I did, but I had. I was an arrogant asshole to her and, for the life of me, I didn't know why.

"What the hell are you doing?" Reece asked, coming up behind me.

"What? What do you mean?" I said, trying to avert my attention to anywhere but Lexi's ass.

Why can't I take my eyes off of it?

"I mean, what are you doing staring at that, when you can stare at this?" he said, shoving his phone with a picture of a naked girl, the one that he stole from underneath me.

"You're a piece of shit. You're lucky I let you have that," I said, pointing to the phone in his hand.

"Well, I think she's officially a Reece fan now. Anyway, are the bags out yet?" he asked, looking around.

"Yeah, they just started coming out."

We walked over to the carousel of bags, waiting for ours. Standing on one side of the carousel, a good thirty feet away, I watched from behind a group of people as the girl I spent the last five hours with held onto some guy who looked like he stepped out of a fucking Ralph Lauren photo shoot. He held her tightly and tickled her sides. I was in some sort of a daze while I watched her face light up with a smile.

Truth be told, behind the tough guy façade, I longed to make a girl smile like that. I wanted to be someone's world, and I wanted to get so lost in theirs that I wouldn't care what others thought, but I had yet to find that.

"Trent!"

I heard my name being called from behind me. I turned around to see a tiny woman with wild blonde hair running at me full speed. She jumped up into my arms and held me tightly around the neck before kissing my cheeks a million times.

"Kitty, really? It's been ten hours since I saw you."

"I don't care, I missed you. That asshole over there just isn't the same, I need you," she faked sobbed in my ear.

"Kitty, I swear to god I will divorce you if you kiss him one more time!" Kane, my friend and fellow band mate called from behind me.

"Shove it, Kane, you're not going to do shit!" she yelled over her shoulder.

I wrapped an arm around her waist so she wouldn't fall, and, when I turned around, I caught Zena, or should I say Lexi staring at me, shaking her head. She reached down grabbed her bag and moved out of sight. I went to move after her. *Damn, I need to clear this up.*

"Trent? Where are we going?" Kitty asked, sitting back in my arms. I was walking with determination to get to Lexi, but I quickly stopped in my tracks. *What am I doing?* Following some girl I wasn't going to see again to explain to her that I wasn't an asshole. It was a lost cause. I placed Kitty on her feet, and we walked back to Kane and Reece, who had gotten our bags.

"You're going to flip when you see the house, dude. The record label didn't disappoint," Kane said, grabbing my hand and pulling me in for a bro hug.

"Well, what are we waiting for?"

It was dark when we arrived at the house but it was lit up like a million bucks. The long driveway had a gate at the end. When we pulled up to the house, JJ and Aiden ran out, beers in their hands and girls at their sides. *They sure didn't waste any time.* I knew the girl under JJ's arm was Piper, Kitty's friend, but the brunette with Aiden was new.

The inside of the house looked like something off of *Cribs*. It was decorated in the latest fashion, modern but comfortable. The kitchen was huge and stocked with food and beer, thanks to the label. They showed me to my room at the end of the house, complete with king-size bed and its own bathroom and balcony. *I could get use to this!*

When I finished tossing my luggage in the room, I went back out to the living area where everyone was sitting around drinking and bullshitting.

"And then he squeezed her ass and called her fat!" Reece said before bursting out laughing with everyone else.

I sat down on the couch and wasn't surprised at all when Kitty got up from Kane's lap to sit on mine. He huffed and tossed his hands in the air, but he knew there wasn't anything he could do about it. His wife, for some odd reason, loved sitting on my lap. It was probably the big bear vibe I put off. Women loved sitting with me or being wrapped up in my arms.

"Trenton Walker, did you grab a girl's ass? And you better pray the second part isn't true," Kitty said, grabbing the collar of my shirt while squinting her eyes at me.

"No, what are you talking about, crazy woman?" I said, widening my eyes and praying that she believed me.

"Don't play dumb, ass hat. You totally smacked her ass and called her fat. For the record, Kitty, I didn't think she was fat," Reece said, trying to cover his own ass.

Not going to work. Kitty got up and walked over to him, kicking him in the shin. "Shut up Reece!" she said before coming back over and grabbing my shirt again. "Trent you're the nice one, the gentleman of the group. Please tell me he's wrong," she begged.

"Why the hell are we talking about this anyway? When do we have to be at the studio to start recording?" I asked, sitting back from Kitty to look around her at Kane. I instantly regretted trying to change the subject. Kitty took hold of my nipple, and I blurted out what happened before I knew I was. "She was a pain in the ass. Do you know what it's like to sit next to a pain in the ass for five hours?" I said in my defense.

"She really looked like a pain in the ass all cuddled up next to you. And let's not forget, you really seemed pissed when you were resting your head on hers. The both of you were snoring like fucking bears," Reece said, rolling his eyes and cowering as Kitty made a fake attempt to hit him.

"Aw, Trent, you were snuggling with her? Why the hell did you call her fat?" Kitty asked, going from nice to bitch in a nano second.

"Kitty, it's really not important. And I didn't call her fat. She misinterpreted what I said. I did grab her ass, though, because she deserved it, and that's all you need to know. I'm still nice-guy Trent with a bad-ass exterior, so sit your ass down and tell me the plans for tomorrow," I said, smiling up at her. "And you!" I said, pointing at Reece. "I thought you were sleeping the whole time."

"Nope, I heard and saw everything, ev—ery—th—ing," he said, hitting every syllable slowly.

Kitty did as I asked, but looked at me differently when she sat down. The rest of the night we talked about what songs we were going to record first and when we had gigs and meetings with the big wigs. An hour later, Kitty was still sitting on my lap, but we had moved outside to the deck that backed to the roaring, dark ocean.

"You're different," Kitty stated. She was quiet when she spoke so only I could hear her.

"What?" I asked, confused.

"You're different, that girl, she did something to you."

"I don't think so, Kitty. She was just a girl I sat next to on a plane. Not unlike any other girl that we meet after shows or when we were on tour," I said, smiling down at her. Her head rested on my chest, her legs crossed over mine.

"No, it's not the same, you're not the same."

"Oh, for fuck's sake, Kitty, I'm the same, I promise you."

"It's not that. I know you're still the same. It's just…I don't know…This girl, does she have a name?"

Why is she pushing me on this? "What does it matter? It was just a girl."

"What was her name, Trent?" she asked, lifting her head from my chest.

I rolled my eyes and rubbed my temples, as I prayed for patience. "Lexi, her name was Lexi. Happy?" I asked, irritated. But I wasn't irritated at her. I was irritated at myself for being so affected by a girl I knew nothing about, a girl who was far from the ones I usually went after.

"Wait, I thought Reece said her name was Zena? I'm confused," she said, raising a brow.

"If you knew her name was Zena, why the hell did you ask me?" I drilled.

"Because that's a stupid name, and someone with a Southern accent would not have a name like Zena. Zena is a name you give someone to piss them off, like Kitty!" she said, shooting a death glare at Kane, who was now sitting inside with the other guys. When she turned back to me, she had a huge grin on her face. "Oh my God! You like her! Like, really like her," she said, standing from my lap and pulling her wild hair back.

"Come on, Kitty. I think you've had too much to drink. Did you not hear me say that she was a pain in the ass?"

"Oh, I heard you. I heard you say that you grabbed her ass, fought with her, snuggled with her, gave her a nickname, and your eyes lit up when you said Lexi. Oh, Trent, we have to find her. You always told me that you want to find the girl of your dreams. I think you did. I think you sat next to her and didn't even realize it." Kitty was pacing back and forth, a huge smile on her face.

Me? I was starting to think that maybe the ocean air was getting to her, because she was talking crazy. I stood, resting my hands on my hips. "Kitty" I said, gaining her attention. "Calm down. She is not the girl of my dreams. I think I'd know if she was."

"But that's just it, you don't know. You're so blinded by this whole she-has-to-look-like-a-fucking-supermodel-with-blonde-hair that you can't see. Trent, you were walking toward something or someone in the airport, was it her?"

Okay, Kitty's gone off the deep end. "Kane!" I yelled over her and into the house. When he came back outside, he leaned up against the door frame, watching his wife pace back and forth. "Kane, your wife is legit crazy," I said, gesturing toward her.

"I could have fucking told you that," Kane said, shaking his head.

"Kane, Trent's in love. He found his soul mate, just like I found you." She ran to him, jumping into his arms, and almost swallowing his face in a kiss. "I love you so much, baby," she said, pulling at his hair and kissing his neck.

"I don't know what you two are talking about out here, but thank you," Kane said, grabbing an ass cheek in each of his hands and pulling her closer to him. He turned with her in his arms and headed back inside.

That night, I lay in bed, staring at the ceiling, replaying everything that happened on the plane. But, for whatever reason, I couldn't get past the memory of her eyes, I couldn't get past the moment when she looked up at me with those honey, silver-streaked eyes. They were exotic and, for the life of me, I couldn't stop thinking about them. *So she had nice eyes, big deal. That doesn't mean I love her or that she's my dream girl. Kitty's just love struck. Her whole situation with Kane has her thinking crazy. It has nothing to do with me.*

Chapter 5

Lexi

Y ou'll be thanking me later," my brother said as he ate the homemade cookies that I brought with me, courtesy of our mother. He had gone out and gotten me a job, a job at a bar.

"Seriously, though, I can't work at a bar," I said for the millionth time.

"You are, and you're going to like it. I worked there when I came here. It's a great way to make money, plus it will give you your days to go on job interviews. Rent ain't cheap, sis," he said, shoving another cookie into his mouth.

"Why a bar?" I asked, eating a cookie myself.

"Well, the woman who owns it owes me a favor. It's really not that bad, Lexi. It's small, and you'll fit right in. I know you will."

I rolled my eyes. I was grateful to have a job, but a bar? "When do I start?" I asked.

"Next week. I'm giving you a week to get your feet on the ground before I start asking for rent."

"I have to pay rent weekly?" I asked, open-mouthed.

He nodded and smiled wickedly across the table.

"You're lying!"

"Not at all, sis. Head shots are expensive," he said, laughing.

∼∻∽

I spent the next week sightseeing and spending time with my brother. I went to the dance classes he taught, surprising the other dancers that I could keep up. Let's just say my brother wouldn't have been such a great dancer if I wasn't the one who went to dance first. I was good, but hobby good, not professional good. That was all Ben.

I went to parties with him, met a few semi-famous people, mostly dancers and some models. I was loving it all. When the time finally came for me to get ready for the job my brother so graciously got me, I felt the butterflies rising in my stomach. I came out of my room in my jeans, boots, and T-shirt.

"All right, take me to my nightmare," I said, standing in front of where he was sitting watching TV.

"You're kidding right?" he asked, staring up at me.

"What?"

"You can't wear that. Oh Lord, help my naive sister," he said, raising his head to the ceiling.

"What's wrong with this? They're the tightest jeans I own. The shirt is stylish and not one of my old ratty ones. What's the problem?"

"The problem is you're not going to get any tips looking like that."

After arguing for thirty minutes, I changed into a black tank-top but I refused to lose the boots. We pulled up to the bar so wonderfully named Lucky's. I had a feeling I wasn't going to be lucky. The parking lot was empty because it was still only three in the afternoon.

We walked in and, immediately, I knew I was in deep shit. Women walked around, moving chairs from tables, in short shorts and corsets, perfectly teased hair, and loads of make-up on their faces. Everywhere I turned, I saw ass and boobs. I turned to my brother, making sure to glare at him.

"Relax, Lexi, you'll be fine," he said, putting an arm around my shoulder.

"Are you kidding me, Ben? I can't wear stuff like that," I said, pointing to one of the girls who walked by with tight jeans and a hot pink corset laced up with black string. *Yeah, I can't do this.* Ben held my hand and kept me firmly at his side. Just then, an older woman, maybe in her fifties, walked up to us. She was dressed casually, jeans and a tank top with a black cropped jacket over top. She was beautiful, like the all the other girls walking around.

"Oh-my-goodness, look what the cat dragged in!" she said, hugging my brother tightly.

"Vick, this is my sister, Lexi," he said, pulling back and introducing me. "Lexi, this is Vick. She's the only reason why I've done so good out here."

"Hey, it's nice to meet you," I said, holding my hand out.

She looked at it then up at my face. Smiling, she shook her head no. "No handshakes here, honey, you're family." She took me in for a big bear hug. "Have you ever worked in a bar?" she asked.

"I worked at the café at my college. Does that count?"

"Not really, but you'll do fine. Oh, you should have seen this one his first week. He was dropping trays and mixing up orders, but we got him straightened out, and look at him now, dancing back up for pop stars."

I felt better knowing that my perfect brother had a rough start, but he had one advantage I didn't—a flawless body to flaunt around. More people walked about. The men and women who worked there were gorgeous. If anything, this would give me motivation to get a real job, the job I came all the way here for.

Before I knew it, my training time was up. All the girls helped me and even did my make-up and hair. I didn't know how they did it, but they were able to curl my hair and make it stay curled. They did my make-up like theirs, dark shadowy eyes and long lashes. As usual, I got tons of compliments on my exotic-colored eyes. I always thought they were ordinary, probably because I couldn't see them.

Two hours in, and I was doing great. The place was packed, and there was a live band playing some really good music. Sandy, one of the girls that I had attached myself to, said that they were an up and coming band. I thought that, if they sounded that good live, I could only imagine what a recording studio was going to make them sound like. *I'd buy their CD.* The customers were great and young and kind to me. There were tons of girls surrounding the stage dancing and singing along to the music. *Okay so my brother might have done good getting me this job.*

Half way through the night, the band stepped down and another went up on stage. I learned from others that this was the place to play to gain an audience. It was like a rite of passage to play here. Everything from rock to pop, soul—they didn't discriminate. I was in the back counting my tips. *One hundred fifty dollars! Okay, I love this job!*

So I messed-up every single order. No one was counting. I guess people felt bad for me, watching my scatter-brained butt run around, drop a tray or two, and forget what I was doing.

"Hey, Lexi, a table just sat down. Can you get them drinks?" Sandy asked. "I know we were only going to give you two tables, but it's packed and I'm swamped."

"Sure, no problem. I can get it for you." I was pumped. I had dollar signs in my eyes and music playing in the background. It was like a dream come true. I walked out of the back and made my way to the table, a six top! *Big money*!

"Hey, guys, I'm Lexi. What can I get for you?" I asked, looking up from my pad of paper and right into the face of asshole from the plane.

"Lexi?" he said, staring at me.

Actually, they were all staring at me, five good-looking men and two beautiful women, one of which was sitting on the asshole's lap. I instantly put her face to memory. She was the same girl who had wrapped herself tightly around muscles down in baggage claim. I didn't know why, but I should have guessed a girl like her was his type.

To be honest, I hadn't even thought of muscles until that exact moment. I made good on my promise and, as soon as I left that airport, he was out of my mind.

"Lexi, like Lexi?" the petite blonde asked, sitting back and looking into muscles's face.

Great, just what I need, some psycho jealous girl-friend coming at me. I was frozen, standing at the edge of the table staring down at him. *Dammit, did he get even hotter since the plane?* He sat there in a black T-shirt, with some faded writing on it, fitted jeans, a sexy scruff on his face, and warm brown eyes. He didn't have his hat on, so I got a glimpse of his hair. It was short and in a buzz cut. *I guess that's why he wears the hat, and, no, I'm not currently thinking about running my fingers around his head and imagining the way that buzzed hair feels against them.*

"Right, fat-ass Lexi," the redheaded, mohawked, jackass from the plane said, pointing at me. "Damn, you clean up nice."

He leaned back in his chair and checked my ass out. I bit my lip hard to keep quiet. I knew I was a second away from drawing blood—his or mine, it was a toss-up.

"Reece, are you fucking kidding me?" the blonde on muscles's lap said, promptly getting up and walking around the table to pull on the redhead's ear, rather viciously.

"Damn, Kitty, let me go," he said, moving slowly, so his ear would stay attached to his head.

"You say you're sorry. Now," she seethed, tugging harder still on his ear.

"I'm sorry, fuck, I'm so sorry," he said, almost crying.

She let his ear go then slapped him upside his head. Again, I just stood there, confused and terrified, and really wanting to get away. But I had a job, and that job consisted of me getting their drinks.

I watched as the blonde went back to muscles and tried to sit on his lap, but he looked at her and shook his head slightly, so she turned and sat in some other guy's lap, kissing his check while he grabbed her ass like they were about to have sex any moment. *Oh-ma-God, I can't be involved in some weird sex triangle or square or hexagon thing that these people clearly have going on. Just get their drink orders and leave.*

I took a deep breath and asked again, "Does anyone want a drink?"

"I'll have a beer," the guy to the left of me said.

I hadn't noticed him before. He had shoulder-length black hair that was pulled back in a low ponytail and the craziest blue eyes I'd ever seen. He was pale, even in the dark lit bar. I almost scooted away. I had a phobia of vampires, and he fit the bill.

"Okay, so one beer?" I asked again, raising my brows at everyone else who was staring at me.

"How about you just bring one for everyone," the blond guy said from across the table.

It's got to be illegal for such a good-looking group of people to be together.

"Got it," I said before shoving the pad of paper and pen back in the short black apron that held such things, along with straws. Before I turned to leave I caught muscles staring at me. Of all the places, he had to show up here at a bar that I just started working at, tonight. *Figures.*

I debated spitting in all their beers. Clearly, he had talked about me. The whole "fat ass" comment had me boiling. It was bad enough when it happened, but to know that he joked about it with his friends hurt pretty bad.

"Sandy!" I called to my fellow worker.

She stopped at the bar before heading out with an order of drinks. "What's up, newbie?" she said, laughing.

"You have to take that table back. I can't do it. Here's their beers," I said, moving the try on the bar in front of her.

"What do you mean?" she asked, scrunching her brow in concern.

"I just can't. I'll take any of your other tables but that one."

"Did something happen?"

"No, I just—it's one of those guys. He and I kind of—it doesn't matter. I just can't go over there. I'm afraid I might slap one of them, and I like this job and don't want to get fired on my first day for beating a customer."

"Say no more. I'll take care of it. Here, these go to

thirty-four," she said, pointing to her tray. "We'll switch."

"You have no idea how grateful I am. Thank you, Sandy," I said as she walked away with the tray full of beers for the good-looking asshole's table.

Chapter 6

Trent

Tonight was the first night we were playing live in almost three weeks. With Kane and Kitty getting married and moving across country to make an album, we hadn't had time to play live. The label set us up to play at the bar, Lucky's. They informed us all their musicians had played there, and it was good luck, so we jumped on it. It also helped that the bar was only a short drive from the house.

It felt good to be back up on stage—my black beautiful bass in my hands, the crowd cheering, and girls screaming and clawing at the stage. We were back in our element. Kane was killing it on vocals, JJ was ripping on the guitar, I had my bass, Reece was going crazy on the drums like he always did, and Aiden was keeping everything in order. We were one hell of a fine-oiled machine.

We were the first to perform that night, so when we were done, we all got a table and settled in for a night of drinking. Kitty sat herself down on my lap while Kane

shot her death glares, Reece was trying to pick up wom-
en, JJ had Piper next to him, and Aiden was eyeing up his
next catch. It was like we were right back at BJ's.

"Hey, guys! I'm Lexi, what can I get for you?"

I felt my eyes grow to the size of saucers. *This isn't
happening.* She couldn't be standing there asking for my
drink order. I wasn't supposed to see her again. She
looked different, good different. Her hair was sexy and
full of thick waves, she had a tight-ass tank-top on, her
tits were huge, and her cleavage had me shifting Kitty on
my lap. She had painted on jeans, and I knew the minute
she turned from the table I was going to lose it.

"Lexi?" I asked, still staring at her like some stupid
kid seeing a dirty magazine for the first time.

A whole conversation went on, but I was zoned out. I
couldn't stop looking at her. How did she go from someone I couldn't stand to someone I couldn't take my eyes
off of?

At one point Kitty got off my lap and, when she
came back, I shook my head no, I didn't want her to think
I had a raging hard on because of her. Kane would kill
me. More talking went on but, again, I didn't know what
the hell was said. Of course, I was right. When she
walked away, her ass looked amazing.

"Trent?" Kitty said, shoving my shoulder.

"What?" I said, snapping out of it and running my
hand over my head.

"I know your secret," she said, winking at me.

I flicked her off, shaking my head.

"Did you see her eyes?" Aiden said to the table. "I
found mine for the night. Calling it, boys," he said, turning his head and watching her at the bar.

"No," was all I said from across the table.

"What do you mean, no? She's not even your regular
flair, Trent. Look, there's a blonde over there, have at it,"

Aiden said, pointing to a girl at another table. I knew I couldn't let Aiden anywhere near Lexi. His slick, dark, brooding thing had women swooning and secretly praying he was a mysterious supernatural creature. But he wasn't. He was an asshole, just like the rest of us. A use-em-and-loose-em asshole.

If I had one mission for the night, it was to prove to Lexi that I wasn't the asshole I was on the plane.

"All right, I have a round of beers for the table," a slender, golden-haired woman said, approaching the table.

My eyes instantly searched the area for Lexi. I saw her over by another table, dropping drinks off.

"What happened to the other girl?" Aiden asked, taking his beer.

"She's working another table. It's her first night so we're trying to give her small tables."

Lies, all lies. She was avoiding me. I took my beer, chugged it, and got up from the table. I left my friends, sitting there talking, to find Lexi and clear the air.

I was pissed and tired on the plane, and now that I was rested and settled in, I knew that I could clear everything up with her.

She was standing near the back hallway. My guess was that it led out back or to an employee's lounge. She was facing down the hallway and didn't see me coming.

"Lexi," I called to her.

She spun around, a huge smile on her face and a phone in her hand. She was texting someone that was obviously making her happy. When she saw it was me, her smile fell from her face and her beautiful eyes squinted up at me. She put the phone back in her apron and crossed her arms under her large tits. *Fuck, why did she have to do that? Now they're bouncing in my face.*

"Can I help you?" she asked, popping her hip out.

I scratched the scruff on my face to hide the fact that I was dying inside. I needed to play it cool. "Can we talk?" I asked.

"Let me think about that…mmm…No."

Her Southern accent was stronger in her anger, and I couldn't help but chuckle.

"See? This is why I don't want to talk to you. You're laughing at me, you called me fat, you're laughing at the way I talk, and now your girlfriend over there is straight-up staring at me."

I turned and, sure enough, Kitty was staring at us, as if she was watching a TV show.

"Come on, give me a chance," I said, taking a step toward her.

She immediately took one back and bumped into the wall. "What are you doing? Give you a chance for what? You have a girlfriend, and I—"

"You have a boyfriend? The guy who picked you up at the airport?" I asked, cutting her off.

She pulled her brows together and shook her head. "You were watching me?"

"No—yes, I just wanted to clear things up, okay?" I said, getting tongue-tied.

"There's nothing to clear up. You're a jerk and I'm over it, like I said on the plane. I haven't thought about it since. Now, if you'll excuse me," she said, pushing past me.

I grabbed her wrist to keep her from leaving. *I shouldn't care, fuck why do I care?*

"What is your deal with grabbing my arm?"

I quickly let her go as she spoke, turning fully back to me and getting up in my face. I had forgotten how tall she was. Her honey silver eyes had black streaks that I hadn't noticed before. Her scent drifted under my nose, and I wanted to pull her even closer and inhale deeply so

I'd never forget it. She pushed on my chest with her hands, and I crashed into the wall behind me. My head hit an exposed pipe and a ringing echoed within it.

"Dammit, Zena, try to remember I'm only human. Fuck, that hurt," I said, rubbing the back of my head.

"Zena! Okay, this conversation is done. Go back to your ogling, blonde girlfriend over there and leave me alone," she said, eyeing me up and down with a disgusted look on her face.

"Wait," I said frantically trying to call her back. *Why am I so bad at this?* "She's not my girlfriend," I said in a rush, thankful that it had stopped her.

She stared at me, her hands on her hips. I was there to explain to her that I wasn't an ass, but fuck, the only thing I could think of was holding onto her hips again and having her pinned beneath me. It all hit me in that one moment of speech. I blurted out that Kitty wasn't my girlfriend because, dammit, I wanted her to know that I was available.

She stood there and then crossed her arms again under her chest. Involuntarily, I licked my lips, and fuck if she didn't catch on to why.

"Are you kidding me?" she hollered, uncrossing her arms and grabbing a try from the table behind her covering her chest with it. "You're a pig! I have no clue what you're trying to prove to me."

"Trust me. Right now, I don't know either," I said, hanging my head in defeat and covering my face with my hands.

Never had I been so blatantly rude to a woman in my life. My game was simple—be the nice guy that protects his woman. It had never failed me before, or at least before her, it hadn't failed me.

"Well, why don't you just stop and go back over to your friends and 'not girlfriend' who is still staring at us, by the way, and I'll go back to work," she said with a fake smile.

Just then her phone went off. She pulled it out from her apron, reading something that made her smile. A wave of jealousy went through me like I'd never felt before. *I shouldn't care. Why do I care?*

"Is that your boyfriend? Let me guess, his name's Hercules?" I asked, not able to keep it in or keep the sarcasm out.

She looked up from her phone, a snarky expression on her face, which quickly changed to something else, something devious. "What's it matter to you?"

"Nothing, it doesn't matter at all," I said, trying to save my ass.

She scrunched her eyes up at me. Out of nowhere, she started laughing—like, genuinely laughing. Her face lit up, her eyes sparkled, and I noticed for the first time that she had one dimple on her left cheek. It became more predominate the harder she laughed. It was sexy, endearing, and, fuck, I wanted to take her in my arms and make her smile like that for the rest of her life—*Wait a minute. What am I saying? She's not my type. Fuck I'm messed up.*

"I—can't—believe—" she said, laughing out every other word. "You like me." She tossed her head back. "Oh 'you're not my type,'" she said in a deep voice, trying to imitate me.

"Will you quiet down, people are staring."

"Oh, God forbid, they see you talking to someone who actually eats. What will the world think?" she said dramatically.

"All right, I've had enough of this," I said, taking her hand in mine and dragging her behind me down the hall and out of view of everyone.

"What are you doing, creep? Get off of me. Oh-ma-

God, please don't kidnap me and cut me up into a million pieces. I want to live. There's still so much I want to do. I can't die."

She was babbling behind me but not really struggling to get free. I pushed through a door, which led to the back of the building. I let her hand go and she withered up against the brick wall of the bar. She looked terrified, and I hated that. I hated that I had that effect on her. It was only making me more pissed off. I stood before her, our faces only inches apart.

"How do I always find the crazy ones?" she said, hanging her head. "If you're going to hurt me, just don't hit my face, I want to look half way decent in my casket."

Is she kidding me right now? "What do you think I'm going to do to you?" I asked, searching her face and cursing myself for doing so. She had perfect skin and full lips that were glistening because she kept sneaking her tongue out and licking them.

"I don't know, but the last time a guy did this it didn't end well, so excuse me if I'm on the defense," she said, looking me dead in the eyes.

"Did someone hurt you?" *How could someone hurt her? Okay, I guess I could see why someone might be annoyed at her. It takes someone very special to deal with scatter-brainedness and a loud mouth.*

"What are you? The knight in shining armor that's going to protect me from all the bad guys and make the ones that hurt me pay for what they've done?" she said, chuckling to herself.

That's when I saw it. The dimple on her left cheek came out as she smiled up at me.

"I could be," I said before it registered in my brain that I had actually said it.

Her smile got wider and the dimple deeper. *I'm done, Kitty was right. Damn, I hate it when she's right.*

Chapter 7

Lexi

F ive minutes before, I thought that muscles was going to drag me outside and have his way with me.

"How do I always find the crazy ones?" I said,
knowing what was going to come next. "If you're going
to hurt me, just don't hit my face. I want to look half way
decent in my casket."

I say things that can be rather inappropriate some-
times. That's why I steer clear of men like the one before
me. They feel entitled and I will not be played a fool
again.

"What do you think I'm going to do to you?" he
asked, searching my face.

"I don't know, but the last time a guy did this, it
didn't end well, so excuse me if I'm on the defense."

"Did someone hurt you?" he asked, instantly going
on the defense for me.

"What are you? The knight in shining armor that's
going to protect me from all the bad guys and make the

ones who hurt me pay for what they've done?" I said, chuckling to myself.

"I could be," he said, in all seriousness.

I couldn't help it. I smiled up at him. The whole situation had gone from, oh-ma-God this can't be happening again to did he really just say that?

"Why are you laughing?" he asked, clearly upset that I wasn't giving into the charm and—

This would be so much easier if he was ugly. He stood his ground in front of me, crossing his arms over his chest. He didn't take his eyes off of mine. It was as if he was looking at me differently, and I didn't like it, not one bit!

I narrowed my gaze and pushed his crossed arms with both my hands. The action made him step back, but his eyes were still tight on mine.

"Oh, 'I could be,'" I said in a deep voice, trying to mimic the way he said it. "Are you kidding me with that shit? I thought I wasn't your type?" I asked, cocking my head and making sure I had my Southern, pissed-off-bitch face on.

"Maybe I was wrong," he said, not backing down and clearly not intimidated by my pissed-off-bitch face.

"Honey, that's sweet and all, but I'd rather crawl into the sewer and live out the rest of my days, than be your type."

Surely, this is going to get him to back off and make him leave me alone. Fuck, what is he doing?

He took the space between us aggressively, pinning me back on the brick wall and between his large strong hands. Without even thinking, I closed my eyes, scrunched my face, and turned it to the side. His lips were at my ear. I could feel his breath swirling around.

"What did he do to you?" He was almost inaudible, but I had heard him. I opened my eyes and glanced up at him. No one had ever asked me that, not even the people who knew me. *How had he figured me out in a five-hour plane ride and a fifteen-minute conversation?* I started arguing with myself. *No one's ever asked you that before, because you've never told them or given any reason to make them question it. Yet, here you are, laying it all out there.*

"Listen, muscles," I said, putting on my mask. I didn't want anyone to know that I could be hurt or that I had been hurt. I was strong and resilient. Call it a Southern thing, call it the female sprit, but I would not show my cards, not even to the sexy pile of muscles in front of me. "Nobody did anything to me." *Liar.* "I just want to get back to work. We both know that this whole thing that's going on right now is just happening because you feel guilty for calling me fat. It means nothing else."

"Right," he said, licking his bottom lip while simultaneously making my heart palpitate. "Because you have a boyfriend."

"Yes," I said quickly, making my eyes huge and loving the lie. *I can run with that!* "Yes, I do. And he would not be happy right now. So I should get back to work." I squatted down and ducked under his arm to get away. "It was nice meeting you, muscles, but it will be even nicer to never see you again," I said, smiling back at him.

"Trent," he said, pushing back from the wall and leaning up against it instead.

"Huh?" I was just outside the door, one foot in when I heard him. I peeked my head back out and raised a brow at him.

"Trent, my name."

"I like muscles better," I said, shrugging my shoulders.

"My name is Trent, and you're a real pain in the ass."

"And you're an arrogant jackass, who thinks the sun raises and sets to your every whim. Ga'nite, muscles," I said, pulling my accent and feeling proud of myself for keeping my head on straight and not falling for his tricks.

As I came around the corner I ran into two women. Both women were blonde and dressed to impress. "Sorry," I said, trying to side step them.

"Did you happen to see a guy over here?" one asked.

"Yeah, really tall, huge muscles, shaved head, and dripping with sexual appeal?" the other one continued.

"I'd stay away from that one, ladies. He's a bonafide jackass." Sometimes I didn't understand the female race. *He's just a man. What is so special about him, that he has women tracking him down?*

The women looked at each other before turning back to me and laughing.

"Do you even know who he is?" one asked.

"I told you, a jackass, a jackass named Trent...I think," I said, rolling my eyes.

They laughed again, giggling into each other's shoulders.

"That jackass that you're referring to, he just killed it up on stage. His band is going to be the next big thing," the other woman added.

"Trust me, he wasn't. He just walked in here," I said, not believing them.

Just then, and as if on cue, muscles walked up behind me. He snaked an arm around my shoulder, making me jump from the sudden closeness of someone touching me.

"What the hell?" I yelled, after catching my breath.

"Hello, ladies," he said, all smooth in his husky voice.

Both women put on their sexy pouty faces, fluffed their hair, and pushed their boobs out. I shook my head at the display of pure desperation to get his attention.

"Hi, Trent," one said.

I turned to look up at him as he smiled down at me then at the women in front of us.

"These nice ladies seem to think that you're some sort of rock star. Don't worry, I cleared it all up and let them know the truth," I said, feeling pleased with my comeback. Besides, there was no way that he was anything more.

"Zena, that's sweet of you," he said, smiling down at me.

What an ass!

"But these ladies are right. I was just on stage and I did kill it."

I felt my jaw go slack. I stared up at him then quickly glanced across the bar at the rest of his table. *Fuck! It was them. I really need to work on being more observant.*

One of the girls took a half step toward Trent. "You were great up there, all of you were."

He raised his brows and smiled at the two women as they made his head get even bigger.

"Yeah, I totally couldn't take my eyes off of you, you were—"

"All right, all right," I said, cutting them off and holding my hands up. Any more compliments and his head wasn't going to fit through the freaking door. "I think he gets the picture."

"Well, do you think we could join you, at your table?" one asked, winking up at him.

Disgusting! Oh, I can't wait to hear his response. I rotated toward him, crossing my arms. Mister I'm-not-a-jackass, you-got-me-all-wrong smiled down at me as he spoke, and not once did he look over at the desperate bimbos.

"I'm sorry, ladies, not tonight. I'm waiting for a very special, very beautiful woman named Lexi. She was hurt by someone, and I know that I'm the only one who can make it better. What can I say? Bitch stole my heart, and now I have to make her see that I'm not a jackass, but actually the complete opposite." Once he finished, he gave me a wink and turned to the two women, who were swooning up at him in their six-inch heels.

"That is the sweetest thing in the whole world," one of the girls said, pulling her hands up under her chin.

"It is, isn't it? You see, this woman Lexi is somewhat of a mystery to me. I've only met her two times, but both times she had me rethinking things—my values, the women I keep in my life and my future in general. Deep down, I know that she has to feel the same way. Living the kind of life I live, it can get lonely and sometimes you just want that one special person to be by your side," he said, scratching the sexy scruff on his face.

The two women were drooling so much I was afraid I'd have to mop the freaking floor.

I rolled my eyes at his little speech. I knew he wanted me to know that he was a nice guy, but, come on, that whole speech was a bit over the top. He had laid it on thick with those women, and turned to me, probably hoping that it had worked on me too. *Not happening.*

"Well, that was enough bullshit to last me for the evening. If you'll excuse me," I said, trying to get away. Just as I was going to walk off, my phone rang from inside my apron. I pulled it out and smiled. It was Ben calling. I stopped and turned in the opposite direction I was going. I needed to get farther down the hall so I could hear him over the music. I stopped at the end of the hall and answered the phone. "Hey!" I said.

"Hey there, sexy!"

"Not funny, Ben. Listen, I don't know if I can work here," I said, leaning up against the wall.

I rotated back to the bar and nearly had a heart attack! Muscles was standing next to me again. I punched his arm and scrunched my face up. I held my hand over the receiver to yell at him. "What is your deal?"

"Is that him, is that your boyfriend?" he asked, blatantly disregarding my question.

"What—" Then it hit me. "Yes, yes, it is," I said, realizing that this was the way I was going to deal with the mound of muscles. "Scoot along," I said, swooshing my hand.

But as I did, he grabbed it. Taking my fingers between his, he brought my hand to his lips and left a delicate kiss upon the top of my knuckles, before letting go and leaving me there alone.

"Lexi! Lexi!" I heard my name coming from the phone that was now off my ear and in front of my chest because I was in shock and staring at the sexiest "man ass" that I'd ever laid eyes on.

૯જ૯જ

"So he's what—stalking you? Should I call the cops?" Ben asked, seeming just as confused as I was.

When I came home from my first night of working, I was two hundred dollars richer and a thousand times more baffled. "I don't know, Ben. You deal with these types of people more than me. Should I be terrified that some want-to-be rock star is following me and trying to prove he's a good guy?" I asked.

"Well, I don't think he's following you. He's contracted under Recycling Studios, which means he's slated to play at Lucky's, all their musicians do, so it's not weird that he was there. Now, it is weird that he thought I was your boyfriend. How did he come to that conclusion?" my brother asked, sitting down at the small table with a cup of tea for himself and really strong black coffee for me.

"I might have led on that you were my boyfriend," I said, cringing inwardly across the table.

"You *what*? Lexi, are you insane? That's low, even for you."

"Oh, whatever. It made him back off," I said, taking a sip of coffee.

"Yeah, and what's going to happen if he sees us together? I do not love you enough to pretend I'm your boyfriend," he said, holding his hand up dramatically and shaking his head.

The reason why no one thought my brother was anything but straight in our hometown was simply because he didn't act like it, but clearly Cali was influencing him.

"Well, that's not going to happen," I said boldly before sipping my coffee.

Chapter 8

Trent

I was right, wasn't I?" Kitty said, plopping down next to me instead of on me for a change.

I glanced over at her, and shook my head.

"I knew it! So what did she say? I saw that she beat you—a woman after my own heart. I think I'm going to like her," Kitty said, smiling.

"Well, she said I was a jackass, she said she'd rather live in a sewer than be my type…let's see, what else. Oh, she thinks we're dating, and she has a boyfriend," I explained, slumping in my chair and drinking my beer.

"Humph," was all she said back.

"Maybe this is a mistake. She really is a pain in the ass. Plus, I don't have time to chase tail around, with the album and—"

"You're giving up already?" Kitty asked, scooting her chair closer.

"Why do you care so much?" I asked.

"Because I care about you, I care about all of you.

Trent, I knew you weren't like the rest of these animals the moment I met you. You're sweet. Now, you're also a little scary, but I know it's just a front you put on. You helped me win the love of my life, and I won't do anything less to help you get yours."

"Love of my life? Kitty, are you hearing yourself? I don't even know her."

"So get to know her, show her what I see every time I hang out with you. Minus the estranged women—you got to cut that shit out."

I spent the rest of the night watching Lexi walk from table to table, delivering drinks and food. I had to come up with a game plan—a foolproof plan to show her the real me. My planning continued at home. I couldn't come up with anything while I watched her walking around the bar and bending over to hand people their drinks. I sat at the huge dining room table. I tried to convince myself I was crazy—or, who knew?—maybe I was falling for someone I'd just met.

"Trent, what are you still doing awake?" Kane asked, walking into the kitchen to grab a bottle of water from the fridge.

"Could ask you the same."

"You could, but then I'd have to tell you about all the amazing sex I was just having with my wife. Need to rehydrate, if you know what I mean," he said, sitting down at the table across from me.

"You're a sick fuck."

"You're just jealous. Could have been you, though. Those two girls were all over you. What happened with them?" he asked.

"I can't do that shit anymore."

"You can't have sex with hot women? What's the matter, your dick broke?" he asked, chuckling.

"No."

"Then what's the problem. The only time I couldn't get it up was when I realized I was—Holy fuck, you're in love? With who? You better not fucking say my wife," he yelled, pointing across the table at me.

"Calm your ass down. I'm not in love with Kitty or anyone. I just—this girl is fucking with my head, and I can't get her out of it."

"Who's the lucky lady, because she is lucky. Dude, you're the gentleman of the group. Women love that shit."

"You remember our waitress tonight?"

"Yeah, the blonde, she was cute—"

"No, not her. The first one, her name was Lexi." My body warmed—well, a particular part of my body warmed when I said her name out loud.

"The tall brunette with the fat ass?" he asked, scrunching his brows. I nodded my response. He frowned. "She's not your type, bro, why her?"

"I don't fucking know. I sat next to her on the plane ride over here. I never thought I was going to see her again. Honestly, she's a pain in the ass. Every time I went to touch her, she pulled back, and she let it slip that she'd been fucked over, in not so many words, and when I heard that, I just snapped. How someone could hurt her so much to actually make her think that I would hit her? Dude, all I saw was red when she said that. I wanted to protect her, keep her safe."

"Trent, that's who you are, that's who you've always been. You always stick up for people who can't do it themselves."

I couldn't deny that. I had a brother Sam, who had special needs, and even though I was younger than him, I stood up for him and people like him and anyone who couldn't defend themselves against bullies, for that matter. I guess that was how I got my tough guy badges.

Even after Sam passed away, I was still that guy to everyone.

"So, what's your advice? Hell if I'm going to ask Reece or Aiden for advice, and JJ is so far up Piper's ass, I haven't even seen him. So you're the only one left."

"I don't fucking know what you should do. What, just because I'm married, I should know all this bullshit now? What am I, some love guru?" he asked, sitting back in his chair.

"No, clearly not—Fuck!" I yelled, standing from my chair and hitting my fist against my chest.

"Dude, calm down," Kane said, standing along with me.

"You don't understand, Kane. I can't get her out of my head!" I was losing it and taking it out on Kane. "I haven't been able to get her out of my head since I met her. On the plane she was annoying and frustrating, but there were moments, moments when I looked at her and I thought she could be *my* Kitty. But the moment would quickly pass, and she'd be a bitch again. Then tonight I wanted to just take her in my arms and kiss her, like I know she's never been kissed before. Then I remember that she has a boyfriend, one who is nothing like me—it's all fucking with my head." I was pacing the room and trying really hard not to punch a hole through the wall.

"Well, fucking win her over, dude. Stop sulking and let her know what's up."

"So you don't think I'm crazy?" I asked, stopping my pacing to look over at my friend.

"You're talking to the man who fell in love in six hours. You're totally sane," he said, grabbing his bottle of water from the table. "Now, if you'll excuse me, I have some things I need to do, all this love talk is...well, I'll see ya in the morning, bro," Kane said, before running up the stairs two at a time.

Lexi was going to see the real me, the nice guy underneath the tough guy façade. I went to bed that night, knowing that when I woke up there was only going to be one thing on my mind—making Lexi see me for who I truly was.

Deep down, I wanted to find someone. I wanted a love like my parents had. I wanted to give my everything to one woman for the rest of my life, and, if that one woman happened to be Lexi, then I was going to do everything I could to see it through.

ფოფ

I was grabbing my keys and phone when Reece came around the corner. He stopped and stared at me. His red Mohawk was combed back and slicked down with gel.

"Where you goin'?" he asked, cocking his head.

"Nowhere," I responded, shoving my phone into my pocket.

"Great, then you won't mind if I tag along," he said, wiggling his eyebrows.

"Where we going?" Aiden asked, coming up behind Reece.

"We're going nowhere," Reece answered him. "Want to come?"

"No one's going anywhere," I said, as my frustration grew. I loved the guys like brothers, but, just like brothers, they had a tendency to get on my fucking nerves.

"What's everyone doing?" JJ asked, entering the room with Piper under his arm.

"We're going nowhere with Trent. You in?" Reece asked.

I tossed my hands up in the air. "Anyone else want to come?" I asked dramatically.

"Where we going?" Kitty asked, walking into the

room, looking a little confused, with Kane right behind her.

"We're going nowhere, Kitty, doesn't that sound exciting?" JJ said, bumping into her shoulder.

"Fuck, I hope we're going to a kink club. Please tell me we're going to a kink club," Reece said, folding his hands under his chin and praying up to the ceiling.

"Sorry, Reece, no kink clubs. You'll have to go there on your own. I'm just going to Lucky's to get a drink, that's it. You all can stay here," I said, walking toward the door.

"Hold up," Kane said, running up behind me. "You doing what I think you're doing?" he asked quietly so no one else could hear.

"I'm trying to."

"Dude, you're going to need back-up. Take a look around. You're not going to find better back up than this lot right here. Well, except Reece, he might ruin it for you, but the rest of us got your back."

"Fine! I'm leaving now so grab your shit and let's go," I said, turning to everyone before I walked out and headed toward my rental truck.

As we entered Lucky's, a wave of anxiousness and nervousness came over me. It was the same kind of nerves I got before we played to a huge audience. There was another band playing, and the place was just as packed as it was the night before when we played. We found a large table for all of us to sit at and, as soon as my ass hit the chair, I started scanning the room. I was looking for a tall brunette with a body I was dying to explore. I'd never been with a woman like Lexi, and I had a feeling that, once I was, I wasn't going to want anything else. I spotted her over by the bar. She must have seen me the moment I saw her because she rolled her eyes and stalked off toward the back.

"Looks like you got some work to do there, bro," Kane said, nudging my arm on the table.

I smiled back at him, nodding in agreement. Our waitress came over and asked for our orders. Kane turned to me and winked then looked back at the waitress.

That look. I knew he was up to something.

"What can I get for everyone?" she asked, glancing around the table, and lingering on Kane a little bit too long for Kitty's liking.

"Beers for everyone," Kitty said roughly, making the cute waitress take her eyes off of Kane and onto her.

"Sure thing," she said, smiling.

"One more thing," Kane said, making her pause. "I'm sure you're great, but we really want to have Lexi as our waitress. We're all old friends," he said, flashing a charming smile.

"Um, sure. I'll let her know."

"Thanks, doll." Kane winked at her and I swear if Kitty's looks could kill, that girl would be dead. But Kitty knew the real reason why he did it—for me. So she kept quiet.

While we waited for our drinks, I was pulled away from the conversation at the table when I heard Lexi's distinct Southern accent from across the room. I watched as she argued with our waitress. She must have lost, because the next thing I saw was her carrying over a tray full of beers.

She stood between Kane and me as she slid the tray onto our table and handed everyone a beer, everyone but me. She left mine on the tray as she picked it back up.

"I don't get one?" I asked, sitting back in my chair so I could look up at her. *Damn, she's hot.* She looked just as she did the night before, except she had a different shirt on. Her honey silver eyes tightened as she stared down at me.

"No," she said, taking my beer and drinking it.

I couldn't help but smile up at her. She was such a pain in the ass, and I might be making the biggest mistake of my life, but I realized that I was willing to. I was done pretending to be someone I knew deep down that I wasn't, and if this sassy-ass woman was it for me, then I had to take the chance. No other woman had ever made such an impression on me before. I'd never wanted to try with anyone else but, for some reason, I wanted to try with the one woman who couldn't stand to be in the same room with me. I had my work cut out.

I watched as Lexi took the bottle from her lips. She licked them and then took one more swig before placing it down in front of me.

I smiled up at her. "Thank you."

"Asshole."

Aww, fuck, the dimple! She smiled so big that it made an appearance. She left me sitting there staring at her ass as she walked away.

"Dude, she hates you," Aiden said, shaking his head. "Why are you even wasting your time?"

I took the beer in my hand, lifting it to see that she had left me one sip. I swigged it back with butterflies in my stomach. I was the tough, take-no-bullshit kind of guy, and I had fucking butterflies because of a woman. I stood from the table, not answering Aiden, and went in search of Lexi.

Chapter 9

Lexi

Y ou forget my drink again?" some lady said as I walked by.

"I'm so sorry. I'm going to get it right now."

I was drowning. I was forgetting things left and right, the bartenders were getting mad at me because I kept telling them the wrong drinks, and the customers weren't so nice the second time around. *This is why I didn't want to be a waitress!*

"You doing okay?" Sandy asked, walking up next to me.

"Doing okay? I'm surprised I haven't been fired yet," I said, making my accent stronger.

"It's fine. Calm down. You'd have to be really, really bad to get fired. I don't think Vick has ever fired anyone," she said, trying to make me feel better.

Just when I was starting to, I looked across the room and, dammit, if my eyes didn't fall right on the heap of muscles that was casually sitting back and staring at me. I rolled my eyes and threw my hands in the air. "I'm getting fired tonight, if not for bad service, then for murder."

"What?" Sandy questioned then followed my gaze. "Oh, you're stalker's back."

"I can see that, thanks."

"If you ask me, I'd let that stalk me all it wants. You realize he's going to be famous, his band is really good. Look around, everyone is waiting for them to play, and they're not even playing tonight. If you ask me, they're going to be bigger than 4Alliance," she said, eyeing the table up like the rest of the women around us.

Of course, I knew about 4Alliance. You'd have to be living under a rock not to. To think that someone slated to be better than the most popular band out there right now was stalking me—*Okay, I guess it's kind of exciting.*

"He's not stalking me. He feels bad for calling me fat, and he's trying to be nice. I'm not buying it. Look at him—all tough and brooding. Trust me, I've been there and done that. It's not worth all the hype," I said, shrugging my shoulders and turning away from the so-called rock star.

Somehow, I got suckered into delivering drinks to their table. Feeling triumphant over drinking all his beer and calling him an asshole in front of his friends, I was really looking forward to the extra ten minute break I earned for taking their table from the other waitress. So maybe I wasn't suckered, but an extra ten minutes added to mine, meant I got twenty minutes of peace and quiet.

On my way to the back of the building, I grabbed a beer from the bar and headed outside. There were a couple of benches that seemed to be calling my name. I wasn't use to running around for hours. *And here I thought I was in shape.* My legs were sore and my arms were tired from carrying trays. I was exhausted, and it was only my second night.

I was stretched out on the bench, my head resting on the seat, my legs lapping over the armrest. I was a second away from catching a speed nap when the back door swung open. I assumed it was a co-worker taking a smoke break so I kept laying there with my eyes closed and my arm over my forehead.

I didn't want to be thinking about it but, damn the mound of muscles looked good tonight. I smiled to myself as I thought back to him grinning up at me while I drank his beer. He did have a great smile, but I, of all people, knew that you could hide a lot behind a smile.

"You have to stop doing that," a deep voice over top of me said.

I moved my arm and opened my eyes. It took me a second to focus, but once I did all those happy thoughts of muscles quickly vanished.

"You're seriously desperate and a bit disturbed," I said, still lying on the bench. I wasn't going to waste my now fifteen minutes on arguing with Mr. Asshole. "For the record, I'm not doing anything. You came out here, I didn't ask you."

"But you are. You're screwing with me," he said, still standing over me.

"Oh, why me?" I moaned, sitting up too fast on the bench. The rush of blood to my head had me spinning so I gripped the side rail. His hand went to my cheek as my head spun, or did my head spin because his hand was on my cheek? *That's not important right now.*

He was standing over me, a look of concern on his face. His hand still on my cheek his fingers wrapped around the back of my neck and, with an ease I didn't know was possible, I rose to my feet as he gently pulled me up toward him. I stared up at him, not able to look away, even though I knew better. *I shouldn't be so frozen under his touch.* I had been frozen by a man's touch before and thought it was what I wanted, needed. I was wrong about that, which meant I was probably wrong about this too.

"What are you doing?" I asked, all breathily. My eyes went to his lips, lips that were wet from his tongue licking them the moment before.

"Lexi, I—"

The way he said my name, made the hairs on my arm stand on end. It was with that chill I was then able to jump back into my body. I took a step away from him. His hand fell from my face and lingered in the air between us before he reeled it in.

"I have to get back to work," I said, tucking my hair behind my ear. I bent down and grabbed my beer bottle.

"I like you," Muscles said from above me.

I rose slowly, with my not even sipped beer in hand. *I don't need this right now in my life.* I was here to build a career not date. I only had a year to make it work out here before I was headed back to my hometown, to a mundane accountant job.

But, hell, it felt good to hear someone say they liked me. I was still a girl, after all, and what did all girls want? To be swept off their feet by handsome men, and muscles sure did fit the bill for a handsome man, trust me. Unfortunately for him, I wasn't so easily swayed. Now, I might have momentarily had a lapse in judgment, but I was back.

"What do you like, muscles, my fat ass or my sunny disposition?" I asked confidently.

"Honestly—both." When he said it, his eyes got all seductive and sexy. "Cat got your tongue?" he asked cockily.

"No, not at all. You're just wasting your time," I said, shrugging it off.

"I don't think I am."

"Bless your heart, you actually think I would… what?…date you?" I asked, chuckling.

"Oh, I think you're going to do more than date me." He placed his hands on his hips. I followed the motion and, before I could stop my stupid eyes, they were pursuing his crotch again like they did on the plane. "Eyes up here, beautiful," he said, tilting his head down.

I set a fiery gaze on him and, for all that's holy, I clenched my fists and bit the inside of my cheek so I wouldn't murder him. "First off, you can go ahead and get whatever image you have in your tiny little brain out! I did not fly across country to work on my dating skills. I'm here to find a job, not date you or anyone—geez men are such pigs. I can't stand any of you. You're all either jackasses, perverts, abusive jerks, or plain old crazy! Maybe I should have—"

"Wait, wait, wait—" he said, cutting my rant off and holding his hands up. "You need to rewind to you're not here to date and abusive jerks."

"Yeah, I'm not and most of you are jerks," I said.

"What happened to your boyfriend? Last night you said you had a boyfriend," he challenged me.

Fuck! God I'm horrible at lying. "I do—I did—I broke up with him last night," I said, crossing my arms and trying like hell to look convincing.

"So you're single now?" he asked, raising a brow in confusion.

"Yes, single and staying single," I clarified.

"We'll see about that," he said, as his lips curled up on one side.

My eyes widened and I stomped my foot down. "I'm serious,"

"Okay, you keep telling yourself that, but I think you wanted to kiss me a few seconds ago."

"Oh, you are so full of yourself! If I wanted to kiss you, I'd just fucking kiss you."

"Really?"

"Yeah, really." I took a dominate step toward him. He didn't scare me. I knew how to handle men like him, I'd done it before. I wasn't frail or wimpy, and I sure as hell wasn't going to back down to him or his wet, plum lips, which were strangely getting closer and closer…

"What do you want now?" he asked huskily.

What do I want now? I want…I want…

I felt his hand rest upon my hip and his fingers tease the skin where my shirt and jeans met.

"Fuck you," I said, before slamming my lips against his.

The beer in my hand slipped away, shattering into pieces at our feet. I was mad as hell at him for challenging me like that. How could a woman do anything but kiss him? *Shit, this isn't good—shit, this is good!* I grabbed the back of his neck, my fingers pressing into the prickly shaved scalp.

I wanted to feel more of it, so I spread my hand up the back of his head. I reveled in the way the tiny hairs tickled the inside of my hand and the way his strong arms wrapped around my body as if I was tiniest of things. The heat coming from his core made little beads of sweat form on my brow.

That kiss wasn't pretty or dainty. It was a reflection of us, rough and wild. I'd never been kissed like that before. As my head fell back, his hand got tangled in my long hair. I felt him tug at the ends—not on purpose, I'm sure—but that was when my past crashed into the present. It went from an awesome kiss to the brutal memory of a man who got pleasure out of my pain.

Pulling back, I placed a hand over his warm chest to hold him at bay. His heart was pounding just as fast as mine was. His hands still on my waist, I took a step back, thinking that he would release me, but if I knew anything about muscles it was that he had a thing for holding onto me. It was then I gained the strength to talk.

"I can't do this with you," I said, trying to make even myself believe it. My head might have been telling me to pull back, but my body, my heart, they were all screaming something completely different.

"I think you can," he said smiling down at me and nodding to my hand, that for some reason was still caressing his warm, strong, and hard-as-a-rock chest.

"Whatever," I said, taking my hand from him and shoving it into the back pocket of my jeans.

"Will you look at me?" he asked.

I followed his request and locked eyes with him. "I'm looking, now what?"

This was all insane—him, me—it was crazy. I wasn't some piece of ass for him to conquer. Yet I let myself turn to mush in a moment of weakness. I was more furious with myself than at him.

"Don't stop, don't stop looking," he said through a half grin.

"Listen, muscles, this is cute, and I'm sure some girls would be flattered to have you stalking them but I'm not some girl."

"So you didn't feel anything when you kissed me?" he asked.

"No…" I said, for the second time tonight sounding like I was trying to convince myself.

"I don't believe you, because I did feel something, Lexi, I felt something that I've never felt with anyone else."

"Oh, you mean, your comparing me to your blonde bimbo type. Of course you 'felt' something different. It's called curves. I'm happy for you. It's good to see men come to the realization that there's more to life than blonde hair, a size zero waist, and big boobs."

"Why do you do that? Go on the defense like this? Yeah, it's true you weren't my type, but—Shit! I can't believe I'm saying this—I like the way you make me feel. I like that I have to work for it. It just feels right when I'm near you."

"Wow. That is so sad."

"See, you're doing it again. I just told you something personal, and you're twisting it around."

"What do you want me to say? 'Oh, my prince has come to rescue me from being a bar maiden?' I don't even know you! You could be a serial killer for all I know."

"Now, that's sad. You know who I am. You wouldn't have kissed me otherwise," he said challengingly.

And there it was. I had nothing smart to say to that. He was right. "How are you so sure about me?" I asked, getting serious for a second.

"I'm not. I'm not sure about anything except how you make me feel."

"And how exactly do I make you feel? Because, a week ago, you were treating me like I was scum on your boots. What changed?"

"Lexi, you make me smile. You get on my nerves, but I like it. I like that you get under my skin and challenge me. So you're not what I usually go for. Maybe that's been my problem all along."

I wanted to believe him but my life wasn't some romantic comedy. The back door swung opened, jostling us back into the real world.

"Lexi, twenty minutes is up. We need you back in here," one of the girls said, popping her head out the door.

"All right, I'll be right there."

"Trent, right?" she asked, pointing to him.

"Yeah…" he said, looking around me.

"There are some girls in here asking all over the bar for you," she said, smiling, before letting the door close.

Chapter 10

Trent

I had her. I had her right where I wanted her. She was listening to me, and I knew that she felt the same things that I was feeling. Whatever it was, it was still a mystery, but I felt it. I fucking had her until that woman had to butt her head in. The taste of her lips still lingered on mine, and I wanted nothing more than to taste them again. As the door slammed closed, Lexi turned back to me and smiled. She didn't say anything as she headed toward the door. I was desperate. I always seemed desperate to make her stay, to keep her from walking away, and just like all the times before, I found myself reaching for her.

"You don't have anything else to say to me?" I asked, stopping her and pulling her toward me.

She looked down at my hand that was wrapped around her wrist then scrunched her brows together before she spoke. "Well...A birdie told me that you like it when a girl plays hard to get. I expect nothing less than a perfect romantic wooing from the self-proclaimed bad-boy-turned-knight-in-shining-armor. So you better bring you're 'A' game if you want to date me. Take notes. I like pink and white flowers, chocolates. I have a serious addiction to tacos and hot mocha coffee. I love all furry animals. I do not like salads, so if you take me out, make sure you have money to pay for a steak dinner and dessert. I'm all about action movies, anything that might make me cry I stay away from, and I only watch scary movies at home, under a blanket. My favorite color is blue, I'm allergic to shell fish, and I don't get dressed up. This is me dressed up," she said, moving her hands down her body.

She smiled up at me. The dimple on her left cheek was present, and I knew that I stood a chance. She was giving me a chance.

"Anything else?" I asked through a grin.

"Definitely, but I don't have all night to stand out her here and tell you. I'm not like other girls, or so I've been told. I will not put up with bullshit and, if I even smell a hint of it, I'm done," she said, pointing at my chest.

"Are you trying to scare me away, because it's having the complete opposite effect?"

"Think whatever you want, muscles, I have to get back to work."

And, with that, she left me standing by myself. I couldn't wipe the stupid grin off my face even if I wanted to. I was going to make Lexi mine, and if I had my way, it was going to be forever.

When you know, you know. That was what my mom always told me. I didn't believe her until I met Lexi. All the other women I'd been with were nothing more than a lay. A way to keep up appearances with the guys. Don't get me wrong. I'm a man, I enjoyed the company of a beautiful woman, but I didn't want to have to see her every day and tell her where I was or what I was doing. In the small town that I grew up in, people just settled for what was next to them. Countless friends from high school were in loveless marriages, on their way to divorce or sticking it out for the kids.

I wanted more than that. I'd never admitted that to any of my friends—well, except Kitty—but my family knew me, and they knew what I was searching for. I sure as hell didn't expect it to plop down next to me on a plane ride across country, but it did and here I was standing next to a dumpster with a shit-eating grin on my face because I had found the woman of my dreams.

෧৩෧

My first night of 'wooing' as Lexi called it wasn't really what I was expecting. As soon as I got back to the table the night before, I wrote down all the things she had told me. I didn't want to forget anything. Lexi was leaning against the bar, waiting for an order when I walked in. She wasn't facing me so I got the pleasure of eyeing up her gorgeous ass as I made my way to her. I had one single pink flower in my hand. Don't ask me what kind it was, I had no fucking clue. It looked good at the flower shop, so I picked it up. I stood behind her, holding the stem of the flower. I let the petals caress her cheek.

"Holy fuck there's bugs in here, get it off, get it off!" she screamed as she smacked at her face, breaking the petals from the stem. When she realized it was a flower and not a bug, she turned around to see me standing behind her with a stem and two petals of what I thought was a really nice flower before she mutilated it. Her face scrunched up in embarrassment when she realized what she'd done. Her hands covered her mouth and the sweetest sound broke out from her. Her laughter was music to me, and I knew that behind her hand that damn sexy dimple was on her face.

"Jesus, muscles, what are you trying to do, give me heart attack?" she asked, removing her hand.

Sure enough the dimple was out. I felt my dick twitch and a grin curve my lips. "Not at all, I'd rather have your heart beating than under attack."

She eyed me up for a second then snatched the stem and two petals from my hand. "Well, that's encouraging," she said before turning back to the bar.

"That's it?" I asked, confused.

She looked at me from over her shoulder and smiled. "Yeah, go sit down. Your waitress will be with you in a minute," she said, waving me away and taking a tray full of drinks in her hand. She went to deliver them to a table across the bar, patting my chest as she walked by. The rest of the night she ignored me, which pissed me off. So I knew that I had to up my game.

Night two, I showed up with a white flower and a hot mocha coffee per her request. She didn't swat the flower to death this time but instead smelled it and smiled up at me. When I showed her the coffee, she snatched it from my hand as if it was a million dollars. Holding it to her nose, she inhaled and sighed. Her eyes rolled and, for the life of me, my mind went to a very, very dirty place. For the second time, she patted my shoulder and ignored me the rest of the night, although I did catch her eyeing me up when she thought I wasn't looking.

Night three didn't happen till a few days later, I tracked her down in the back outside the bar. We had rehearsed late that night so she was on break by the time I was able to show up at Lucky's. That night, I had a few pink and white flowers, plus I had stopped by a taco truck. When I walked out back, she was laying on the bench.

"Muscles, I'm not in the mood tonight," she said from the bench. Her arm was over her eyes as she spoke.

I walked over, even though I knew she was pissed. I couldn't help but to smile as I stared down at her. She sniffed the air once, then twice.

"Is that—" She moved her arm to see me standing over her, the flowers in one hand and a box of tacos in the other. "Tell me those are tacos in your hand and not a taco scented candle," she pleaded, sitting up on the bench.

I didn't have a moment to answer her before she took the box from me. The first taco was in her mouth before I could sit down.

"Are they good?" I asked from beside her.

She moaned and nodded over at me. "I haven't had a taco since I got here. This is exactly what I needed tonight," she said, moaning again around another bite.

I leaned forward, my elbows on my knees, trying to cover the raging hard on I was sporting from listening to her moan.

When I had myself under control, I sat back and went to take a taco from the box. There were four of them in there, and they smelled fucking amazing. There was no way she was going to eat all of them. My hand was just inside the box when she slapped it, hard.

"No! These are mine, hands off," she practically growled.

"You're not going to eat all of them, give me one," I said, wiggling my fingers.

"The hell I'm not! I had a horrible day and these tacos are the only thing keeping me from moving back home right now," she said seriously. *Moving back home? She can't move back home. I need her here.*

"Tacos are the only thing keeping you here?" I asked, raising a brow.

"Yeah, these tacos and maybe those flowers," she

said, flashing a smile my way and nodding at the flowers
still in my hand.

The next two nights, she wasn't working. I was so
close to asking where she lived, it was borderline stalker.
Not seeing her for those two days was horrible. The moment I found out she wasn't there, I hopped into my rental truck and went home. There was no point in me being
there if she wasn't.

The fourth night of wooing commenced. I brought
chocolates which she devoured, plus I did get a kiss on
the cheek. By then she was talking to me a little more.
*Maybe she missed seeing me as much as I missed seeing
her.* That fourth night I watched as she got to know my
friends. Instead of going out back for her break she sat at
our table.

"So you all are from the same town?" she asked.

"Yeah, we grew up together," JJ answered.

"And you two are married?" she asked, pointing to
Kane and Kitty.

"I was tricked into it, but, yes, we're married a little
over a month now," Kitty said, smiling across the table.

"I did not trick you," Kane said, defending himself.

"You ambushed me in front of a room full of people.
I couldn't really say no."

"Damn right, you couldn't!"

We all laughed as Kitty swatted Kane upside the
head for that remark.

"What about you two? Are you guys married too?"
she asked in JJ and Piper's direction. Piper shook her
head vigorously, laughing it off. JJ, not so much. Those
two had been on since Kitty and Kane got hitched, but it
was difficult for them, Piper was still so young and living
in New York at Kitty's old apartment most of the time.
She'd usually be with us for long weekends but then have
to head back to New York for work. Trust me, you didn't

want to be around JJ for at least two days after Piper left.

"We're just hanging out, definitely no marriage on this side of the table for a long, long, very long time," Piper said, laughing. She turned to JJ, expecting him to be laughing too, but he wasn't. You could tell he was forcing the smile on his face as he turned back to Piper.

"What made you guys start a band?" Lexi asked, genuinely interested.

"Honestly, we were bored," Aiden said from beside her.

We all laughed and carried on easy conversation while Lexi sat with us. It was like taking a glimpse into the future, except in my image of the future, she would be sitting on my lap and I'd be rubbing her ass…A guy could dream.

The fifth night, I brought her a blue ONS T-shirt. That night was the best thus far. We arrived late, after working on the album. Lexi had the early shift that night and even though she could have left, she sat with us till the bar closed down. I sat next to her, watching her interact with my friends and laugh at Reece as he tried to pick women up. That night, she told me she wasn't working the next day, but that she looked forward to the sixth day of wooing.

Now, I had big plans for the sixth night. I was going to ask her out. I was nervous as hell. She was unpredictable and, as much as I loved her spunkiness, it scared the shit out of me that she might turn me down.

It was a Saturday night and we were onstage at Lucky's. The place was packed. There wasn't a table available, and the staff was running around like crazy, trying to keep up. Lucky's had become our home. In the four weeks that we had been going there, we knew all the locals and the staff. The owner had told us that she hadn't been as busy as she had been, ever. We were bringing in business just sitting there. So the staff loved/hated us. It was busy and they were making tons of money, but there were no slow days anymore. People came, even if we weren't there, just in case we showed up.

"Dude, Lexi looks good tonight," Aiden said from beside me as Kane talked to the crowd in-between songs. I followed his sightline to her. Of course I knew she looked good, I'd been staring at her all fucking night. She was dancing around the bar in her jeans, boots, and black tank top that said *Lucky Girl* on the back. Her hair was straight and pulled up in a ponytail. She stood to the side of the room, leaning up against the wall watching us play.

"Why the fuck you looking at my girl?"

"She's not your girl—"

"The fuck she isn't!" I smiled back. "Look at her. She can't keep her eyes off me."

I held the neck of my bass in one hand and hit Aiden on the back with the other. She was laughing up at us, and I remember winking at her and feeling fucking awesome when her face lit up. My eyes were solely on hers, so when another man came up to her, tossing his arm around her shoulder and pulling her into his side, my heart took a one way trip to my gut. It was the fucker from the airport.

"Wow Trent, she really looks like she's into you," Aiden said, commenting on the two of them snuggling on the wall. I could see her dimple as she smiled up at the man that was holding her tightly.

I tore my bass off and shoved it into Aiden's arms, not caring if he was going to hold it or not. I had one thing on my mind, and that was to get that fucker off my woman. As I jumped off the stage and headed toward Lexi, I saw the confusion on her face along with the jackass next to her. I cracked my knuckles and neck as I prepared myself for a fight. If the whole music thing hadn't worked out for me, I'd most likely have been an MMA fighter. Lucky for everyone the music worked. I was ruthless when I was in the zone. Just ask the assholes I left behind in my path. The crowd cleared for me. Obviously not wanting to get in an enraged man's way.

Chapter 11

Lexi

What is he doing? What is he doing? That was what ran through my head as I watched the smile fade from his face and an angry pissed-off glare replace it. When he took his bass off and shoved it at Aiden, I remembered scrunching my brows. Then, when he jumped off the stage, I could only stare at him in shock like the rest of the crowd. *What is going on?*

I looked up at my brother and then at his hand that was on my shoulder, and that's when it all clicked into place. I took Ben's hand, shoved it off my shoulder.

"Lexi, why is he storming over here?" Ben asked through clenched teeth. "Lexi, you did tell him who I am, right?"

I cringed, scrunching my shoulders up to my ears.

"Lexi!" he yelled, grabbing my arms tightly. "You better fix this before your terminator boyfriend messes my money maker up!"

He moved me around so I was now in-between him

and the very pissed off pile of muscles that was coming full speed at us.

"He's not my boyfriend," I said back over my shoulder.

"Does he know that?" Ben said from behind me. "Because it looks like he's coming over here to rip my head off!"

"Just calm down. It'll be fine." *Yeah, it'll be fine. Oh God, it's not going to be fine!*

Before I knew it, muscles was pressed up against me, and I was then pressed up against my brother.

"Tell him, Lexi!" my brother growled in my ear.

The smell of testosterone coming off of muscles had me so confused. I was scared for my brother's life, but, oh ma Lord, did muscles look a sweaty, sexy mess all up in my face. I was finding it hard to form words, so I just stood there and inhaled the aroma coming off of him.

"Lexi!" my brother yelled in my ear again.

"Sorry, I can't—" I moved my hands up on muscles's chest, a hand on either peck.

They were hard and damp from his sweat. His heart was pounding away underneath my hands. He was warm, like I remembered from the night we kissed. Sweat glistened on him from being up on stage all night. I didn't know what else to do in that moment. I couldn't talk, I had no strength to push him away because I was too busy trying to keep my knees from buckling so I did the one thing that I knew I could to get him to back off. I grabbed his jaw, turned his face down to mine away from my brother's, and kissed him, I kissed him as if I was quenching a thirst—a thirst that I had been denying myself for over three weeks.

For weeks, I watched as he brought me everything I asked him to. He was patient and gave me space but kept a watchful eye on me. In those weeks, I went from rolling my eyes when I caught him watching me from across the room to getting a warm, fuzzy feeling in the pit of my stomach. The days he didn't show up, I found myself watching the door for his large frame to walk through, and the days I didn't work, I spent them trying to come up with stupid reasons to show up. I enjoyed hanging out with his friends, and to be honest, I really enjoyed all the gifts and goodies.

I never thought you could fall for someone so fast, but I was. I knew that it wasn't what I had come here for, but there I was, falling for a man that I should have been steering clear of. Was he good looking? *Yes*. Was he making an effort? *Yeah, he was*. Was he everything that John wasn't? *So far, yes, but he was also just like him, and that's what terrified me*.

I held onto his face, my hands caressing the stubble that was turning into more of a beard with every day that he didn't shave. The people around us erupted in applause and cheers. I remember hearing Kane the lead singer saying something about his friend finding the love of his life. I opened my eyes and pulled my lips from his. He was staring down at me, and I could do nothing but smile up at him. His thumb ran over my dimple before he kissed it and took a step back from me. He made sure to take my hand in his as he pulled me next to him and away from my brother.

"Muscles, this is my brother, Ben," I said, cringing up at him.

"Your *what*?" muscles growled down at me once he realized what he was about to do to my brother.

"My brother," I said, smiling sweetly up at him.

"Lexi, you do realize that I was getting ready to murder your brother for touching you, don't you?" he said, taking my shoulders in his hands.

"Don't be so damn dramatic. It's not like we're dating anyway," I said, shrugging his hands off my shoulders. I'm not sure why I said it, maybe to prove a point that I wasn't so easily swayed, or maybe it was because, deep down, I knew better than to get involved with alphas like muscles.

He stood there, studying my face a moment. I moved my eyes around nervously because I didn't know if he was going to yell at me, or who knows what? He looked pissed and hurt all rolled up into one. He couldn't honestly stand there and believe that I was dating him. He hadn't even taken me out and, although he was bringing me treats and flowers, that didn't mean I was dating him.

"Dramatic?" he questioned me. "Lexi, that's the second time you've kissed me like that, I wouldn't call that a 'friend' kiss. What else do I have to do? Throw you over my shoulder like a caveman?"

"First off, don't ever do that. Second, you haven't even taken me out. All you do is stalk me at the bar. You haven't even asked for my number. Why would you think we were dating?" I snapped back.

"Fine, give me your number. We're going out to dinner and a movie tomorrow. Are you happy?" His eyes bore into me, waiting for a smart-ass answer and sure enough I had one.

"I can't tomorrow I have job interviews all day," I said smugly, holding my chin up.

"Fine, the next day."

"I work," I said, shrugging my shoulders as if I was bored.

"The day after that?" he asked, raising just one perfectly thick brow.

I grabbed my long ponytail then flicked it. "I have to wash my hair."

"Alexis Lynn Ford! Stop being such a pain in the ass!" my brother yelled from beside us.

I turned to him, eyes scrunched. *He's my brother he's supposed to be on my side.*

"She'll go out with you. She's lying. She doesn't work till mid-week," he said, flashing a million-dollar smile. "You can pick her up at six tomorrow. We live off Sunrise Lane, in the condos on your left. We're in the big cream colored one in the middle. Tell the main desk you're there to see the Fords, he'll let you up. We're on the third floor, room three-oh-seven."

My brother smiled at muscles, who seemed grateful for the help. Me, on the other hand, I was ready to kill. *How could my brother betray me like this?*

The crowd was starting to get rowdy, waiting for the band to start playing again. They had begun chanting O-N-S over and over. Muscles held up one finger to his band then turned back to me. "I'm getting your number as soon as we're done up there, so don't think about sneaking away. You might need me to prove to you that we're dating, but I've been dating you since you plopped down next to me on that plane. Somehow you've managed to break me, in a good way. I'm not going anywhere, and neither are you," he said before leaving the softest most romantic kiss at the corner of my lips.

I stood there, my mouth hanging open as he walked away from me and jumped back up on stage. I turned to the stage, watching him grab his bass and sling it over his shoulder.

"You're welcome," my brother said, coming up behind me and slinging his arm around my shoulder.

"Why would you do that, tell him were we live? He could be an ax murderer and you just gave him all the information he needs to come attack me at home. I hope you're happy. You probably just killed your only sister," I said, still staring up muscles. The music started up again and, for the life of me, I couldn't stop watching him play that damn bass. His muscles flexed with each note and every couple of strokes he'd look up and lock eyes with me. *I am in serious trouble.*

Ben snorted. "Stop lying. It's sad and, quite frankly, you appear a bit crazy. You're saying one thing and acting a completely different way. You really think I would give him our address if I hadn't done an intensive background check on him. He's a good guy Lexi, no record, close loving family, plus he's going to be famous."

As promised, I gave my number to muscles, but the rest of the night I kept my distance. The next day, I was going on six interviews. My brother had hooked me up with a few contacts in the weeks I had been there. I knew that I had to get serious, and having muscles trying to whisper sweet nothings in my ear was a distraction I did not need.

෨෮෨

In typical Lexi fashion, I was a hot mess. I woke up late, because I wasn't able to get to sleep. I blamed muscles. He had to pick the night before my big interviews to…I don't even know what he did but it messed me up. My emotions were all over the place and it was *all* his fault.

My first interview was with an up and coming actress who was younger than I was. I had a feeling I bombed it because I wasn't up on all the current slang. The second interview was for a sixty-year-old film editor who seemed like he wanted an escort more than an assistant. The third and fourth were okay, but again I thought the two women wanted something that wasn't an assistant. One wanted a nanny for her kids and the other one wanted me to take care of her dog. Not at all what I had come across the country for.

The fifth interview had me going downtown to a posh office building. The place was sleek and modern. I was interviewing for a publicist assistant position. The client was a bit of a socialite/entrepreneur from the east coast. He was building a team to help with, not only his publicity, but the advertisement of his companies.

"So, Miss Ford, what kind of experience do you have?" the tall, slender, extremely good-looking man asked, looking up from the resume I had handed him.

"Well, Mr. Monroe, to be honest, I don't have much. I just moved out here four weeks ago, but I'm ready to work and eager to learn everything I can. You can call me Lexi," I said, smiling across the table.

We were in a large conference room. The table we were sitting at could have easily held thirty people. My papers were lying on the table in a manila folder. I glanced down and saw that they were all facing different direction and some were sticking out and crinkled. One paper on top caught my attention. It was tattered and the ink was a little smeared. It was the piece of paper that was stuck to my back when I was on the plane. As I tried to straighten it, I chuckled to myself. *Damn muscles, he's messing up my interview. Why does he have to be so...everywhere!*

"Lexi—" he said, smiling across the table.

"I know I don't have experience, Mr. Monroe, but I know I can do the job," I said, cutting him off rather abruptly.

"You remind me of someone I hold very dear to my heart. Call me Teddy, please."

"May I ask who I remind you of."

"My sister. She can be very persuasive and determined when she wants to be, and I feel like you have the same qualities as her, plus you kind of resemble her."

"Well, then she seems awesome...Wait a minute," I

said putting two and two together. "Is Elizabeth Monroe you're sister?"

"Guilty," he said, holding his hands up.

Elizabeth Monroe was someone I looked up too. The media had ran her through the mud and back, but she kept on moving forward, and now she was dating the hottest man on the planet. So yes, I envied her.

"Lexi, I would love to hire you, but I have to go with my gut on this. If you had even a little bit of experience, I'd take you on, but I'm afraid I can't just now."

I felt like an idiot. One for not recognizing Teddy, and two for even thinking someone like him would hire someone with no experience. This just went to show how much research I did on my future employer before my interview.

"I understand, Mr. Monroe, it was a long shot," I said, standing and gathering my papers.

He stood with me, his hands sliding his suit jacket back and going into his pant pockets. "Lexi, get some time under your belt and get your bearings. I'm not going anywhere. I'll leave a spot on my team open for you. I can promise you that," he said, smiling across the table. I returned his smile, shook his hand, and said my good-byes.

I walked the streets of LA sulking. *Maybe I made a mistake coming out here*. I was so done with all the interviews, I just wanted to go home and curl up in my bed. But I had one left. I looked down at my phone, checking the time. *Five o'clock! How is it five o'clock already! I* was supposed to be at the office building at four-thirty for the last interview. I ran down the sidewalk, my hair flying in the wind behind me. I sprinted inside, pushing the up button for the elevator a million times...Nothing. I checked my notes to see what floor I was supposed to be on. *It would be the eighth floor*.

I gave up on the elevator and ran toward the door marked stairs. What felt like an hour later, I made it up to the eighth floor. I limped to the door marked eight-oh-five. Bursting in, I hit someone with the door. I heard the distinct thud of someone falling on the other side.

"I am so sorry," I panted, while I tried to help the innocent woman up off the floor.

"Dammit," the woman yelled from the floor. "Watch where the fuck you're going." She looked me over and laughed to herself. "If I were you, I'd leave now. I already got the job." She stood and fixed her tight black pencil skirt, flowing blonde hair, and low cut shirt. "Good luck following me," she said, giving me the finger and walking out the door.

What a bitch! I was furious, not only at her but at myself for thinking I could beat out someone like her. *Women in LA are vicious.* I stood in the middle of the room, still panting from running up eight flights of stairs. I was bent over, my hands on my knees as I tried to catch my breath. The door opened and I heard a male voice.

"I think she was the last one, there wasn't anyone left in the room when I came to get her, but I'll check." An older man walked out and spotted me. Rushing over, he asked if I was all right.

"I'm fine, really. Can I still interview?" I asked in-between breaths.

"Yeah, come on in," the older man said, gesturing toward the door across the room.

I walked in, knowing that my face was most likely red and sweaty and my hair was a mess, and I was clearly overdressed because I had on a black stylish pantsuit, instead of cleavage-showing, ass-hugging outfit. *If I remembered correctly, this was an interview to be an assistant for a record company. I think?* I sat down in the given chair and pulled out my folder of crunched up papers and a pad of paper and pen, just in case. I fixed my hair and placed both hands flat on the table to calm my nerves and steady my breathing. I expected the interviewer to walk in any moment so I closed my eyes and looked up to the ceiling. When I opened them, I expected to be alone in the room while I waited.

But I didn't have to wait. I was so wrapped up in myself I didn't even realize that they were already in the room watching my every move. Across the way, five men sat at a long table studying me. The one in the middle had a smile a mile wide on his face and a fucking twinkle in his eye.

"Oh, hell no," I said, shaking my head in disbelief.

Chapter 12

Trent

Five hours we had been sitting, with only a half hour break to scarf down some lunch. I was more than ready to get the hell out of there. We were told by our record company that we needed to hire a person to be in charge of roadie stuff, a publicist who was going to take us in the right direction and an assistant to take care of tour stuff, advertising, radio appearances, plane tickets, hotel arrangements—you name it—that one person we were to hire was going to be our coordinator from here on out. We had been using 4Alliance's while we were on tour with them but, now that we were on our own, the record company thought it appropriate for us to get our own posy of people.

We had found someone to fill every position, but the last was the hardest—the one we were going to have to interact with the most. In other words, this person was going to be our babysitter, make sure we were where we needed to be. The first two guys were older and seemed dull. The next girl was way too hard-core. We'd never have any fun with her. The last one was a perfect picture of a wet dream, so it looked like we'd come to a stand-still.

"I say we hire the last one," Reece said, sitting back in his chair and crossing his arms.

"No, Reece, we can't hire her because you'll be fucking her to death, which means she won't be working and we won't have any gigs or places to sleep while we're on tour," Kane said, leaning over the table to look down at Reece, who was on the other end.

I don't know why they put me in the middle with Kane and JJ to my right and Aiden and Reece to my left. Kane should have been conducting the interviews. He's the lead singer, but somehow I got voted.

I slammed my head on the table as the two of them fought back and forth. I had one thing on my mind the entire day, and that was getting the hell out of that room and picking Lexi up for our first official date. She could deny it and ignore me all she wanted, but I knew what she wanted, and I knew for a fact that 'it' wanted her too. After tonight, there was no going back. She was going to fall for me and all the charm that I had been holding onto for just the right woman.

She wasn't going to know what hit her. I just had to make her see me and not the tough guy façade that I put on. I was so good at having it up all these years, it was going to be a challenge to make sure that I kept it down. I was still figuring Lexi out, only knowing her for a short time and not really knowing her at all. I knew that some-thing or someone from her past had fucked her over and that was why she was so resistant to me.

With my head still on the table, I heard the door open and someone walk in. The room was silent. You could have heard a pin drop. I assumed it was either a really hot woman or a big wig checking up on us. When no one said anything, I lifted my head from the table. There sitting in a chair across the room, a red faced, wild haired, woman of my dreams sat organizing the disheveled papers in front of her. She tried to fix her hair, and we could all hear her taking deep calming breaths. Kane nudged my arm a few times but said nothing. I watched in wonder as she fiddled like she had on the plane. She was so unorganized but, fuck, it was turning me on watching her. The smile on my face hurt and the strain against my jeans made my heart beat faster. She must have thought she was alone because she didn't address us or ever look up at us, until she did.

"Oh, hell no!" she said, making eye contact with me and then the rest of the guys. "Is this some kind of joke?" she asked, looking at each one of us. We all shook our heads no in unison. "Well this is just icing on the cake, I'm outta here." She gathered her papers and stood from the chair.

"Wait a minute, we didn't even interview you," Aiden said.

"No need. I don't need a job that bad," she said, still packing her stuff up.

"Aw, come on, Zena, we're not that bad. You are dating our boy here, we'll go easy on ya," Reece added, probably thinking that he was helping, but only digging me deeper in a hole.

"Yeah? No, I can't do this," she said, shaking her head.

"Lexi, wait!" I called as she turned to leave.

She stopped and at least gave me a moment to speak my peace. "Will you please sit back down? You came here for a job, did you not? This could be your job."

She stood at the door, arguing with herself. I could see it all over her face. She wanted a job like this, and she knew that we might be her only opportunity to make those dreams come true.

"Fine," she said, letting go of the handle and sitting back down.

We all sat there silent, no one wanting to speak up first.

"Um, this is the part where you ask me questions?" she said, raising a brow.

"Oh right, um. Do you have any experience?" Kane asked, trying to sound professional.

"Nope," she said, making the word pop.

"Have you ever worked for a band?" JJ asked.

"No."

"Have you ever done any event planning?" Aiden asked.

"Does planning birthday parties' count?" she asked, shrugging her shoulders slowly.

"What about threesomes, do you do threesomes?" Reece asked in a serious voice. His hands folded under his chin.

"What? No!" she yelled in frustration at Reece.

"Well, I don't know about you guys, but I think she's perfect," I said, grinning at her.

She was ogling me in disbelief, her head shaking back and forth. "You all are insane. Even if you wanted to hire me, your record label would fire me. I have no experience and this whole trip moving over here was a huge mistake. Do you realize I just had an interview with Teddy Monroe? Not that you all know who he is, but working for someone like him is what I've wanted. He turned me down simply because I don't have any experience. How the hell are you supposed to get experience if no one will hire you?" She kept on talking about all the interviews she had gone on, rambling like a mad woman.

I couldn't have her leaving. If she left and went back

home, I wouldn't stand a chance to win her over. "Lexi," I called, interrupting her.

"Trent, this is all sweet, but I should go and pack and buy a plane ticket."

I stopped her there. *No way is she leaving, not on my watch.* When she called me Trent instead of muscles, I knew that she was done, beyond playing around with us. She was serious about leaving, so I got serious about making her stay.

"You're not doing any of that," I said, looking to my friends, my band mates. They knew where I was going with this and they had my back. They all knew how much I liked her and how I was dead set on making her like me.

"Trent, please I'm finished here. Just let me go with whatever dignity I have left," she begged.

"You're not leaving, you're not finished, and I won't let you go. You need us," I said, a little more cockily than I wanted.

"I need you?" she questioned me.

"Yeah, you want that dream job with Teddy...bear...or whatever his name is, you need us. We're your experience. Sign on with us, learn the ropes, gain your experience, and when you're ready, we'll let you go so you can ask him for a job again, with a glowing reference from us of course."

"Why are you doing this for me? You, of all people, should know how scatter-brained and disheveled I can be."

"We'll make it work, so can we hire you? Will you be our flight booking, appearance scheduling, and hotel arranging assistant?"

She stood across from us contemplating our offer. The few minutes she took to think it over seemed like an eternity. "I guess I don't have a choice," she said, tossing her hands in the air.

"There is one condition," I said slyly.

"Oh, do I even want to know?" she asked, her accent drawing her words.

"The one condition is that you have to move in with us." I watched as her face fell.

"Listen, muscles, if this is some diversion for you to do god knows what—"

"Not at all, we're going to need you around to schedule things and work with the record label, book flights. You need to be where we are, all the time. Think of it as taking on a bunch of foster kids. You're our new mom," I said through a cool grin.

"I—but—really?" she squeaked.

"I'm afraid Trent's right," Kane added, backing me up.

"I just want you to know, sometimes I get afraid of the dark and need to snuggle with my mommy," Reece added, again not making things any easier.

"Don't pay him any mind. He's the runt of the litter," JJ said, winking at Lexi. "Someone should have taken him down to the river, if you get my gist."

"Hey, asshole! Fuck you!" Reece yelled from the end of the table.

The next thing I knew, cuss words were flying back and forth and I had a feeling that soon or later someone was going to end up with a black eye, because that's how we solved our problems, by beating the shit out of each other. So I was shocked when a loud, ear splitting whistle split the room in half.

We all froze and gaped at Lexi, who still had her fingers in her mouth from whistling.

"All right listen up, assholes! If I'm going to do this, you all need to know that I'm not going to put up with shit like this. Y'all are as bad as a bunch of loose fucking sheep."

"Maaa-ma," Reece said, imitating a sheep.

"I better not fucking regret this," she said, walking across the room and holding her hand out in front of me.

I took her hand in mine and shook it firmly. "I guarantee you, you won't," I said, before kissing the top of her hand.

She rolled her eyes, took her hand from mine, and began shaking everyone else's. We had her sign some papers and the label explained in detail to her over the phone what they expected. She sat there, dutifully taking notes and getting numbers and information that she was going to need. They told her that they were going to supply her with a phone, laptop, and tablet and that they would be delivered to the house as soon as possible. She also had to attend a few meetings during the week, a sort of crash course in the music business.

When the phone call was over, she stood and packed her stuff up to leave.

"All right well, I guess I'll see you all tomorrow," she said, waving to us.

"Wait a minute where are you going?" I asked from my seat.

"Home."

"What about our date, it's six," I said, pouting up at her.

"Are you kidding me, muscles? I just agreed to live with you, give me one more night of freedom, before I'm stuck with y'all twenty-four/seven. Tonight I need to process what I just signed on to do," she said, seeming a little overwhelmed.

I knew it was a lot, so I backed off.

"Can you at least give my boy a kiss goodnight?" Reece asked, trying out his puppy dog eyes.

"Yeah, tell him to come and get it."

I honestly didn't know whether to slap him or fucking kiss him. I put a hand of the table and jumped over it to get to her. I took her in my arms, loving the way she felt between them, soft and warm. She was looking up at me, a devilish smile on her face. I couldn't help myself, my lips touched hers, sparks flew, and the room spun, *I could get fucking use to this.*

"Did you like that?" she asked, gazing into my eyes. I nodded my response and kissed her lips softly once then twice. "Good," she said, "because you can't do it any-more. If I'm working for you, then this—" She pointed between the two of us. "—can't happen. I work for you now, and I'm pretty sure I just signed a paper saying that I wouldn't fraternize with any of the band members."

She smiled up at me before patting my chest with her hand and leaving me standing there, wondering what the fuck I had just done.

Chapter 13

Lexi

I *guess I killed two birds with one stone tonight.* I had a job that didn't involve me running around a room carrying beer, plus I managed to put a nice thick wall up between muscles and me. There was one huge problem. I didn't want there to be a wall anymore. I had signed the contract stating that I was not going to sleep with or be romantically involved with any of the band members. I had no clue how I was going to go about even beginning to deal with that situation. I was moving into their home the next day and being thrown into a world I knew nothing about. I was excited to learn the business, but I was going to be forced to be around a man I didn't expect to have feelings for every minute, of every loving day, and I couldn't do a damn thing about it but sit back and admire him.

So as I lay in bed in my brother's apartment, I thought of every possible excuse's I could use to get out of working for ONS. I went through everything, from I had to leave to take care of a sick family member to, I had a serious case of crabs that was going to keep me from moving in, to just skipping town and jumping on a plane to go back home.

I couldn't do any of those things. Nevertheless, I knew that I had to stick it out. This was why I came out here. I came here to work for famous people, and although ONS hadn't truly broken through to mainstream, it was only a matter of time. I was ecstatic that I was going to be able to witness their rise and help them gain the recognition they deserved, even take care of them, but I was scared I'd screw it up for them too. Add the growing feelings I had for Trent, and I was a worried rat.

I wanted to go back to picturing him as the asshole who called me fat. It was easy to hate him then, but I saw the change in him, the real him, as he explained over and over to me, and as much as I wished that I could say otherwise, Trent was totally my type. I had to figure out how I was going to keep a professional relationship with him when what I really wanted to do was jump his bones. *Ugh I'm so screwed.*

ↄ∕ↄↄ∕ↄ

I stood outside the door to the ONS rental home, my bags at my feet. The house was huge and stunning from the outside. I could hear the sound of waves crashing against the shore in the back of the house, seagulls making noise overhead, and the distinct tone of Reece's voice yelling from the inside of the house. Of all the men, I was most concerned about him. If there was one guy who was going to give me a hard time, I had a feeling it was going to be him. I knew that Kane was fine. His wife Kitty kept him on a tight leash, which he seemed to love, and JJ, who I found out was Kitty's cousin, was pretty even tempered. He had a long distance thing going on with one of Kitty's friends back in New York. Aiden was still a mystery. He seemed a bit dark and brooding but, from what I knew of him from seeing him and hanging out at the bar, he was chill too.

Of course, looking in from the outside, I would have thought that Trent was going to be another problem. His sheer size alone was enough to scare the pants off a burglar. He came off like the take-no-shit kind of guy, and I guessed he was like that, but I had a feeling he was just very protective of his friends, his family, and anyone that he cared for, which included me—cue him trying to kill my brother for touching me.

So that left Reece again—the dirty little animal that left every night with a different woman from the bar. I had a recurring nightmare the night before about dragging him from an orgy to make sure he was at a gig.

"Why the hell would she stay with you? I'm the one with two beds in my room!" I heard Reece yell from the other side of the door.

"You must be high as fuck if you think I'm going to let her sleep within twenty feet of you, little man," Trent's distinctly deep voice boomed from inside. *Trent, it's going to be strange calling him by his name instead of calling him muscles.*

"Will you two knock it off?" I heard a female voice, Kitty I assumed, then the obvious sounds of someone getting slapped upside the head. I figured that was my cue to ring the doorbell.

The door opened slowly with Kitty standing just on the other side. She was short and perky. Her hair was almost as big as she was, and she had big blue eyes. She might have looked nice, but she could keep all of these guys in check. I'd seen her in action, and I knew that we'd get along.

"Hey, Lexi, please come in," she said, stepping aside to give me room to walk past her. "Reece, Trent, can you get her bags, please?"

Both men were standing in the foyer staring at me as I walked in. Both of them rushed to the door, each taking a bag. I followed Kitty into the large family room where everyone else was sitting watching TV or messing around on their phones. They gave me a tour of the massive house, but as Kitty was dragging me around I was mentally counting, *only five bedrooms? Where the hell am I going to sleep?* By the time we made it back to the family room the TV was off and phones were put away.

"This place is amazing," I said, smiling at everyone.

"You know what makes it even better? We don't have to pay for it or fix it up," JJ said from a chair across the room.

"Why would you fix it up?" I asked, raising a brow. *Like any of these "rock stars" could be handy enough to even change a light bulb.*

"Before we hit it big we were a remolding team of sorts," Kane answered as everyone nodded at his explanation.

"Remodeling team? No way, none of you look like you've ever lifted a hammer," I said challengingly.

"Believe it, Lexi. Beneath the rock star personas, they are actually average construction workers," Kitty added.

"Average? Woman, I made your bedroom a fucking five star hotel room," Kane objected from the couch.

Kitty rolled her eyes and, apparently, Kane didn't appreciate that much. He reached behind him to where Kitty was standing and grabbed her arm, pulling her over the couch so he could trap her on his lap and tickle her.

"Say it, say I'm a master carpenter," he yelled, tickling her more.

Her laughter was loud but cute and her face was red as she tried to fight against him. "Never!" she howled through her laughter.

"That's it! Lexi I'm happy to have you here, make yourself at home, I need to go talk with my wife." Kane stood from the couch with Kitty still trapped in his arms. He took her by the waist, heaved her over his shoulder like a sack of potatoes, and headed toward the stairs, Kitty kicking and hitting him the whole way.

I nervously looked around the room, not sure what to do so I rocked on my feet, scanning the room.

"You should get use to that," JJ said, breaking the silence. "They're fucking animals, the two of them. I had to listen to it for two weeks straight. My room was directly below theirs. Worst two weeks of my life after they got married."

I smiled or maybe I cringed at the image, yeah, I definitely cringed at the thought of hearing them all the time.

"So where am I sleeping?" I asked to the room. "When I was on my tour I only counted five rooms and clearly there are five of you so what? Am I sleeping in a closet or something?" I nervously joked.

"Looks like you're shaking up with me," Reece said, wiggling his eyebrows. "My room has two queen size beds in it."

What? No way.

"Reece shut up," Trent said, hitting him upside the head. "You're going to take my room," he said through a sexy half smile.

"Where are you going to sleep?" I asked.

"Looks like me and the couch are going to become very familiar with one another," he said, slapping his hands on the pillows of the couch in front of him.

"Are you sure? I can sleep on the couch, you're going to need to be well rested, I don't know if you've seen the schedule they have for you guys but it's packed. I don't want to be responsible for a lackluster bass player because I made him sleep on the couch."

"I'll be fine," he said, winking at me.

Oh Lord, this is going to be rough, especially if he does sexy shit like winking at me.

I followed Trent up the stairs. As we passed Kane and Kitty's room, a loud bang hit against the wall just as we walked by. I jumped away from it, clutching at my chest.

"You'll get used to it," Trent said, smiling back at me.

"Right," I said, following behind him.

Trent's room was at the very end of the house. He opened the door and I was hit again with a view I had only seen on TV. He had a huge sliding door that faced the ocean. The moon was large that night and it fit perfectly in the middle. I felt my jaw drop at the view and the sound of the waves coming through the opened door.

"I'm never leaving—"

"Good, I don't want you to," he said from beside me.

Oh shit, I said that out loud? I turned to look up at him. His face was smiling down at me, and I knew what he was thinking.

"I didn't mean that to come out," I said snidely.

"But it did." He took my bags and carried them to a dresser. I shook my head as he did. "I'm still going to keep my stuff in here," he said. "I packed a bag for the first couple days, but I'll sleep on the couch."

I nodded to him and then walked around the room. It was bright, even though it was dark outside. Crisp white bedding and fluffy blue throw pillows made me want to run and jump on the bed. It was beach themed, but very elegant and rustic looking.

"I guess I'll let you unpack. You can use the dresser

and I moved my stuff to one side of the closet so you can hang things up. I took the right side of the bathroom so the left is all yours," he said, pointing toward the door that had a bathroom behind it.

"Thanks, Trent."

He nodded back and clapped his hands once before awkwardly rocking on his heels.

I touched the soft covers on the bed, "Seriously Trent, thank you."

He shook his head. "For what?"

"For getting me a job, for believing in me, for saving me from having to share a room with Reece," I said, laughing.

"I am pretty awesome."

"All right, muscles. I think I've made your head big enough for one day. Get out so I can unpack," I said, pushing him toward the door. He held his hands out on the door frame so I couldn't push him anymore. He turned around in the doorway, tilting his head to the side and looking all smolderingly hot.

"No good night kiss for your knight in shining armor? I did save you from a life of filing taxes. The least you could do is kiss me. No one's looking. It can be our little secret." His thick brow raised and the corner of his lips curled up.

I wanted nothing more than to kiss him in that moment, but I knew better, plus I had signed a contract saying that I wouldn't. *Oh, who am I kidding*? I walked up to him, my hand curled around his thick neck. I reached up and left a kiss on his cheek, his stubbly, sexy cheek.

"Now get out," I said.

Taking him off guard, I was able to push him and close the door in his face. I turned to rest my back on the door. I had the biggest, stupidest smile on my face.

I didn't want to admit it but muscles was breaking me. He was breaking me down, and it was only a matter of time before I was begging him to kiss me.

Chapter 14

Trent

ঙৄৎঙৄৎ

I got her into our house. She was going to be sleeping in my bed, and I was going to be able to see her every day. I stood there in the hallway after she closed the door in my face, still feeling the warmth of her lips on my cheek. Everything was coming up Trent.

ঙৄৎঙৄৎ

It was four days later, and I hadn't seen Lexi once. We were like passing ships. I was with the guys at the studio all day and late into the night, and she was at meetings and learning the job that she had signed on to do. She quit her job at Lucky's, but we still ended up there after a long day at the studio. She never came with us. Instead, she barricaded herself in her room.

I wanted nothing more than to bust into the room and make her mine, make her see that she was my type and that nothing else mattered, but I had fucked up. Here I thought that having her work for us was going to be my master plan to have her be mine. Unfortunately, it back-fired because I didn't read the fine print. She had signed a contract stating that she would keep all relationships with us professional. That meant no kissing, no dating, and no fraternizing, which meant I was going to have some seri-ous blue balls.

Every day since she signed the contract, I had been calling the studio and doing all that I could to change that one small aspect of the deal. After being told no, time and time again, I was finally put in touch with the legal de-partment. I was waiting for them to call back with an an-swer, when I heard a high-pitched screech come from my bedroom. No one was home, except Lexi, so I knew it had to be her. The rest of the house was at Lucky's. I had come back, knowing that there was an important call coming. I didn't want to be on the phone in a loud bar as I tried to convince whoever was on the other end that I was mature and could handle dating my touring coordina-tor.

I took the stairs two at a time and ran down the hall-way. Busting open the door, I stood in the doorway, sur-veying the scene. *What the fuck happened to my room?* It was destroyed, as if a fucking tornado had come through the French doors and torn the place apart. There were pa-pers, clothes, food containers, empty cups, dirty towels everywhere. It was a fucking mess. The bed was all di-sheveled, the pillows were at the wrong end, the blankets and sheets were all twisted. I didn't even want to look in the bathroom. I was too scared. I had to hold onto the door frame to keep from stumbling back in disbelief. *How could one woman make such a huge mess in four fucking days?*

I had packed a small bag of things to keep down-stairs until she got comfortable with sharing a room with me. Since I had a bag of stuff, I hadn't gone into my room since she moved in. Boy, was that a fucking mistake, for more than one reason.

I never considered myself a neat freak by any means. That was Kane. That fucker couldn't go to sleep until everything was put away in its proper place. The sink even had to be clear of dishes before he ever called it a night. But this, Lexi, she was on a completely different level of messy.

The bathroom door opened and Lexi walked out in nothing but a towel. She had ear buds in and her eyes closed as she danced out of the bathroom. That's when I heard it.

The screech, that I thought meant something was wrong, turned out to be Lexi, signing. She cautiously danced around the room making sure to tip toe around all the shit that was on the floor. Her hair was wrapped up in a towel like a turban atop her head.

Oh god there it is. I cringed as she sang at the top of her lungs. *Was that one of our songs?* She spun around with her hands in the air and began playing an air guitar, or I guess it could have been a bass, but as she jammed out she lost her balance. Stepping on god knows what, she stumbled and held her foot.

"Holy shit! Goddammit!" she screamed, hopping on one foot.

I couldn't help laughing to myself. She really was fucking perfect—mess and all, she was perfect.

"Trent—Trent—muscles," she yelled at me.

I must have been somewhere off in my mind as she screamed my name because I didn't remember seeing her notice me. Who was I kidding? I sure as fuck was off in my own head. I was picturing her dancing around and that crisp white towel slipping from around her body and cascading on the floor at her feet. I imagined her running to me and jumping into my arms as we fell back on a soft fluffy bed.

"Are you deaf? Trent!" she yelled again.

"Sorry," I said, shaking my head and the perfect image out of it.

"What are you doing in here?" she asked.

"I heard you scream and thought something was wrong."

"What? That is the lamest excuse I've ever heard. You've got some nerve, buddy," she said, tripping over more shit as she walked closer to me. Her finger was erect and pointing up at me.

"Don't point that thing at me," I said, gesturing to her finger.

"I'll point it all I want to," she said, waving it in my face.

"Don't get a fucking attitude with me. If anything, I'm the one that should be pissed. Look at this place. It's a fucking pigsty. How the hell are you getting anything done up here?" I asked, giving it right back to her and not feeling a bit ashamed.

"I—I—What's the big deal? It's a little messy, so what?" she said, nervously looking around the room.

"Lexi, I can't see the floor! That's what's wrong!" I said, baffled that she didn't see the problem in it.

"Fine, I'll clean it up. Relax, muscles," she said dramatically. "What are you doing here anyway? Shouldn't you be at Lucky's with everyone else?" she asked, turning from me and grabbing a pile of papers and clothes from the floor.

"I'm not. I'm here."

She turned to me, cocking her head and squinting her eyes in disbelief.

"So since I'm here, can we have an actual conversation?" I asked, taking a step into the room.

"Conversation?" she questioned me.

"Yes, conversation. You know, where I talk about me and you talk about you."

"Why do you want to know about me? Nothing can happen between us, Trent. I signed a contract. Believe it or not, with only four days under my belt, I love this job. I'm not giving it up." She tossed the stuff in her hands on the floor and then crossed them under her chest. I watched in awe as the force of her hands loosened the knot in the towel just enough so even more cleavage showed.

"You really think I give a fuck about a contract? Lexi, you and I both know that something else is going on between us. And ignoring me and locking yourself in the room isn't going to change that. Look at you," I said, pointing to her.

She was staring at me, chewing on the inside of her lip, crossing her legs tightly. Her eyes were wide and taking me in from top to bottom. I'd seen it a hundred times before. It was the look I got from women when they were thinking about fucking me. Trust me, I'd seen it, a lot. I'd come to know all the signs and Lexi was displaying all of them.

"You're really that confident that I feel the same way?" she said, challenging me.

She was heading toward me a step at a time, and I to her. We met in the middle of the room. The only clear spot on the floor, the one she had just picked up. We stood there toe to toe, her in her towel, me in a pair of gym shorts and black sleeveless shirt.

We were like magnets, always being pulled toward one another. I'd never felt a pull so hard as the one I felt for her. So, yes I was confident. I licked my lips as I stared down into her face, readying myself for the moment when I was able to taste her again. I was going to touch her face, feel her soft tan skin beneath my fingers. I was going to take it slow because that's what I thought you did when you cared for someone. Boy, I was wrong, and, fuck, I was glad.

Cool arms wrapped around my neck and shoulders. Her body pressed up against mine, and her mouth gave me what I had been wishing for from the moment I swung open the door. Her towel fell free from her head and her hair spilled down her back, touching my arms and leaving drops of water along them.

We stood there kissing, feeling each other's closeness. By then, I had figured that maybe this was our way of talking, having a conversation, because that kiss meant so much to me. It meant that she did feel the same and that she wasn't going to let a stupid contract come between us. As the kiss slowed, I got to caress her cheek the way I had planned earlier. It was flushed pink and her dimple was smiling back at me.

"You're right, Trent, something else is going on, and I don't want it to stop. I don't want it to end," she said in a breathy sigh against my ear.

That was all I needed to hear. I held her tighter in my arms, kissing her, our tongues dancing back and forth. She was cool against the warmth of my body, cooling my rising temperature. Her fingers held onto the bottom of my shit. The tips of them grazed my skin, sending chills throughout my body. I let her go only to reach behind me and grab my shirt, pulling it up and over my head. I tossed it on the floor with the rest of the mess.

Her hands splayed on my chest, running up and down, driving me crazy, making me want more. The knot on her towel had loosened even more. It was only a matter of moves before it fell from her body, a body that I'd been fantasizing about for weeks. As if answering my prayer, the knot finally gave way and the towel fell. I felt her pull her hands from me and cover herself. Grabbing her writs before she could, I brought them up to my lips, kissing the insides of her palms and down the tender skin of her wrist. Her eyes closed and her head fell back as I switched and did the same to her other hand.

I knew she could feel me against her. I was in gym shorts but fuck if they weren't tight. My dick was begging to be released from the restraints of my shorts and boxers, and if I didn't let if free soon, I was certain I was going to die from dick strangulation.

"I want this, Lexi, tell me you want this and I'll never have another type but you," I said releasing her hands and making her look up at me.

"I lied," she said. My heart shuddered as she shook her head. "I lied to you on the plane when I told you that you weren't my type. You're so fucking my type, it's sad, it's so fucking sad."

I kissed her then with a smile on my face. *I fucking knew it!* I kept my cool because I didn't want to ruin the moment with my gloating.

She pushed against my chest until I hit the bed behind me. My knees buckled against the bed, making me fall back. I sat on the edge of the mattress staring at the woman of my dreams. She was perfect. The light from behind her outlined the curves of her body. Her breasts were large, and I knew that they were going to spill over my hands before I even touched them. They were perky and plump as fucking melons.

"I need you to promise me something," she said, pausing and covering her voluptuous body with a sheet from the bed.

I fell back, clutching my hand over my heart. "You're killing me, Lexi," I said from the bed as I stared up at the ceiling.

She hit my thigh once and then pulled on the waist

band of my shorts. That little move got me to sit right up.

"I'm serious, Trent, I need you to promise me that—that you're not gonna—I can't do this unless I know you're not going to hurt me," she said, stuttering nervously.

I sat a little straighter. The way she said it made me believe that she didn't mean matters of the heart. With all our past encounters and the way she freaked out when I touched her and when I pinned her against the wall, she had to be talking about hurting her physically. My hands made fists against my thighs, I was seeing red. *Someone had fucking hurt her, and if I ever find out who, they're going to wish they had never laid a hand on her.*

I took her free hand in mine. Her other was still clutching the sheet against her body. I quickly and suavely switched places with her. She was laying on the bed as I leaned over her. My hands resting at either side of her face, I watched as a doubt moved across it. She doubted herself, her decision. I cupped her face, making her eyes lock onto mine.

"I will never hurt you and, from here on out, I'll make sure no one ever hurts you again." My words seemed to calm her, clarify to her that I wasn't the bad guy.

"I know you won't. You're my knight in shining armor. How could you ever hurt me?"

"I couldn't if I tried," I whispered before kissing her lips softly.

Chapter 15

Lexi

Twenty minutes before I was in the shower, foolishly fantasizing about a man that I wasn't allowed to be with. Never did I imagine it was to come true. For four days, I had kept myself locked in his room, only coming out when I needed nourishment or had a meeting to go to. The label had me meeting with others who held the same job position as I did. I learned a lot—from how to get a drunken rock star sober for a gig to keeping the groupies to a minimum.

I was given a rough copy of the guys' music. It wasn't all the songs, just the first three that they had recorded. I was in the bathroom rocking out and, when I came out to grab some clothes, I almost fell on my ass when I saw muscles standing in my doorway being all peeping tom. He insulted my singing, but I couldn't disagree with him. Singing wasn't my thing but that didn't stop me from belting in privacy, or so I thought. Then he called me a slob because I might have neglected to clean anything up. I was in the zone and didn't have time to clean. He had to understand that.

I still don't remember exactly how I ended up laying on the bed with him over top of me, promising me that he was going to take care of me and keep me safe from any and everything. I guess I figured in my head that even if I did get fired for breaking the contract I signed, I'd still be around, I'd still be able to learn the business by his side. So I guess that's how I reasoned with myself. I had held out for four days and, quite frankly, that was longer than I thought was possible with a sexy, alpha, beast of a man right under my feet. Holing up in my room was most likely the only reason why it didn't happen sooner. Either way, I was so fucking glad that it *was* happening.

He was sweet and kind, strong and sincere. A bit of an ass but, hey, everyone had their faults. I couldn't keep making excuses for not giving him and me a chance. I was done fighting and done with being terrified that he was going to be like John. I was able to get away from that situation, so I knew that, if shit did hit the fan, I'd be able to walk away from Trent too.

"Are you sure about me, about doing this?" I asked, searching for any sign of hesitation that might make him back off me and leave me lying there alone.

"I don't think I've ever been surer about anything in my life."

"I'm not going to change for you," I said, running a hand up his thick, strong, tatted up arm. I was loving the way his skin felt under my fingertips. "This is me. I'm loud and messy, I speak my mind. I'm never going to look like Kitty, or the girls that follow you around. I'm not ashamed of my body or how I look. I've been in a relationship like that before, one where I was made to change who I was for someone who wanted me to be what they thought I was supposed to be for them." I found myself spilling my guts under him. He had a way of making me feel secure enough to do so. I'd never told anyone about the way John treated me. From the outside we appeared to be the perfect couple, him the star football player and me the dutiful girlfriend, but there was so much more going on underneath the personas we played in public.

"I don't want you to change. I want you just the way you are."

"But what if you find—what if you've made a mistake? What if you realize I'm not really your type at all? What if you—" *Dammit, I hate it when I doubt myself!*

"Lexi."

He moved from over me, taking my hand and pulling me up to sit on the bed, while he knelt between my legs. For once, I had to tilt my head down to read him. His hands rested on the curves of my hips, his broad shoulders flexed as he held onto me tighter.

"I don't know what he did to you, but I am not him. You have to know that by now. Lexi, I'm not doing this just because I want to sleep with you, I'm doing this because I want to know you, love you, and take care of you. I've been waiting my whole life to feel this way about someone, so why would I ever want to change that?" he said, studying my face.

He is perfect. How could one man be so perfect? Whatever doubt I had went right out the freaking window. *I'm doing this and I'll just have to worry about the consequences later.*

The sheet fell from under my arms as I rested my hands on his shoulders. Moving at a snail's pace they drifted over them and up his neck. The pads of my fingers grazed up the back of his neck and into his hair. My thumbs wrapped under his jaw, turning his head up to face me.

"Kiss me."

My voice was brittle as I begged for him to make good on his word. His arms wrapped my waist and as he went to his feet he lifted me from the bed with ease. I clung to him, my legs wrapping his core, my arms engulfing his neck. I didn't want to let go of him. I knew, in that moment, I wasn't ever letting go of him.

Over a month of sexual tension had built up to that moment. As we fell onto the bed, I kicked his shorts off with my feet. His gray boxers were the only thing preventing me from the Holy Grail. He kneeled between my legs, I sat up the best I could, grabbing him through his boxers. His head fell as I snuck a hand down the waist band of his boxers. His soft, velvety skin was heaven in my hand, and I wanted so badly for it to be inside me already.

I'd never been with anyone but John. Only knowing one man in the biblical sense was a bit dull for a twenty-four-year-old, so I was more than excited to add to the list. With that excitement came a wave of nerves. I pushed his boxers down and continued to stroke what I knew was the largest penis I'd ever held. *Sorry, John.*

Trent's hand splayed over my stomach, pulling on my hips. He looked down at me with a fire in his eyes, and I knew that same fire was behind mine.

"You're so soft," he said as his hand came up, cupping my breast.

They instantly began to tingle as his thumb ran over my nipple, back and then forth. I had to remember to breathe as he sucked it to an even larger peek. *Oh god, more. I need more.*

I grinned up at him as I tugged on him again. "And you're so hard."

"You have no idea," he said before going for a taste of the other sister.

I never liked when John kissed me there. It always felt weird. *Maybe John didn't know what he was doing?* Muscles, on the other hand, knew. He knew damn well what he was doing and if felt fucking amazing. His tongue swirled and flicked in all the right places, as his hand squeezed and massaged. I felt the tightening of my core and knew that I was closer than I thought to coming. *If he can do this with only kissing my tits, what the hell is going to happen when he gets a hold of my girl?*

"Oh God—" I breathed, clutching him tighter in my hand while digging my nails into his shoulder. He had done it with just his tongue and my tits. He made me lose it, lose all of it. *I'm in so much trouble.*

Releasing me, he kissed me as I came down from the high, but I never came all the way down. I stayed up there, ready for more of him, ready to fill myself with him.

"Take your boxers off," I demanded as he kissed down my neck.

He pushed up on his arm in a side plank and shoved them down. The muscles in his shoulders and arms bulged. I swallowed the dry lump in my throat as I watched the muscles move under his tan skin. They caught on him. *His fucking penis is so large he can't get his boxers down. Now that's one for the record books.*

He moved back off of me, kneeling between my legs so he could properly take his boxers off.

Gasp.

Yes, I gasped at the full sight of him. I decided then that he wasn't real. No man could be that well endowed, and that hot, and that perfect. He knelt there his thick thighs between my legs. His torso and chest spanned mine, and a half. He might not have had a rippling six-pack, but, fuck, if you couldn't eat off of it. I had to touch him to make sure he was real. I stretched out a hand feeling my way up his body. He mirrored my moves, as if doing the same thing—making sure this was all real.

"You know that I'm done, right?" he said, cupping my breast again, while covering me with his body.

"Oh, you're far from done, muscles," I said as my stomach fluttered with anticipation.

He held himself between me and I knew that it was only a matter of moves before I was filled to the brim. He was slow and steady as he pushed himself in. I remember arching off the bed and biting so hard on my cheek that the taste of copper filled it. His hand cupped my cheek, his thumb caressing it as he pushed farther.

"You all right?" he asked softly.

I didn't want to talk, so I nodded and smiled a dreamy smile, because that's what it felt like to have him in me. It felt like a dream.

An hour later, we lay in bed panting. I couldn't help but notice how comfortable I felt resting my head on Trent's shoulder. I didn't know why it surprised me so. It wasn't the first time I'd snuggled up on him and felt totally comfortable.

"Tell me something about you, something that no one else knows," I said, resting my chin up on his sweaty chest. His hand was idly brushing the hair that fell down my back when I broke the silence between us.

"Something no one knows, huh?"

I nodded up for him to go on.

"How about this, when I was eight, I stole a bag of chips from the convenience store," he said, raising his brows, knowing full well I wanted something deeper than "I stole a bag of chips."

"Not good enough?" I shook my head no.

"Okay, let me think about it, I'll get you something good," he said before sitting up a bit to kiss the top of my head.

"Why don't you tell me about your family while you think of something?" I said, smiling up at him.

"Family? All right, my family is the absolute best. My mom Jane and my father Tom met in high school and have been together ever since. They love each other every day like it's the last day they have together."

As he spoke about his parents, I realized that he had been searching for what his parents had for each other. It scared me a bit that he was considering that we might have that same kind of forever love, but I'd be lying out my ass if I said I didn't want that too. *Isn't that what everyone is searching for, to find that one person you can't live without?*

I learned that he had two older brothers. One was married with two little girls, the kids that I had seen in the pictures when we were on the plane. He told me about losing his other brother too and how hard that was for him. He told me about how he stuck up for his brother, even though the kids that were teasing him were sometimes four years older. His past perfectly explained his need to protect the people he cared for by being the tough guy.

It seemed that the more Trent talked about himself, the harder I was falling for him. *What will he think of my past when he finds out about it?* There was no talking about my past without talking about John. He was in every single part of it.

"What about you? I've been blabbing about me. What's your family like?" he asked, sitting up even more so as he could see me better.

"Me?" I questioned, raising my brows.

"Yes, you," he said, pulling my arm so that I'd move to straddle his lap. When I was comfortably sitting on him, I panicked, covering my face with my hands, I didn't know what I was thinking. Maybe I was hoping that when I put them down, he'd move on to another question, but that would probably also lead me back to John. Everything always led back to him. *How the hell am I going to explain this to an overbearing alpha that seemed to have a bit of a temper?*

"Come on, don't get shy on me now, this is the easy part," he said, tugging my hands from my face.

"I have a brother," I said, even though I knew that wasn't going to be enough, but it still didn't stop me from praying that it was.

"Yes, I know that. What about your parents? Or other siblings?"

"I have a mom, Cathy," I said, still trying to keep it short and sweet.

"Do you have father?" he asked.

"I did."

"Lexi, come on you gotta give me more than that. What are you trying to hide? Do you have a wicked stepfather? Or, oh, I got it, you were in love with your stepbrother. No wait, a cousin!" he said, laughing.

I knew he was teasing because of the fact that I lived in West Virginia, but when my face fell and the only person laughing was him, he sat up straighter, pulling his brows together he studied me. He had figured it out without me saying a word.

Chapter 16

Trent

I was joking. I was making a fucking, smart-ass joke, and it fucking bit me in the face. Everything had been perfect up until that moment. I was so pissed I wanted to punch a fucking wall. My smart mouth had ruined the moment.

Lexi was sitting on my lap and I could feel her shaking with nerves. I sat all the way up in bed and, as I did, she moved back resting between my legs on the mattress. She reached to the side of us grabbing a cover, pulling it over her shoulders, and wrapping it tightly around her body.

"What's the matter?" I asked, even though I knew I was pushing a button I wasn't sure I should be.

"Nothing," she said, shaking her head.

"Please tell me, don't push me away," I begged.

"Trust me, it won't do any good for either of us, for me to spill my guts."

"Do you want to do this with me?" I asked. If I was

going to put my all into this, like I knew I wanted to, then I needed to know her, know all of her, good and bad.

"Of course I do. I thought that we already established that?"

I tilted her head up with a finger on her chin. "We did, but now you need to keep good on it. I told you about my family and now I'd like to learn about yours."

She jerked her head to the side. My finger fell from her chin as she glared up at me. "Why do you need to know so badly? Isn't it enough that I gave into you? You got what you wanted."

"Is that really what you think? After all this?" I said, looking around the mess of a room. *How could she still think I was doing anything but trying to get to know her better?*

"I don't know what to think." She didn't say anything more as she scooted away from me.

"Lexi." I moved toward, her grabbing her arm before she could walk away from the bed. I was on my knees. She was standing at the edge of the bed, my hand firmly around her arm. She glanced down at it, then back up at me. Her brows pulled together. "This—This is the problem," she said, moving the arm that I had a grip on. "Every time you do that it reminds me of him, and then I want nothing more than to run away as fast as I can. He did that to me all the time, and I can't stand it! And you look just like him, and then you do this and I freak out…" She kept on rambling like she always did, but I didn't let go of her, for I was afraid, if I did, she'd walk away and never let me back in.

"Who is he?" I asked.

She finally shut up, biting down on her lip. I could see her shaking an image out of her mind. Her eyes got red and a single tear ran down. "Lexi, just tell me," I begged, letting her arm go and grabbing her waist with both hands so I could pull her closer to me. I tucked a strand of loose hair behind her ear, caressed her cheek, and pleaded with my eyes for her to let me in, let me help her get over it—him, whoever it was.

"You're going to regret this," she seethed, grasping my shoulder and shaking her head.

I winked up at her. "Try me. I've got thick skin, I think I can take it."

She rolled her eyes and took a deep calming breath. "John, his name is John Ford. He's my stepbrother, and we fell madly in love, like disgustingly in love with each other."

I tried to process what she was saying but the only thing that stuck out was, one he had the same last name and two, that they were madly in love.

"See? I told you it wouldn't do any good," she said, shrugging her shoulders.

"Well, you're being a little short sided with it," I said, following her gaze.

"What more is there to know? I loved my stepbrother and he was an abusive jerk."

I dropped my hands from her waist and moved them through my shaved head as I stared down at the bed in shock. That's the only way I could describe it. I was in shock over what she just told me.

"Still think you like me?" she asked as she pulled on a pair of sweats and a shirt from the floor. "Exactly, I mean, why would you? I'm a freak that loved her stepbrother. I think you should just go," she said, exhaling.

"I need you to tell me more. What did he do to you?" I asked, taking her off guard.

"Are you serious?"

"Yes."

"Fine, you want to torture us both, I'll give you the full run down. John lived on the farm next to us. We were best friends. His mother ran off and my father died when we were eight. Our parents found comfort in one another. They moved in with us. Five years later, his father died of a heart attack. John didn't have any other family so my mom adopted him. As we became teenagers, we realized we were falling in love. It was super convenient that he was a room away back then, by the way. We were inseparable, the golden couple in high school. But when we went to college, things changed. He started drinking, and it got bad. He wanted me to be his arm candy, and I wasn't going to change who I was, so he would push me around to get his point across."

The more she spoke, the more I saw red.

"He never did it in public, and he was never anything but a gentleman in front of my mom, my brother, everyone. So I stayed with him, because I loved him. He was my best friend, and he was only bad when he drank. He asked me to marry him after we graduated and, obviously, I said no. That was two days before I came out here," she said, nervously looking around the room.

"Wow," I said, sitting back on the bed.

"Yeah, that's my family. Aren't you happy you asked?"

"So what made you leave?" I asked.

"Honestly, I knew there was more for me. I loved him but I had this drive to come out here and give my dream a shot, and I knew that being with him wasn't a part of my dream anymore."

"So all the times I grabbed you—"

"I saw John. I'd be right back there."

She was being honest with me and I was so happy and proud of her. "And no one knows what he did to you?" I asked.

"No one but you. My mom thinks we're still going to get back together, the whole town does, actually."

"Well, that's never going to fucking happen. Sorry to your mom and the town, but I'm not letting you go back there, not if he's around," I said with determination.

"You see that's the problem. He's always going to be there. He's always there. He lives in my home, he works on my farm. He's been a part of my family since I was eight. There's no getting away from him. He's every-where!"

"He's not here," I said, taking one of the hands that she was swinging around dramatically.

"Aren't you grossed out? How can you be so okay with all this?" she asked.

I pulled her back onto the bed with me. I shook my head no to her questions. I kissed her lips and held her face close to mine.

"You're not real," she said against my lips. "How can you be real?"

"I'm real and I'm here for you. Just promise me you won't hold anything back from me. I'm falling so hard for you that I don't care about your past, as long as I'm in your future."

Was it sappy? Did it sound like a fucking romance novel? Hell, yeah, it did. I was a sappy, love sick man, and I was going to make the woman in front of me be-lieve every word that came out of my mouth, even if it sounded ridiculous.

"There's nothing else to hold back, that's the worst of it," she said, shrugging her shoulders.

"Oh, that's not the worst. The worst is that you're a fucking slob." I smiled down at her, kissing her cheek I fell back on the bed, laying down arms stretched out.

"What are you doing?" she asked through a giggle.

"I'm going to lay here while you clean this fucking place up. I'm not leaving the bed till it's clean," I said, propping my arms behind my head so I could watch.

"In that case, I'm never cleaning." Lexi moved seductively up my body, her hand went from my legs, up my abdomen, over my chest, and around my neck. She was so beautiful. Her hair fell around us like a curtain, shielding us from the rest of the world. I didn't want her to move. I didn't want the curtain to open and for reality to come crashing back around us.

We still had one problem, I didn't want this to end, but I wanted her to keep her job. I wanted her to be happy. I needed the lawyers to call and give me the full go ahead and everything would be perfect.

"You're so beautiful," I whispered near her ear.

Her face lit up in a smile and her dimple appeared, making my heart melt even more. *I'm a fucking goner.* She held my cheek in her soft hand and kissed my lips tenderly.

"You've broken me, muscles, you've broken me in the most splendid way."

Chapter 17

Tue story—I did not clean my room that night. We lay in bed, talking and getting to know one another even more. I was in the middle of explaining what we do on our farm when his phone rang from somewhere on the floor. Muscles jumped out of the bed, butt-ass naked, and started tossing things in the air.

"Get down here and help me find my shorts!" he hollered from the floor.

"Why? It's probably just the guys checking up on you," I said, getting comfortable on the pillow.

"Or it could be the legal department calling to tell us that they have added an addendum to the contract that you signed saying that we can date one another." I sat straight up in bed, brows scrunched in confusion.

"Why would they do that?" I asked.

"Because I asked them to! Now get your fine ass down here and help me find my phone!" he yelled.

I jumped out of bed with him and dove head first into

the mess, tossing this and that over my head. The ringing was getting closer and closer, and then—

"I got it! Here," I said, tossing the phone across the room to him.

He looked at the screen and smiled. "It's them," he said before answering. "Hello…yes this is him…I see, well…And you're positive…" His face was unreadable. I couldn't tell if he was getting his way or not. "All right, I will talk to you later. Thank you," he said, hanging up the phone. He was sitting next to the bed, his shoulders slumped over. *The call wasn't good. They aren't going to let us date.*

"Well?" I asked from across the room.

"Well, looks like I'm moving in," he said, wiggling his eyebrows.

"They're going to change the contract?" I asked in disbelief.

"You better believe it!" Crawling across the floor like a child, he tackled me onto my back, pinning me beneath him. Kissing me, he paused just over me. I loved the way he looked at me. He was staring at me as if he wasn't going to get the chance to do it again. I loved that. I thought that I had been someone's everything before, but even with all the history I had with John, it was never like this. He never looked at me the way Trent did.

ഐഐ

"Lexi, where's the bus?"

I was well on my way to chewing the inside of cheek off, as five angry men and one very tired woman set laser beam stares at me. We had been on the promotion tour for four months, and I thought I had been doing a good job. That was, until I lost the bus. *Now you must be thinking how can a girl loose a huge touring bus?* It's not as

easy as it looks taking care of all the guys and the roadies, and wives. I was tired, and I hadn't been sleeping, I
felt like I was being pulled in eighty different directions
all the time.

If it wasn't the manager calling to make sure we
were hitting all our stops, it was Reece asking me if he
could have his own hotel room, or Aiden asking me when
we'd be stopping to go sightseeing. Then I'd have JJ in
my ear asking if there was room for Piper. Don't even get
me started on Kane and his "We have to say hello to every fan."

I stood in the rain for over an hour while they all
greeted fans outside of a mall, which of course was a stop
we had to make for Kitty, who couldn't live without her
weekly shopping spree for more lingerie.

Then there was Trent. Now he wasn't so much of a
pain in the ass, but he was a huge distraction, huge in all
the right ways. If I wasn't working or trying to keep the
peace between everyone, I was with him. The two
months we were in the house, it was easier because he
was working on the album which gave me time to focus.
But on the bus—that was a different story. He might have
kept me from being focused, but I was usually able to
pull it all together. I had some serious last-minute-panic
skills.

For instance, the first week we were on the road, I
forgot the legal papers that basically gave them the go
ahead to promote. But I was quick on my feet and found
a way around it. Then I might have been sneaking off
with muscles instead of booking a hotel. That one landed
us in a motel that could have been the backdrop for a horror movie. But we made the best of it.

*So the bus was missing? It wasn't as if I couldn't just
call the driver—I can't call the driver because all our
stuff is on the bus.*

"Guys, calm down. Dave couldn't have gone too far," I said nervously.

"Lexi, if I have to sleep in another haunted motel, I'm going to strangle you," Kitty said from beside Kane.

Muscles stood next to them his large frame was emoting the pissed off vibe as well. To be honest, if he hadn't been helping me, we wouldn't have been able to play anywhere. It was he who figured out a way to have the legal papers sent to us, and it was he who usually booked the good hotels, so everyone knew it was me who booked the run down ones. My excuse every time was "It looked cozy in the pictures." No one bought it.

They should have fired me, hell they should have never hired me, but I'm so glad they did, because I was able to spend every day and night with the mound of muscles that seemed royally pissed as we all stood out-back of the venue they just played in.

His huge, tattooed arms were folded over his chest, making him appear larger. His warm brown eyes were boring a hole into me, and not in the good way—the bad way, the I'm-going-to-make-you-pay-for-this kind of boring. He'd never hurt me. No, he had a completely different sick and twisted way of making me pay for lost papers, mess ups, and bad hotels. He'd have me on the edge ready for the end and just leave me there. He'd leave me all hot and bothered and simply walk away. Worst. Punishment. Ever!

"Lexi, earth to Lexi!" Reece yelled.

I snapped out of the image I knew was going to come true that night, *Hell, the look on his face, it might be two nights.*

My head fell at the realization that the man who held the precious keys to my orgasms was going to hold them captive, because I had lost his bands bus.

"Where's the bus, Lexi?" Trent asked.

"The bus—it's on its way?" I said more in the form of a question.

Just as I thought the group of people I had come to call friends was about to jump me, the back door opened and another band came out, distracting the angry mob. I swear I could have kissed every single one of them.

It was the band Fallen from ONS's hometown. We'd met up with them here and there for the past two months, since they played the same kind of music but weren't as big as ONS, they'd open for them every once in a while. I ran over to Gabe, their tour manager and asked to borrow his phone. I hung back as I made the call and watched the two bands interact.

Fallen's lead singer was a girl named Chloe who could have easily been a super model. She had long legs and long black hair, tattooed arms and, as Reece said, a banging body. The phone was ringing against my ear, as I waited for Dave to answer. *Had I told him to leave? Who knows?*

Dave answered groggily. "Hello?"

"Dave, where the hell are you?" I asked, skipping pleasantries.

"Who is this?"

"Who is this? It's Lexi, where the hell are you? We're standing outside the venue and there's no bus!" I yelled into the phone. I must have yelled pretty loudly because all heads turned in my direction.

"Oh, no! You're not going to pin this on me. You told me to 'go ahead,'" he said defensively.

"What are you talking about? I said no such thing! Why would I say that?"

"I called you before the show and asked where to park the bus. I asked if I could just park it at the hotel and get some sleep before we left and you said—"

"Go ahead," I said finishing his sentence. *Fuck!* I

quickly remembered talking to him, I remember lying on a couch, my legs spread in the air, Trent between them and my phone ringing at the worst possible moment. "So you're at the hotel?"

"Yeah, do you need me to come pick everyone up, or you guys going to take a cab?" he asked through a yawn.

"No, no, no, we'll catch a cab, you get some rest we have a six-hour drive ahead of us and we can't have you tired. We'll see you in the morning at the bus."

"All right, Lexi, see you then," he said, hanging up.

I wanted to ram my head into the brick wall but as I went to hand the phone back to its owner I caught Chloe with her arms wrapped around Trent's neck and his around her waist, not to mention her lips were on his cheek. *What the fuck?*

I stomped across the parking lot ready to kill. She was tall but I was just as tall, plus I had a few pounds on her. It would be nothing for me to put her in her place, which was not near Trent.

"Oh, shit!" Reece said when he saw me walking over.

All heads turned in my direction.

"Chloe, I'd back up if I were you," Kitty said sincerely.

"Why?" she asked with an attitude.

"Because my girlfriend is going to break your arms off," Trent said, taking her arms from around his neck.

I'd never had to deal with other women. When I was with John, everyone knew, everyone saw how good we were together, there was never any competition. I'd never been jealous before. It was all new to me. But since being with Trent, I was having insecurities over the smallest of things. It had gotten really bad in the past month. I'd wake up, my heart racing from nightmares of him leaving me for…well, his "type," the tall, blondes that always fit so perfectly against his large body. It was getting border-line stressful, and I hated stress.

"Step away, Chloe!" I yelled, my accent pulled on the word away.

"Calm down, West Virginia," she said snidely. "Trent and I have a bit of a past. I can hug him if I want to."

Red—all I saw was red!

I went to lunge at her but Kane held me back. He was big like Trent but not as strong. I shoved farther, trying to break his grip. JJ joined in, holding my other arm as I swung it free from Kane's grasp.

"Oh come on, guys, let her go," Reece said. "I'm all about watching the Amazons fight. Hey does anyone have a hose or some Jell-O laying around?"

Kitty smacked Reece upside of the head.

"Damn Kitty, I'm just joking," he said, rubbing his head.

"No, you're really not, Reece. We all know you're not," Kitty said.

"Babe, come on, she was just saying hi," Trent said, defending her. *He is actually defending her?*

"You—did you sleep with her?" I asked in a rage.

I'd never flown so far off the handles as I did in that moment. I didn't know what it was but I had blinders on, and all I could see was Chloe straddling *my* mound of muscles, her long black hair falling down her back and him with a stupid grin on his face. I was losing my mind!

"Lexi, don't—"

"Did. You. Sleep. With her?" I asked, pointing to Chloe and talking slowly just in case he didn't understand me the first time.

"I can answer that," Chloe said from beside him.

He turned to her, his eyes went huge, and I swear I saw 1 bead of sweat form on his brow.

That fucker slept with her! "You don't have to, he just did," I said, shaking my head in disappointment.

"Dude, you slept with Chloe? When?" Kane asked.

"That doesn't really matter," Trent said, shrugging his shoulders.

"You're right, Trent, it doesn't matter," Kitty said, crossing her arms and staring up at Kane.

"Oh, we slept together about four or was it five months ago? Anyway it was when your dick was broke. You remember right, Trent? Kane couldn't get it up and we were both horny and alone on the bus and...well, fucking happens," Chloe said nonchalantly. "Speaking of busses, where is yours?" she said, looking around, as if a huge pile of shit hadn't been bumped down in front of all of us.

"It's at our hotel. Come on, Kitty, let's get a cab. Clearly, they all need to get their stories straight." I yanked my arm from Kane and JJ, took Kitty's hand in mine, and stalked off to find a cab.

"Lexi, wait a minute," Trent yelled, running up behind us.

"Can't, I need some space," I said, not turning around to address him.

He grabbed my arm, making me and Kitty stop in our tracks.

I looked down at his hand wrapped tightly around my arm then glared up at him. "You need to let me go," I said through gritted teeth.

"What is going on with you?" he asked concerned.

What is going on?

Chapter 18

Trent

*W*hat *the hell just happened?* I glanced next to me. Chloe had an evil grin spread across her face while Lexi and Kitty walked away.

"Wow, I guess your girls can't hang," she said, picking at her nails.

"What's your deal?" Kane asked, shaking his head.

"What? It's not my fault. You're the ones that fucked me, and, if I remember correctly, both of you liked it. What's to be ashamed of?"

"Oh, Chloe. You're going to be miserable for the rest of your life with a fucking attitude like that. Don't try to destroy what we all have, just because you're jealous," Kane said, getting up in her face.

I ran after Lexi and Kitty, who were halfway across the parking lot. "Lexi, wait a minute," I yelled, running up behind them.

"Can't. I need some space," she said, not turning around to address me.

I didn't want to but I had no choice. I needed her to stop so I grabbed her arm, making them stop in their tracks. She looked down at my hand that was wrapped tightly around her arm, and then glared up at me. Her beautiful eyes were glossy as they burned into mine.

"You need to let me go," she said through gritted teeth.

"What is going on with you?" I asked, concerned.

Lately, she had been restless when we slept, tossing and turning. She was watching my every move. Not that I cared, but something was bothering her. Something was weighing heavily on her mind.

"What's going on? What's going on is that I just had to watch some skank hang on you. Then I had to watch as you tried to lie to me about sleeping with her. That's what's going on," she yelled at me.

"Trent, maybe you should just ba—"

"No, I'm not going to back off," I growled, cutting Kitty off. "Lexi, something else is going on. You've been acting weird, and—"

"Don't you stand here and try to make me feel bad for acting the way I just did. Anyone in my position would have."

"What is that supposed to mean?"

"It means that—that, fuck! Trent, I'm terrified you're going to leave me and go back to your original type of skank. There I said it, it's out there. I have insecurities, and I don't think I'm good enough to be with you. You happy?" She started off yelling but, by the end, her voice was low and brittle.

I didn't know what to say. She had always been so confident in us, in herself. I was baffled. *What changed?* It couldn't have been Chloe. Her acting like this had been going on for a week or two.

We were two months out from going back to our

hometown and I was stoked to have her meet my family. I had been gushing about her to them. She had met my brother and his family as I skyped with them, but she wanted to meet my parents in person. I knew they were going to love her because I loved her. I loved her more than I knew was possible.

I was panicking. I didn't want us to fall apart but, fuck, if we weren't falling apart right before my eyes. "Why would you ever think that? Lexi come on, I would never—"

"Trent, just stop. I can't do this right now. I need some space, I need to clear my head, and I can't have you being the knight in shining armor, right now," she said, tossing her hair around.

"Okay, fine," I said giving in and hating every second of it.

"I'll stay with her tonight. You and Kane can bunk together," Kitty said. She was clearly pissed that her husband was curious about when I slept with Chloe, which was back when they were on the mend. I guess Kane and I had both fucked up.

"Yeah, okay," I said, hanging my head. "Lexi," I said, tilting my head so I could read her face. "There's only you. You have nothing to be insecure about."

I had to at least say that. I had to make sure she knew I had moved past hooking up with the type of woman I used to covet.

She wouldn't look at me. Her eyes were fixed on the ground. She wasn't giving me anything. Before anything else could be said, Kane came running up beside me.

"Kitty—"

"Don't you Kitty me. You're flirting with disaster. Why don't you and Trent here room tonight? You can swap sex stories of Chloe, since you just had to know who she was sleeping with!"

"Baby, come on."

"I'm warning you, Kane, back up!" she said, getting in his face. She was trying to be tough but I saw her wink up at him. She was just acting out for Lexi's sake. I guess chicks feel better when they're both pissed off at their men.

"Fine, we'll talk tomorrow. Let's go, Trent," he said, looking down at her and winking back.

He nodded once, placed a hand on my shoulder, and tugged me to head back to the rest of the guys. I didn't say anything else to Lexi. I figured she was too pissed to hear reason at that moment, so I decided to save it for the next day when she'd be more level headed.

Not happening. We had been on the bus for six hours, and she still hadn't come out of the back room. She and Kitty were holed up in there the whole freaking time. When we arrived at the next venue, the roadies were already there setting up for the show. We were at a college festival. The place was packed with people and musicians of all kinds. It was the last night of the festival, and we were the grand finale. We'd always been big with college kids, and this festival proved it.

As soon as the bus came to a stop, Lexi came storming out of the back room. She stopped at the couch where we were all sitting playing video games and addressed us. "Ya'll have a meet and greet before you go on at nine. You have to be at sound check by six and in the meet and greet room by seven. If you are not there, you will be sleeping on the bus for the next week while everyone else is in a nice luxury hotel room. Everything has been booked for the next two months, and you'll all be happy to know that we will not be staying in anything less than a four-star hotel. Congratulations, your label gave you a raise so we can spend the extra money on nice hotels. If there's nothing else, I will see you all at six for sound check." She was like a robot—no expression, no change in her voice. It was fucking scary.

She waited a moment to see if anyone had a question and when no one spoke up, she gave a fake ass smile grabbed her papers and stalked off the bus. The five of us sat on the couch in disbelief.

"Dude, your girl is not herself," Reece said, leaning forward and making eye contact with me.

"What happened between the two of you?" JJ asked.

"You think I have a fucking clue what happened? I'm just as confused as you fuckers," I said, rubbing my eyes with the palms of my hands.

"Maybe it's a good thing. She's on top of her shit. Maybe you've been the fucking problem the whole time, distracting her with your limp dick," Reece said, standing and stretching his back.

I reached over the guys and punched him in the gut. He fell back on the couch, holding his stomach.

"Fuck you, Reece," I said, standing to go after Lexi.

"Oh God, I think you ruptured my spleen," he said, writhing on Kane's shoulder.

"You deserved it," Kane said, pushing Reece off of him and into Aiden's lap.

I ran off the bus to find Lexi, but she was so damn fast I couldn't find her through all the other busses and venders. I spent the remainder of my time trying to find her, asking around. No one had seen her. By the time we were scheduled for sound check, I had lost hope of talking to her. The only thing that gave me peace of mind was knowing that she couldn't go anywhere without us. I knew that at least I'd have time to talk to her tonight after the show, if not the next day when we were all stuck on the bus for another eight-hour drive across country.

I was standing stage left next to Kane, like I normally did, as we ran through the set. I glanced in the wings, expecting to see Lexi standing there like she had been for the past three months but the space was empty. I could hear her through my earpiece so at least I knew she was in the area, most likely near the soundboard.

Kane was singing, we were all playing, but I was distracted as I listened to her through the earpiece.

"That is not true," I heard her say then laugh.

"Oh, but it is," a male voice said, a little too fucking seductively for my liking.

"You're bad. You trying to get me in trouble?" she asked.

It was her voice but she sounded different. She sounded like the women she always made fun of for flirting with us.

"I'd love to get you into some trouble."

At that, I hit a sour note, knocking everyone off their game. Kane stopped singing and Reece quit drumming. JJ stilled his strings, and Aiden just stood behind me silently.

I never missed a cord. I never had a finger slip, and I never fucked up. The talking in my ear stopped as well.

"Umm, should we do that one again?" a voice said from over the loud system.

"No, we're good, let's just go on to the next song," Kane said, answering for us all.

I didn't know if they heard what I heard but, if they did, they knew I was getting angrier by the moment.

The lights went up in the venue and, out in the middle of the crowd, the sound booth sat. A group of people stood around taking notes, with Lexi among them, she was standing next to some guy I'd never seen. He wasn't on our team, which meant that he worked for the venue or some other band. She was standing too fucking close to him, and he was looking at her in the wrong fucking way. As the music started up for the last song of our set, she looked at the stage, her beautiful eyes were pinned on me, but her expression wasn't the one I wanted to see. I wanted to see her smile, I needed to see that dimple as a sign that we were fine, that everything was back to normal. *Hell, I'll take "kind of normal."* But she just stood there staring at me, no expression on her face. My heart twitched in my chest. It wasn't over. Whatever insecurities she had about us were still there.

The man next to her placed his hand on the small of her back and whispered in her ear. If I stared any harder at them, fucking lasers were going to shoot out of my eyes. She smiled over at him. *She fucking smiled at him!* Kane looked over at me as he sang, his eyes wide and his expression one of concern. I just shook my head and kept playing. There was nothing I could do in the moment. Well, that was I lie, I had thought about jumping off the stage and bashing the guy's face in, but I didn't. I kept my cool and kept playing, because I'm a fucking professional. But I never took my eyes off of her.

"What was that about?" Kane asked once our practice was over and we were headed to the meet and greet.

"I don't fucking know. Did Kitty tell you anything?"

"No nothing," he said, slinging an arm around my shoulder.

We were the last to arrive in the room. I scanned it, searching for Lexi. She was standing behind Aiden rubbing his shoulders harshly and punching him, probably because he said something rude.

"Ha, I guess you're getting a little bit of the silent treatment. She seems pretty comfortable with Aiden," Kane said.

I shouldn't feel jealous. Aiden was one of my oldest friends, but I was ready to knock him out. She was smiling and laughing at something Aiden said, and as much as I wanted to be pissed, I was glad she was having a good time. I walked across the room and stood in front of the table where Aiden sat and Lexi stood behind him. My hands on the table, I leaned across it getting in her face with Aiden between us.

I didn't say anything. I just stared into her eyes, making a mental note of all her features. Being on the road and running around all the time, her face had lost some of its roundness and her eyes looked tired. Her hair was down and tucked behind her perfectly proportioned ears. Her nose was button like and her lips were full and tinted with pink lip gloss.

"Can I help you?" she asked, her accent pulling, after a few moments of me staring at her.

I caught her lick her lips as she watched the muscles in my arms flex as I leaned over the table a little more.

"What are you doing?" I asked.

She looked around the room, scrunched her brows and found me again. "Waiting for the meet and greet. What are you doing?"

"Trying to figure out why my girl is acting like someone I don't even know," I said, cocking my head to the side as I waited for an answer.

She took a deep breath and started messing with Aiden's hair that was pulled back in his signature low pony tail. She wouldn't look at me as she twisted the hair around her fingers.

"Dude, just give her some space," Aiden said from below me.

"Aiden, I love ya, man, but stay the fuck out of this."

"Hey, don't talk to him like that," Lexi yelled, pushing my shoulders so I was forced to take a step back and stand straight.

"Really, Lexi?" I huffed, getting angrier that she was sticking up for him, protecting him. I walked around the table to where she stood, but as I was about to be toe to toe with her, Aiden stood from his seat and blocked me.

"Trent, stop it," he said, holding his hands up.

Maybe it was the fact that I knew Aiden found Lexi attractive or maybe it was the fact that she had ignored me and found comfort in others, but I was pissed. Without knowing I was doing it, my chest puffed up and I braced myself for a beat down.

"Look at you," Lexi yelled from around Aiden. "What are you going to do, beat up your best friend because I'm talking to him? This is exactly the reason why I pushed you away in the beginning." She shook her head and tossed her hands in the air. Turning from us both, she walked out of the room.

"What's wrong with me?" I said, hanging my head.

"I think you just gotta ride it out, man. She'll come around. Listen, I need to tell you something," Aiden said shoving his hands in his pockets. "I was with Lexi last night." My face jumped up to his. He quickly shook his head no and crossed his hands in the air. "Not like that, bro, I'd never do that. But I was with her."

"What are you talking about? She was with Kitty last night," I said anxiously.

"I went to the bar in the hotel last night and saw her sitting there, so I joined her. We ended up talking till we left this morning," he said, pulling his hair tighter against this head.

"Well, what the hell's wrong with her? Why is she keeping me at arm's length? I don't fucking get it, bro," I asked in a rush.

"Calm down, take a breath."

Aiden had a calm about him, always had. He'd usually be the one to bring me down after a fight and even stop me from getting in fights in the first place. Aiden was a listener. He was levelheaded and never lashed out like the rest of us had a tendency of doing. If I was the physical enforcer of the group, Aiden was the calm presence that kept us all focused, but that didn't mean he was any less of an ass.

"What did you talk about?" I asked as we sat down.

"Dude, everything. She told me about John," he said, shaking his head and turning a pen between his fingers. "She also told me that she cares about you. She's just in a rough spot right now, and she doesn't know why. You know what he did to her. You can imagine what's going through her head."

I knew that John, her ex, tried to morph her into what he thought was perfect, even though she was perfect all along. I knew that, when he drank, he got sloppy and took everything out on her. She was so fucking brave. She took it and took it with a smile on her face, because she thought she loved him.

"Did she tell you he used to tell her she wasn't pretty? Can you believe that?" he asked.

Someone saying that Lexi wasn't pretty was like saying puppies were vicious animals.

"Why is she doubting me now? We've been fine for months, and now she's what...having flashbacks?" I asked, trying to wrap my head around it all.

"I think that seeing you with other women is messing with her head—"

"But I'm not. I'm not with anyone but her," I said, cutting him off.

"I know that. And I think she knows that deep down. She's just second-guessing herself. Give her time. She'll figure it all out," Aiden said just as the doors opened and the line of fans started trickling in. Lexi ushered in the first group. I couldn't take my eyes off her. She had become my everything, and I wasn't about to lose her over doubt.

I was the first at the long table. The rest of the guys

were to my right. Lexi stood next to me the whole time
we greeted fans and signed pictures and memorabilia.

Chapter 19

Lexi

The last twenty-four hours of my life had been a whirl wind of emotions. Seeing Trent with Chloe, staying up all night and talking to Aiden, who I thought for the longest time was mute because he was always so quiet, I had gone from being on a high after their show, to embarrassed for losing the bus, jealous after seeing Trent with his arm around Chloe, to pissed off at Trent for letting that happen, then back to embarrassed as I spilled my guts to Aiden. I'd never had that many emotions in such a short period of time. I was usually pretty even keeled. *Don't get me wrong, I got mad and could be loud when the time called for it, but this was ridiculous.*

Of course I was stuck standing next to Trent for the hour-long signing before the show. There was a break in people streaming in the room, and that's when Trent took the moment to gain my attention. His large hand ran up the back of my jean-clad thigh, stilling just under my ass cheek.

I flashed him a warning look but he kept his hand steady. "What are you doing?" I asked, looking down at him. My clipboard over my chest, I held onto it tightly.

"Nothing," he said, raising his eyes up to mine.

I moved on my toes and craned my neck around to look at his hand securely on my thigh. "That," I said, pointing to his hand with my pen. "What is that doing?" I questioned him with brows raised.

"This?" he said, wiggling his fingers on the back of my thigh.

"Yes."

"Do you want me to move it?" he asked, raising one perfectly thick brow.

Did I want him to move it? That one thought had a pool of warmth spreading from my core. *Yes, I did want him to move it...North and then east.* His hand moved up a little more. I wanted to give in, I wanted to let my head fall back, and I wanted to give in to his soft and kind touch.

Again, my emotions were going haywire. I wanted my boyfriend. I needed him to give me that reassurance that, up until a day ago, I never needed. He sat casually back in his chair, his handsome face staring up at me. I longed to touch the now-two-day-old thick scruff that grew on his face. I loved the way it felt under my hand and against my body. *What am I doing?*

It was clear that he loved me, and I was a fucking idiot if I couldn't see that I loved him. I bit the inside of my cheek as his fingers spread around the back of my thigh. The whole time I had been talking to myself I never quit looking at him. His broad shoulders were covered by a black shirt, but I knew that underneath of them, the tattoos I loved to trace with my finger were waiting for me.

His index finger was on its way to the motherland when the door opened and the last of the fans came streaming through. I let out a breath I hadn't known I'd been holding.

"You all right?" he asked, smiling up at me.

I smiled back and shook my head, before smacking his shoulder. "You play dirty," I quipped.

"I'd do anything to make you smile like that. And if that includes playing dirty, eh, I'm going to do it," he said, slapping my ass. He turned back in his chair to the eager fan in front of him without missing a beat. "Hi, sweetie, what's your name?" he asked, taking the picture of them from her hands.

"Hi!" she squeaked. "I'm Cameron. I absolutely love you and your music of course," she gushed.

It was a known fact among the ONS fans that the guys loved them. They were quickly becoming a household name and it was all because of their report with the fans, and their music was pretty sweet, too.

"Well, thank you, I'm glad you love our music. Hey, can I tell you a secret?" he asked, leaning forward over the table.

This Cameron, who looked sixteen, nodded and knelt down a little to get closer.

"You see that girl right there?" he asked, nodding in my direction.

"Yeah," Cameron said giggling and looking over at me.

"I'm in love with her," he said all seductively.

The fan smiled back, because what else can you do when a hot ass man looked the way he did, whispering in your face.

"Do you think you could help me tonight?" he asked. The fan nodded and smiled wider. "I need you to tell everyone you meet tonight to yell 'Trent loves Lexi' after we sing 'Found.' Can you do that for me? I need to make her see just how much I love her."

Found, of course, being my favorite song that the guys sang. He was truly playing dirty.

"Yeah, I can do that," she said, nodding and smiling.

"All right, if you can get that done for me, I'll send you the very first copy of our CD before anyone else gets it, signed of course by all of us. Give me your name and address."

We both watched as the girl scrambled in her purse for a scrap of paper, which ended up being a receipt to some clothing store. She scribbled her name and address down and shoved it at Trent. He took it from her, read it, and then sat up a little and pulled his wallet out, placing the paper securely between a few dollar bills. He stuck his wallet back in his back pocket and, I kid you not, the fan was about to faint.

"I won't let you down," she said, winking.

"I know you won't, because we have the best fucking fans in the world," he yelled, getting everyone else in line all fired up.

The room erupted in cheers and screams. I covered my ears and squinted my eyes at the noise.

"You really think that's going to work?" I asked after the girl had moved on down the line.

"Fucking right it's going to work. Not that I need it to make you see how much I need you, but I don't think it'll hurt."

He smiled up at me. I hit his shoulder and rolled my eyes.

We were back. Thank fucking God, we were back to normal. *Maybe it was just a speed bump?* I was feeling good, and any doubt I had was gone as fast as it had come. *Maybe I should go to the doctor just to make sure I'm not turning bi-polar?*

ぐぬぐ

Sure enough, after the guys played "Found," the crowd screamed "Trent loves Lexi."

Trent helped, of course. He went up to his microphone as the last of the music trailed off. "Cameron...Cameron..." He reached in his back pocket and pulled out his wallet and the piece of paper. "Cameron Reynolds from Wichita Kansas?" he said into the microphone.

I stood in my usual spot off stage, just next to him with the biggest smile on my face. He was going to make the poor girl have a freaking heart attack calling her out like that. I wished that Kitty was here to witness it but she wasn't feeling well so she stayed on the bus.

The crowd got quiet as Cameron screamed and jumped up and down with her friends. The spotlight found her and she screamed even more as her face was plastered on the big screen.

"Ah, there you are," Trent said. "Time to make good on your promise."

She yelled as loud as she could. "One. Two. Three..."

"Trent loves Lexi!" The whole crowd yelled. It was so loud I covered my ears like I had in the signing room.

"I don't think she heard you," Reece said from behind the drums.

Again the crowd yelled even louder. Trent stood on stage with his hands up in the air, his bass slung around his shoulder. He was the perfect picture of a rock star, and he was all mine.

"Did you hear them, baby?" he asked, holding the microphone in one hand and his bass's neck in the other.

He smiled over at me and I melted to the floor. I was a puddle of Lexi mush on the freaking floor. But I wanted to hear it one more time. So I shook my head no with a smile on my face.

"She doesn't believe you," he said, addressing the crowd again. The crowed sighed collectively. "Let's make her really believe it this time," Trent said, holding up his hand. He held up his fingers, one, then two and finally three.

"Trent loves Lexi."

The crowd was so loud the walls and floors vibrated. I covered my face, happy as I had ever been. I felt the sting of happy tears prick at my eyes. I wiped them with my fingers and when I was able to focus I saw that Trent had run off the stage and was standing in front of me. He moved his bass strap so it slung over his back.

"What are you doing?" I asked, wiping my eyes again.

"Do you believe me? Do you believe it's only you?" he asked, tilting my chin up with his fingers.

I smiled up into his face as he searched mine. "Yes, I believe you."

"Good," he said, leaning over the short distance to kiss my lips.

What I thought was going to be a quick peck on the lips swiftly turned into a full on make out session. *Who knew that one day of not kissing would lead to needing him so much?* My arms draped around his sweaty neck as he held my hips, pulling me closer.

"Excuse me, we still have music to play, shows not over," JJ said into his microphone, making the crowd erupt in cheers.

"I have to go," Trent said, resting his forehead on mine.

"Stop sucking her face off and get back out here, lover boy," Reece hollered from his drums.

"I'm going to kill him," Trent said against my lips.

"Don't, he's just jealous. You can get him back when he's the one all love struck and stupid." I held Trent's face between my hands, kissing his lips one last time before pushing him back out on stage.

The crowd cheered again. Before he fixed his bass, he adjusted himself, lifting his shirt so the world could see his amazing torso, next he fixed his zipper and belt. I could have killed him.

Kane walked over, giving him a high five and bro hug. They said something, but I couldn't hear over the screams and cheers coming from the crowd. A few moments later, Reece started up the next song, and they were right back at it, doing what the five of them had dreamed about since starting the band in Aiden's garage when they were nothing more than a bunch of horny, pimpled faced thirteen-year-olds.

I sat happily on a stool just off the stage, watching the man of my dreams and his band play. I always watched them. They were simply that good. The crowd was cheering and the music was blaring, but even over all of that, I noticed my phone ringing from inside my pocket. Assuming it was one of the big wigs checking up on us, I decided to let it go to voice mail. Two minutes later it was ringing again. I reached in my back pocket, pulling my phone out. When I checked the screen, my heart sank to the pit of my stomach. It was my mom calling. *Something's wrong.*

"Hello?" I answered, covering my other ear so I could hear her.

"Lexi? It's Mom."

"I know, caller ID silly. What's up?" I asked, standing from my stool and moving back to a quieter space.

"It's John, he was in an accident," she said in a sob.

I heard her take a shaky breath and knew that she was either crying or about to start crying. "Mom, are you okay?" I asked.

"Yes—Yes, I'm fine but John—Lexi, he's back in surgery right now and I'm all alone, and it would be nice to have some family here." She was crying, sobbing into the phone.

My heart broke for her. "I can't just leave, Mom. I have a job, responsibilities." *A man I'm in love with.* I wouldn't dare say that. She'd get even more upset because she still had it in her mind that I was going to marry John.

"I understand that but family needs to come first. Even though you turned him down, John is still a part of this family, and he needs you." I rolled my eyes at that one. "I need you, Lexi, how am I supposed to do everything on my own. Your brother is coming as soon as he can, but he's overseas."

"Oh, so it's okay for him to have a job and not be there but I have to drop everything?"

"Alexis Lynn Ford! That is not what is going on here, and you know it. I don't know why you left John, probably because you've never told anyone, but you need to put that aside. He is your best friend, if nothing else. You two have been through everything together, and he needs you now. I need you now. I can't do this on my own. I lost your father, then I lost Tim, I can't lose John too." She was full-on crying, begging me to come save her.

I held my forehead in confusion. I didn't know what to do. Stay? Go? "How bad? And what happened?" I asked, hoping that maybe she was being over dramatic.

"He was on his bike and got T-boned by a pick-up truck. The paramedics said he flew over twenty feet in the air before landing on a guard rail. I know he broke his left arm and right leg. They said they are trying to stop the internal bleeding now. Lexi, it's not good. The nurses said that he kept saying your name over and over again so much that they thought you might have been on the bike with him."

My back rested on the cool concrete wall, as images of the man I loved my whole life flashed past my eyes. I picture him lying in a room alone, because that's what he was, alone. No family, except my mom, no friends because they all moved away for work. He'd stayed and took over the farm after college, expecting that we'd get married and start our own family there. The more I thought about it, the more anxious I became.

"Lexi, are you still there?" my mom asked.

"Yeah, Mom, I'm here." I felt the sting of tears behind my eyes for a man who I loved so much. Even if it wasn't in a romantic way, he was family and I did care.

"Oh, wait the doctors are coming out, I'll put it on speaker—"

"No, Mom, don't—"

"Ms. Ford?" I heard the doctor ask.

"Yes…um…my daughter, John's um…"

"Sister," I said, knowing that if I didn't, my mom might say that I was his girlfriend or fiancée.

"Okay, well, we have an update. He had the broken arm, which we've corrected. His leg was a bit more complicated. We had to put a rod and plates in, to repair it properly."

My first thought was of him working on the farm, and how it was going to be a while before he could. He loved that place. He was going to be crushed.

"Now, the internal bleeding was bad. He lost a significant amount of blood, but we were able to give him a transfusion. He had a collapsed lung and a small tear to his heart. We were able to fix both, but we did have to shock him twice to bring him back. We ended up taking out his ruptured spleen, and we had to take out some of his intestines, because they were so shredded from the guardrail. Now, thankfully, he had his helmet on so there was no brain damage, or head injuries. Because of the extensive exploratory surgery, we're going to keep him in the ICU until he gets around the bend."

"What does that mean, around the bend?" my mother asked, through a sob.

"Ms. Ford, John is lucky to be alive. If we can keep him stable and keep any infections at bay, watch to make sure there are no more hidden problems, he should make a full recovery. But I'm going to warn you, it's not easy and any support system he has should be here to help him make the turn. We see it a lot when young men come in and don't have that support system, they give up and, once they give up, there's not much we can do," the doctor said.

Again, my heart thudded against my chest. It was weird to think that a man so strong and brave was weak and frail, and at the mercy of everything.

"All right, thank you, Doctor. When can I see him?" my mother asked.

"We're going to keep him heavily sedated for a few days because the pain is going to be too much for his body to take, so in a few hours you'll be able to see him. But just remember he'll be out of it, and not able to communicate."

"Thank you, thank you so much," my mother sobbed.

"Yes, thank you," I added. I could hear my mother move the phone as if she was hugging the doctors. It went quiet for a moment before I heard her very distinctive sigh. "Mom, are you okay? Why don't you find somewhere to sit down for a minute?" I said, praying that she wouldn't pass out on me.

"Please come home, baby," she said, crying and hyperventilating through the phone.

"Mom, calm down, he's fine. Did you hear the doctor?" I said, trying to sooth her from over a thousand miles away.

"No, Lexi, I can't calm down. Tim asked me to watch over his boy and here he is in the hospital clinging to life. I can't do this on my own," she cried.

"All right, just please calm down. What good is it going to do if you're in the bed next to him, having a heart attack?" I said, shoving my hand through my hair.

I knew deep down what I had to do. I just didn't want to do it. I glanced out on stage. Kane and Trent were back to back singing and having the time of their lives, while I stood there drowning in decisions that were going to change everything.

Chapter 20

Trent

Everything was right in the world. I was on a huge stage with my best friends, making the music we'd always dreamed about and playing to crowds we never thought imaginable. The love of my life wasn't ignoring me, but sitting on a stool just off the stage. My family was healthy and—what more could I say? My life was fucking amazing.

After the show, I ran off the stage, sweat rolling down my face. I grabbed a towel from one of the roadies and dried my face, head, and neck. I tossed the dripping, sweat-filled towel in its designated basket, took my bass off, and handed it to the roadie who was in charge of all our instruments.

Taking a bottle of water from a table, I drank it all in a matter of seconds. Glancing around, I noticed Lexi's stool was vacant.

"Hey, man, where's my woman at?" I asked James, one of our roadies.

"I saw her take a phone call a while back. I guess she walked out to hear better," he said nonchalantly.

"Thanks, man," I said, clasping his shoulder as I walked past him in search of Lexi.

We had a long night ahead of us, and I was more than ready to get it started. Going without her for one night was one fucking night too long.

I felt like I ran from one side of the building to the other, looking for Lexi. On my way back to the holding room to check if she was there, I stumbled on some waiting fans. A group of four women stood between me and the door.

They were decked out in their ONS shirts, tight ass jeans, and long blonde hair. Their heels were high and their bodies were flawless. I came to stop a few feet from them, but it was no use, they'd seen me and came clicking their way over.

"Trent!" one of them yelled as she shimmied over.

"Hello, ladies," I said politely. The last thing I needed was for Lexi to come around the corner and see me with four stunning blondes throwing themselves at me.

"Where's the fire, sweetheart?" another piped up when I tried to skirt around them.

"Ladies, I'd love to chat but I'm kind of looking for someone," I said charmingly.

"What's the matter? You don't see anything you like here?" the third girl asked, taking a step toward me.

"Trent!"

I heard Reece calling me. For once in my life I was thrilled.

"Ladies, ladies, ladies, mmm, you all look mighty scrumptious," Reece said, joining the gathering in the hall. He slung his arm around my shoulder and cocked a wicked grin at the women in front of us.

"We were wondering where the party was, and if we

could join, of course?" the first one asked, draping her arms around Reece's neck.

Five months ago, I would have been all over these women, but right then all I could think about was getting the hell away from them and finding Lexi.

I crossed my arms over my chest and put on the best get-the-fuck-away vibe I could, without being rude to our fans, of course.

I covered my mouth with my hand to keep from saying something rude to our nice fans.

"What's wrong, big guy?" the second one asked, rubbing my shoulder.

"Nothing's wrong, skank. He's just trying not to burst out laughing in your face because you look like a hooker searching for her next ticket." Lexi stood in the doorway down from us, her long legs crossed casually and her arms folded over her chest.

"Excuse me?" the second one said with a head roll.

"Nobody talks to my friend like that!" the third fan said, joining her friend in a weird unison head roll.

"Oh, well then, I guess I'll talk to you." Lexi straightened from the door jam, staring down the women in front of her. "Get your grubby, little, fake hair, fake tan, slutty hands off my man."

"Who the hell are you?" the fourth one piped up.

"I wouldn't do that if I were you," I said, shaking my head vigorously.

The women looked at me then back at Lexi. They looked at her as if she wasn't at their level, as if she wasn't good enough for us.

"Wait a minute, you're Lexi, aren't you?" the one asked, once it started to click in her tiny brain.

"That's the Lexi you're in love with?" another asked, raising a brow as if it was the hardest thing to imagine.

"Your goddamn right I am," I said sternly.

"What about you? Are you free?" they asked Reece with wanton eyes.

"No, he's not," Lexi said, answering on Reece's behalf.

"What the hell, Lexi?" Reece said through gritted teeth.

She made her way down the hall and over to us. Busting through the wall of blonde, she stood between Reece and me. Snaking her arm around both of us she pulled us closer to her. Our bodies formed one as she reached up, grabbed my face with both her hands, and kissed me. Then to my surprise and Reece's, she turned to him, took his face in between her hands, and kissed him as well. We're not talking about a peck on the cheek either, we're talking about a full-on I-saw-his-fucking-tongue-in-her-mouth kiss.

When she pulled back, Reece looked like he was going to pass the fuck out.

"These two are taken tonight, go find some roadies," Lexi said snidely, draping her arms around us again.

Both of us held her around the waist as we stood there in the brightly lit hallway.

"Are you serious, you're going to take her over us?" the loudest one of the bunch asked, popping her hip out and crossing her arms over her chest.

I swear if her eyes had any more make-up on them, she wouldn't have been able to keep them open.

"I'm good," I said, pulling Lexi closer to me. She smiled up at me and gave me dimple for days.

"Oh, I'm definitely good. I've never been fucking better, actually," Reece said, reaching over and kissing the hand that rested on his shoulder. He smiled over at Lexi as she did the same.

"Well, I think that's your cue to scurry along," Lexi said, wiggling her fingers for them to move on.

The four of them huffed as one as they turned and walked out of sight and around the corner. The three of us stood there laughing once they were out of sight.

"Oh, man, that was—"

"So much fun!" Lexi said, smiling over at Reece.

"I think you just saved me from getting an STD, Lexi. Thank you, my dear, I am forever in your debt," Reece said, stepping in front of her, taking her hand, and bowing to kiss it, as if he was addressing royalty.

His lips lingered on her hand, and I finally had enough. "All right get your filthy lips off my woman."

"Calm down, muscles," Lexi said as I shoved Reece so he was forced to let her hand go and back away.

"Dude, I just made out with your woman, and it was fucking amazing!" Reece yelled, making a celebratory fist in the air.

"It was pretty nice. I can see why the ladies love you, Reece. The tongue ring is surprisingly good."

"Finally, someone understands. You have no idea what I go through," he said, biting his lip and doing a horrible job of acting like he was suffering.

"All right, you need to go wash your mouth out with fucking bleach before I kiss you again," I said, pointing to Lexi. "And I better never catch you kissing my woman again or I'm going to rip your arms off and use them as fucking drum sticks," I threatened Reece.

"Calm down, big boy," Reece said, holding his hands up. He stuck his tongue out and clicked his tongue ring against his teeth. "She kissed me, bro. I was just an innocent bystander."

"Right...that's why I saw your tongue in her mouth?" I said, cracking my knuckles.

"I'm not going to lie. I'd do it again, with your permission, of course. So, may I join you tonight?" Reece asked, in all seriousness, wiggling his eyebrows and folding his hands in prayer as he awaited our answer. "I promise I won't look at your junk, bro. Trust me, my eyes will be elsewhere." He took that moment to ogle Lexi and lick his lips seductively.

"Run, Reece," Lexi said as Reece kept staring at her tits.

"Why?" he asked, *still* staring at her tits.

"Because Trent's going to kill you, and I don't want to have to tell the label that one of the members is dead and the other is in jail for manslaughter," she said evenly.

It finally registered and as he turned to look at me. I made a mad dash toward him, but the little fucker was fast, and he managed to bolt down the hallway before I could get my hands on him.

He continued to run down the hall yelling at the top of his lungs. "I made out with Lexi and it was fucking awesome!"

By the time he rounded the corner, I started to make my way back to Lexi. "You created a monster, you know that right?" I said, jogging toward her.

"I know, but it was fun and I needed a pick me up."

"Monster—M. O. N. S. T. E. R," I said, spelling it out while taking her in my arms.

"He really isn't that bad of a kisser," she said, grinning up at me. I shook my head no at her, the corner of my lips turning up. "What? He is. But, seriously, all jokes aside, it was just what I needed."

"So you weren't jealous of the blonde gang bangers?" I asked

"No, I was more determined to put them in their place, which is out with the garbage," she said smiling up at me. She reached up to kiss me, but I put my hand over her mouth. Her brows drew together as she stared up at me. "What's the matter?" she asked from behind my hand.

"I told you, I'm not kissing you till you wash your mouth out." A determined look washed across her face as she went to kiss me again. I held her shoulders so she couldn't get closer.

"Oh come on, really?" she begged, trying to get closer.

"No way, baby. I'm not going near you till you wash whatever Reece put on your lips off."

She kept coming at me and, finally, I turned from her and ran down the hallway, with her hot on my heels.

"Come here, muscles!" she yelled from behind me. "Don't you love me anymore?"

"I do, but I'm not going near those lips till you wash them!" I said over my shoulder.

She chased me all the way to the bus, where everyone was waiting so we could head over to the hotel.

I ran onto the bus a good minute or two before her, and as I came around the corner, Reece was standing in the middle of the bus with a fucking grin on his face. *He must have told everyone what happened.*

"You let *him* kiss your girl, but when I talk to her, you're ready to beat me to a fucking pulp? I don't get it, dude, what the fuck do I gotta do to get one planted on my lips?" Aiden said, laughing.

"Ha, ha, very funny," I said just as Lexi ran up on the bus. Her face was red and, as she came around the corner, she didn't stop, she just kept charging. Reece jumped out of the way as I pushed by him and barricaded myself in the back bedroom.

"Trenton! Get your ass out here and fucking kiss me!" she yelled from the other side of the door.

"Not until you wash that mouth. You can forget it, baby, it's not happening."

"Fine I'll just find someone else to kiss," she said, sounding like she was backing away from the door.

"I'll do it. I will kiss you," Aiden said from the front of the bus.

The fuck he was! This wasn't pass-Trent's-woman-around-so-everyone-could-get-a-fucking-kiss night. I swung the door open and there, leaning against the bunks was Lexi, a sly grin on her beautiful face.

I narrowed my eyes in on her long frame draped against the bunks. I reached out, grabbing her arm and pulling her toward me. Her body smashed into mine. Pressing my hand against the small of her back, I kept her flush against me.

"You realize you're my fucking kryptonite, right?" I said, inches from her lips. "I don't want these lips kissing anything but mine. And please, for the sake of my health and yours, don't ever kiss Reece again."

"I can hear you, asshole," Reece said from the front of the bus.

"We have an agreement?" I asked, ignoring Reece.

"I guess. I mean it's going to be really hard to keep myself contained around Reece, now that I know what that mouth can do," she said, snickering and shrugging her shoulders.

"Must I remind you what my mouth can do to you?" I asked confidently.

I think I took her off guard, because she didn't have a quick comeback for that. Plus I felt her nipples harden against my chest, proving that she knew exactly what my mouth could do to her. *Discussion over, score: Trent 1, Reece 0.*

જીભજી

"Please, please, please, I can't hold on anymore!" Lexi moaned in my ear.

"I can get it, just give me a second, it's being difficult," I called to her.

"Oh, just give it here, let me do it."

"No, I got it, babe, I just need to concentrate."

"Muscles, just give it to me. I need to go, *NOW!*" She was panting now and rocking back and forth.

"Damn, woman! I'm working on it!"

"It's not rocket science, just give it to me."

She was screaming now. I turned to her, narrowing my eyes. I was the fucking man, and I was more than capable of handling it on my own.

"Stop looking at me and fucking open the door, Trent! You know damn well I've had to pee for the last half hour!" she hollered while simultaneously doing a jig to keep from peeing herself.

"I know, Lexi, but the card isn't working!" I huffed, shoving it in her face. She ripped it from my hand and pushed me out of the way. By the time I turned back to the door, she had it open and was bolting for the bathroom and slamming the door once she made it. *Dammit, Trent 0, door 1*

It was a short ride to the hotel, but fuck if it didn't feel like hours. I needed to be inside Lexi. I needed to feel her flesh against mine and, let's be honest, I wasn't doing that on a bus full of horny men. With my luck one of them would bust in and try to join. I loved my boys but not fucking enough to share my woman with them.

After dragging our overnight bags into the room and tossing them on the dresser, I waited on the bed for Lexi to come out. I sat there twiddling my thumbs to keep from getting started on my own. When the door to the bathroom opened, my dick jumped against my pants in anticipation. *Calm down, buddy, we got all night*.

She walked into the open bedroom/office/kitchen nook/living room in her underwear and stylish ONS T-shirt, which she always wore when we played gigs, she called it her uniform. I watched from the bed as she tossed her jeans and shoes next to her overnight bag. Her hair was down but she stood in front of the large mirror on the dresser and pulled it back into a hot mess atop her head. Once done with that, she caught me watching her in the mirror from behind her.

She was perfect. The way her black lacy underwear laid on her ass was every man's dream, and, if it wasn't, then they must still be locked in the closet. The shirt was tight enough so it hugged her body the way I planned on hugging her the entire night. She reached up her back and under the shirt, unclipping her bar she slipped it off, her tits bounced under her shirt as they were released. Seductively, she pulled the black bra through the armhole of her shirt, letting it slip from her fingers. It fell flawlessly on top of her pants and shoes on the floor.

She was still facing the mirror and giving me the hottest ass shot known to man. My pants were becoming tighter, I had to lose them or face the possibility that I might actually cut off circulation. I stood from the bed and unbuckled my belt. I pulled it out of the loops of my jeans and tossed it on the floor. I went to unbutton my jeans. Taking a glance, I wasn't surprised to see Lexi in the same position watching me from the mirror as I undressed. I kicked my jeans to where my belt lay on the floor. I reached behind me and added my shirt to the floor.

Grabbing myself, I adjusted to the freedom of just having my boxers on. They were tee-peed to the max but it felt a hell of lot more comfortable then the confining jeans. Crawling onto the bed, I sat back on the head board, my arms going behind my head. I stared at Lexi's ass and, God help me, the tent grew another inch. Lexi's hands were practically white knuckling the dresser as she watched me watch her. I crossed my legs and settled into the bed as I waited for her turn around.

Her eyes dropped from the mirror and me, to stare at the dark wood on top of the dresser. She looked worried about something, like something was on her mind. But as she looked back up in the mirror, she smiled at me, dimple and all, and I knew that whatever it was wasn't enough to pull her totally away.

"You just going to stand there all night?" I asked, raising my brows.

She didn't answer, just shrugged her shoulders and pouted her lips.

"I mean that's fine with me," I said, " but this guy's getting a little anxious and if you don't do anything about it, then I'm going to have to. I'll just need you to bend over a little, maybe bounce a bit—jiggling is always good -and I'm going to need you to lose the shirt and flash some tits toward the end."

She shook her head and whipped around to face me. "Oh, is that all?" she asked.

"Yeah, that should do it," I said, smiling from the bed.

She smiled wickedly. "All right."

What the fuck did I just do? She reached for the bottom of her shirt, pulling it up and over her head as she turned back around to face the dresser. *This is happening...oh shit!* I undid my hands from behind my head, shoved one into my boxers, pulled myself out, and indulged.

As requested Lexi bent over, bounced, jiggled, and felt her way up her body. About ten minutes in, the room was silent except for my hand moving.

"This good for you?" she asked, still watching me from the mirror.

"Yeah, babe, it's good," I said struggling to talk

while I stared at her ass as she swayed back and forth.

"So you don't want me to lose the underwear?"

Oh God, stop, stop moving your hand before you explode in it. I slowed my movements to a stroke every other second. "I never said that."

"You never asked either," she teased as she threaded her thumbs under the lacy fabric.

"Take them off," I demanded. Her brows drew together in a scowl. "Please take them off?" I said, adjusting my request.

Down they went, and up went my dick. I picked up the pace to every second. Kicking the underwear from her feet, she turned to face me. Her eyes were fixed on mine for a moment before she took in the rest of me. I saw it in her eyes, that worried, anxious air about her. But as fast as it appeared, it was gone again, but I'd seen it. It was there.

Regrettably, I tore my hand from myself and sat up a little, scratching the now longer than scruff but not quite a beard upon my face. "You wanna talk?" I asked. She shook her head no, but before she did, I saw it for a third time. "Lexi, I don't want to lose another night without you, so if something is on your mind, you need to spill it before it blows up like it did two days ago."

She chewed nervously on the inside of her cheek. *I knew I was right.*

"I do want to talk but not right now. Right now, I want to put everything else aside and just enjoy you, us," she said, slinking from the dresser and coming closer to the bed.

I tried to gauge her, but, for some reason, I couldn't get past her tits bouncing in my face as she crawled over top of me. The warmth between her legs made common sense fly out and desire to have her ride me like a fucking bull replace it. My hands when to her hips and I moved her down over top of me. Heads fell, breath was sucked, in and a warm slick heaven surrounded me.

"Never again," I moaned from beneath her.

"What?" she panted back.

"I'm never letting you walk away from me again," I said, holding her hips and meeting her with each motion she made against me.

I expected her to agree with me the way she was riding me, but she kept quiet, apart from for the moans, screams, and screeches of pleasure. So I didn't think anything of it.

Chapter 21

Lexi

I fucked Trent that night as if it was going to be the last time, because I knew, deep down in my heart, that it might very well be the last time. He wasn't ever going to understand why I had to leave, and, to be honest, I thought about lying or coming up with something else entirely to tell him.

I was safe between his arms. His damp body was flush against mine. I wrapped my arms around his chest the best I could and just held him, listened to his heartbeat, took in the aroma of him, that special aroma that only came after we'd made love. That was what it was, I thought. It wasn't fucking, or rough. Every single time since that first encounter when we'd made love to one another, it was kind and sensual. *Was I falling in love with him?*

I felt the tear roll down my cheek and stick to his skin before I was able to wipe it away. *Did he notice? Damn, he noticed.*

"Hey?" he asked, trying to move me from his chest so he could see my face.

I cursed then got to my knees. I sat next to him mentally preparing for a fight. "All right," I said, holding my hands up in defeat. "I need to tell you something and I need you to keep in mind that there are more people involved than just us. I need you to stay calm, and level headed."

"What the hell's going on?" he asked, sitting up himself.

I took another deep breath before I began. "I received a phone call today," I started. My mouth instantly went dry. "From my mother."

"Is everything okay? Is she all right?" he asked, reaching for my hand and finding it. He held it tenderly between his, stroking the top with his thumb.

"Yes, and no," I said, shrugging.

"What's that supposed to mean?" he asked, brows scrunched.

I let my hand slip from his as I dragged them through my hair anxiously. "My mom needs me to come home as soon as possible. There was an accident, John was in an accident." I stopped there to glance up and gage his reaction, which I should have known was going to be sheer confusion. He narrowed his eyes and seemed to say "go on," so I did.

"He was on his bike and got T-boned by a truck. He's hurt pretty badly—a couple broken bones and some more serious internal injuries. My mom needs me to be there, not only for her but for John and the farm. She can't do it all on her own, not anymore," I finished, and again glanced up to gage his response. It was the same, he was staring at me, or through me, I couldn't tell. He was blank faced and unreadable at that moment. "Did you hear me?" I asked, making sure he was getting everything.

His eyes kind of glazed over as he looked past me and, then seconds later, he was back in the room, eyes hard on mine.

"I fucking heard you," he hissed through a clenched jaw.

"Do you have anything else to say? I mean you always seem to have something to say," I said, getting a little frustrated.

He just sat there. He fucking sat there dragging out the already awkward moment. I wanted to know what was going through his mind, what he thought about it, about me leaving. *Was he happy? Is that why he hasn't said anything? Was he pissed? Probably? Was he just as confused as I was?* I thought the last was my best option. At least with that we could work things out together.

"Trent, please say something," I begged, needing to hear his calming voice, *that's not happening.*

"When did you get this call?" he finally asked.

"During your show."

"And you're just now telling me?" he questioned.

Wait a minute. This isn't my fault! "Yes, I'm telling you now. Would you've rather I'd ran out on stage and told you I was thinking about leaving," I raved. "I didn't think so," I said, chuckling to myself.

"Jesus, Lexi, this isn't something to fucking laugh about."

"Trent, I don't know what to tell you. I don't know what you want to hear, but my mom is begging for me to come home and help her, and John is going to need help too, and even if I'm not romantically in love with him, he's—I can't just—I can't just turn my back on them!"

"You still love him, don't you?" Trent questioned me.

I stilled all movements and just stared at him. *How do I fucking answer that?* "Trent, I'm not going to argue with you about this, it's ridiculous," I said, tossing my hands in the air then crossing them over my bare chest. As we both sat in silence, it was glaringly obvious when my phone started going off across the room on the dresser. I glanced over at him, but he wouldn't look my way. He just stared straight ahead with his jaw clenched tightly. I huffed once then left the bed to retrieve my phone. I was hoping it was anyone but who it actually was—my mother.

I grabbed one of Trent's shirts from his suit case, knowing that it would be long enough if I was forced to step outside and talk with her.

"Hey, Mom," I said, answering the phone. I turned around to face Trent, my back resting against the dresser, and propped a foot up on the bed.

"Lexi, he coded again. I can't do this alone," she cried into the phone.

My heart broke for her. She was one hell of a strong woman, losing not only one love of her life but two. She was the strongest woman I knew, and to hear her breaking down was shredding my insides. "Mom, you've got to calm down, is he stable now?" I asked.

Across from me, Trent was rolling his eyes. I pushed down the urge to throw the phone at his face. None of it was easy to take in, but it was fucking annoying as hell to have someone rolling their eyes at the fact that a human life was hanging in the balance. I lost a little respect for Trent then.

"Yes, he's stable, but Lexi I'm so scared," she said, sucking in a breath as if trying to calm herself down.

"I know it's scary, Mom, but John is strong and he won't go down without a fight," I said, trying to give her as much hope as I could through a phone call.

"Oh, he's strong enough, strong enough to hit your daughter!" Trent said from the bed, loud enough for my mother to hear through the phone.

"Who's that? Who's with you at three-thirty in the morning?" my mother questioned me. Now remember, my mother still thought that I was going to marry John, so to hear another man in the background at all hours of the night kind of screwed with her plans to marry me off.

"Will you shut up?" I yelled, covering my hand over the receiver.

"Excuse me? Alexis Lynn Ford, I know that you did not just tell me to shut up!" My mother's scolding voice came booming through the phone, loud enough for Trent to hear.

He sat back and chuckled to himself. *Jerk!*

"No, Mom I didn't say that to you," I said, trying to save my ass.

"I should hope not. Now who the heck is with you at all hours of the night?" Her accent was getting thicker the longer I kept her on the phone.

"Go ahead tell her who I am, because clearly I haven't meant enough to you, for you to tell your own mother you're dating me," Trent said, crossing his arms over his huge chest, the action made his pecks flex and his arms bulge. Then he deliberately uncrossed just one and scratched the sexy, scruffy, beard along his jaw, because he knew that I loved it when he did that. He was playing so dirty, and I hated him for it. This wasn't about us. It was about my family and had nothing to do with him and his sexy scruff that he kept on touching. *Why does he keep doing that?* I dropped my foot from the bed and crossed my legs tightly to keep my mind focused on anything other than the pounding that was going on between them. *Fucking, dirty ass player!*

"And what was that about someone hitting you? Did that man I heard hit you?" she huffed.

"No! Mom, please just stop talking. Everyone, stop talking and, you—" I said, pointing to Trent. "—you stop doing that." I turned from Trent and went into the bathroom, slamming the door behind me. I needed to be alone, to be able to think straight.

"Lexi, what is going on with you?" my mother asked, switching from needing help herself to over protective mother in a heartbeat.

"Mom…I…" I was struggling, I wanted to tell her about Trent, about how much I cared for him and how I wanted her to meet him. But I also thought about her state of mind, knowing John was in limbo and how much she wanted us to be together. It might just be enough to send her over the edge and into an even more depressed state of mind. *No, she didn't need to know about Trent, not yet at least.*

"It's one of the people I work with mom. We were just working late."

"Did you inform them that you were leaving?" she asked.

I could hear the desperation in her voice, and it was breaking me down. *How do you say no to your mom, when she needs you?*

"Not yet, but I'm going to tell them. I have to stay here for at least two more days. Then we have a break, I guess I'll just tell them I'm not going to be able to come back after the break." I hated saying it out loud, because saying it out loud made it real. I was going to leave Trent, the guys, my job, all to go back to West Virginia and take care of my ex-boyfriend and mother.

"Okay, I feel so much better, knowing that you're going to be coming home, baby. I called Karen and Bob. They're over at the farm, checking on the animals."

"Good, why don't you go home and rest, Mom?" I suggested.

"Yeah, I guess I should. I think I'll stay till the morning and get someone to drive me home, Bob drove me here last night because I was too upset."

"Okay, do you want me to call him and have him come pick you up?" I asked

"Yeah, honey, that's fine," she said, yawing into the phone.

"All right, I'll call him." I hung up with my mother and called our other neighbor Karen. She and my mom were best friends.

"Karen, it's Lexi, I'm sorry to call so early, or late. But can you or Bob pick up my mom from the hospital tomorrow morning and make sure she gets home all right?"

"Yeah, darling, that's fine. How's she doing?"

"She's a wreck," I said, hanging my head, and that was when it all hit me. In that moment, it hit like a freight train coming at me full speed. The tears ran down my face and the breath I thought I had under control started to escape me. The sobs and ugly crying came next.

"Why don't you get some rest too, Lexi? This is tough on everyone. We all love John, and we have to be strong for him, just like he's always been strong for us."

"Yeah, okay," I said through intakes of breath. I hung up with Karen.

Dropping the phone, I sank to the floor and lost it. I curled up into a ball, pulling my knees as tightly as I could to my chest and cried like a baby. I cried for my mother, John, and then I cried for myself, for all that I had been through and all that I still had to endure. I'd lost my father, then I lost my second father, who I loved just as much as my biological one, and suddenly I could lose two more important men in my life.

How much can my heart take, how much longer will it keep working? Will it ever work again if it loses any more loved ones?

Chapter 22

Trent

*H*ow can she just drop a fucking bomb on me like that? I sat in bed as she stormed off into the bathroom, dramatically slamming the door behind her. I punched the air then slapped my face a few times. I was furious. I couldn't understand how she could leave me to go back to the bastard who took advantage of her. I'd given her all of me the five months we were together, I told her all my secrets, I told my family about her. I was fucking ready to marry her. Put a fucking gun to my head and I would have married her and never looked back—*fifteen minutes ago, that is.*

I jumped off the bed and paced back and forth, punching the air as I went from one side of the room to the other. I was hot and needed to calm down before I said or did something that I knew I was going to regret the moment the morning light came through the window. I pulled on my jeans, not bothering to button them. They hung on my hips as I continued to pace back and forth.

Stopping in the middle of the room, I realized I needed to get out of there. I grabbed my shirt and left the room, the door banged behind me as I huffed down the hall, bare feet and all. I went to the bar in the hotel, which was closed, so my next stop was over to the front desk and mini mart next to it. I grabbed a six-pack, two mini captains, and told the man to put in on the rooms bill. I wasn't even done telling him to do that before I took the two captains down and popped the top off the first beer bottle.

Beer in one hand, refills in the other, I made my way back to the empty, dark bar. I placed my five pack on the bar and pulled out an elegant stool to sit my ass on. *Two captains, One beer down.* I reached over and took another, taking a long refreshing swig. For some reason it tasted better than ever before. I took the bottle to my lips again. *Two captains, two beers down.* Again I reached next to me, and again I sat there enjoying the cool liquid that was rushing down my throat and warming my insides. *Two captains, three beers down.*

The whole time I sat there, I thought about how was I going to keep from leaving the tour and going with her? She was it for me. There would be no one else. So how was I going to fight the need to be with her and stick it out with the guys? Sure, before Lexi, my dream was to be a rock star, but I always knew that, even if I was to achieve that dream, I'd never be satisfied. I'd always be searching for the one, the perfect version of my type, blonde, petite, sexy, someone who stood behind me quietly. I never thought I'd be willing to give everything up for someone like Lexi. Even though she was sexy as hell, she wasn't quiet and she'd never stand behind me. No, she'd be right next to me, my equal, and I never thought I'd be with someone like that. *Am I willing to give everything up for her? Would she do the same for me?*

Two caps...Three...no four beers down.

I couldn't get the image of Lexi and John out of my head. I kept having this flash of him with his hands around her arms, him yelling at her, and her cowering down to him like she did the night I first got in her face. Then the image would flash to them in bed together. Although I'd never seen a picture of him, I knew he was built like me, and even resembled me, so it wasn't hard to picture a pretty boy adaptation of me, one with no tattoos or beard. *Caps?...Five beers down.*

I lined all the bottles up one after another along the bar. I was drunk. I hadn't eaten that night and downing the shots and beers so fast had my head spinning and my cheeks flush. I tilted the sixth and final beer up, finishing it off in three huge gulps. Twirling the bottle in my fingers, I let it clink against the ones on the bar, each one an image of Lexi with John.

First clink, her by his bedside as she stroked his face, second her helping him and them having a moment. Third bottle was him smiling at her, running his fingers through her long dark brown hair. Fourth bottle, she closed her eyes and fell deeper into the hand that rested upon her face. Fifth bottle was them looking into each other's eyes, him saying he was sorry, her accepting his apology. Sixth bottle—Fucking, all I saw was them fucking each other. I sat the last bottle on the bar neatly in line with the others. I stared at it for a moment then stood.

Raking my arm as fast as I could across the six bottles, I hit them so hard they crashed together and broke into shattered pieces of glass that scattered the bar, my arm, and the floor.

"Fuck!" I yelled at the top of my lungs. Slamming my fists on the bar, I could feel the glass slicing into my hands, but I was so numb it didn't hurt. Blood dripped down my forearms as I raised them and slammed my fists down again and again. The glass bounced off the bar with each bang of my fists.

I yelled again. "Fuck!" This time it was for the shards of glass that stuck in my hands. I plucked out the large pieces and shook the small ones off my hand. I staggered away from the bar, the alcohol going straight to my head. I needed to lie down. I needed to get back to the room and fucking pass out. I held my hands up. My eyes went in and out of focus, but it was clear that I'd fucked up my hands. I knew I had to clean them up, so I left the mess at the bar and headed for the elevator.

I couldn't remember which button to push so I pushed them all. When I figured out which floor was mine, I staggered out of the elevator and looked for the door I'd come out of. I found it propped open by the extra latch. I remembered doing that, because I didn't have a key.

Shoving the door open, I stumbled in. The bed was still empty, still cold as when I'd left it. The dripping blood from my hand hit the top of my bare foot. It was then I remembered I needed to clean them, wash them off, maybe bandage them up if I could see straight enough to find my toiletries bag that housed a few first aid things.

"Dammit," I cursed as I remembered I'd only brought Lexi's up and not mine.

I pushed open the bathroom door, the movement sensor for the light went off as I walked in and the bathroom lit up. I scrunched my eyes, bringing my hand up to shade them. The blood dripped onto my face. I tried to wipe it off but only added more to it. My hands were covered in blood. I leaned closer to the mirror and saw the blood smeared over my face, I didn't recognize myself. As I went to take a step toward the sink I hit something with my foot. *What the hell?*

It didn't register in my drunken mind until I looked down, what I had just kicked on the floor. A moan came from below me and, as I stepped back, my eyes focused on a blob on the bathroom floor.

I rubbed my eyes once, then it hit me. It was Lexi, curled up on the floor in a tight ball. Her hands were over her head, and her legs were pulled tightly into her chest. I stood there watching as she shivered on the floor. She turned her head then and opened her eyes. They were wet and black from her smeared make-up and crying. She scrambled and sat up. Resting her back against the wall, she wiped at her eyes and attempted to pull herself together in front of me.

The Trent I had suppressed with alcohol wanted to kneel down and hold her, comfort her, but that Trent wasn't in control. The drunk, mad, hurt Trent was in control, and he didn't feel bad at all.

"What the hell are you crying about?" Drunken Trent slurred.

She stopped fixing her hair. Her eyes made their way up and met mine. "Are you—Trent what the hell happened to you?" she asked as she saw the blood on my face, hands, pants, and shirt. She got to her feet quickly and came over to stand before me.

"Cute," I said, shaking my head at her. "You're what happened to me. You've been fucking with my head since the day I met you," I said, stabbing my right temple with my finger a few times.

"Me?" Her brows rose as she looked me over. Her hand went to take mine, once she realized that was where the source of blood was coming from.

I moved it just as she touched me. I held my hands up in front of my chest and shook my head no. "Don't touch me," I seethed.

"Are you fucking kidding me right now?" she yelled and then sniffed my face. "You're drunk?" she asked, placing her hands on her hips.

"Oh, don't act like you suddenly care about me," Drunken Trent said.

Normal Trent was pounding from the inside, putting up a good fight to get out and take over. But I was too far gone for him to break out.

"Don't do this," she warned me.

"Oh, you mean, don't start a fight? Too fucking late, baby." I turned from her and smacked my hands down on the counter, before turning the water on. I let it run for a moment before I put my knuckles under it. The pain was intense but not nearly as bad as hearing Lexi say she was leaving me to take care of her jackass, abusive ex-boyfriend. "So when are you leaving?" I asked from the sink.

I splashed water on my face to rid it of the blood. I watched her in the mirror as water droplets fell from my face onto the sink. She was stalling, messing with her hair, fixing *my* shirt.

"Not yet," she said. Looking up at me through the mirror, she was begging me to end it end the fight.

So I did. But not in the way she was expecting. "So you are leaving?" I asked, making sure that I heard her right.

"Yes, in a few days, but I'm here now," she said.

I paused for a moment. Wiping the dripping water from my nose, I stared at her before I looked away and continued with my thought. "Well, maybe it would be better for you to leave now," I said, taking a towel from the counter to dry my face and hands before I wrapped them tightly around my cuts. "You know, you should be there for John when he wakes up," I said, turning around to face her.

"Why are you doing this?" she asked, shaking her head in disgust.

She should be disgusted, running after a man who used her and treated her like shit! Drunken Trent was pissed.

"I'm not doing anything. You're the one who's leaving. I'm simply suggesting that you do it sooner rather than drawing it out for later," I snapped back. I wanted to kick Drunken Trent in the fucking balls for saying that.

"You don't mean that," she said, shaking her head more. "You're drunk and you're going to feel like a fucking asshole in the morning for saying that to me."

"Am I? You see, I don't think I am. You knew I was an ass coming into this, and I knew you were a pain in mine. Did we really think this could work? I mean it might have, had you not still been in love with your fucking stepbrother!" I roared, the veins in my neck popping out with rage.

"Shut up! Shut—up!" she yelled covering her ears. "You know what? Fine! You want me gone, I'm gone," she screamed, getting in my face.

She pushed my chest and, because I was so drunk and she was a fucking Amazon, I fell back onto the sink, my back hitting the mirror, sending a crack down the middle of it. "Good, get you fat ass out of here, baby, because clearly you never gave a fuck about me," I yelled as she left the bathroom in a hurry.

I pushed myself off the counter and slipped on the tile floor, falling on my ass and hitting my head against the back of the sink. I sat up and, finally, Drunken Trent was taken down, leaving me to pick up the fucking mess he left behind. "Lexi!" I yelled, holding my head as I fought off Drunken Trent one last time. I pushed myself away from the sink and stumbled toward the door frame. "Lexi, stop," I called to her.

She was by the dresser, shoving her things into her bag and grabbing anything else that she might need from mine.

"Save it, asshole," she spat over her shoulder.

"You're right, I'm drunk, don't listen to me," I said, trying to convince her to stop packing.

"Yeah, you're right, you are drunk, and apparently you only speak the truth when you're drunk. Tell me what you really think," she yelled.

"No, I didn't mean any of that. I was just upset, baby, come on," I said, moving toward her and wrapping my arms around her from behind.

She grabbed them and tried to break free from my grip. "Get off of me, Trent," she said, fighting against my hold.

"Lexi, can't we just forget about this and figure it out in the morning?" I asked, my face next to hers.

She turned her head as far as she could and stared at me. "Trent, it is the morning!" she said, pointing to the early morning light coming through the curtains.

When the hell did that happen? "All right fine," I said, letting her go, taking a step away from her, and stumbling to the bed.

Chapter 23

Lexi

I finished stuffing everything into my bag and turned around to see him sitting on the edge of the bed, his body slumped over and swaying. He was so drunk, I wouldn't be surprised if he didn't remember anything the next morning. He was the picture of pathetic—a large, strong man succumbing to alcohol. I'd seen it before, plenty of times. I'd only seen *him* drunk like this once before.

I walked over to the bed. His hands were on his thighs, the blood from his cuts spilling onto his jeans and spreading across the denim. I shook my head then went to find my toiletries bag. I grabbed a few Band-Aids and a wet and dry rag from the bathroom. I knelt down in front of him and took his left hand in mine. I cleaned up the blood and applied three Band-Aids to the side of his hand. He sat there the whole time I patched him back up. His head hung down, and a couple of times, I thought he'd passed out sitting up.

As I finished putting the fourth Band-Aid on his right hand, he finally came to. I was picking up all the pieces of wrappers from the Band-Aids when he reached for my hand. I was on my knees between his legs, so when I looked up at his face and saw tears in his eyes I was in shock. I sat back on my heels to stare up at him.

"I'm sorry. I'm sorry I fucked this up," he said quietly.

"I know you are," I answered back.

I did know he was sorry. He was hurt and I should have known he'd react like that. This wasn't him, the man who fought with me in the bathroom wasn't my Trent, and that sacred me. It took me right back to being under John's thumb. He held my hand in his for another second then let it go to cover his own face. His shoulders shook and, for the life of me, I didn't know what to do. No grown man had ever broken down like that in front of me.

I sat up on my knees and pulled his head to my chest, because I simply didn't know what else to do. Part of me wanted to leave him there to stew over all the nasty things he'd said to me. But another part of me, the selfish part, wanted to hold him one last time. It was clear that even if we did work it out, I wasn't going to be able to forget the things he said. He still thought I was in love with John, and maybe deep down I still was. Maybe Trent was my rebound, and the accident John had was our wake up call to make things work again. *Who knows?*

We had worked before, we worked really well, so well that I was able to overlook things, things I shouldn't have. But now I was stronger. Trent had made me stronger. I wasn't afraid of John anymore, and I had Trent to thank for that. He was the first man I'd stood up to, put my foot down, and, unfortunately, I was going to have to do it again.

I rocked with him. His head on my chest, I held his face between my hands—his handsome face, a face that I loved waking up to each morning for those last five months. It was going to be hard to let him go, but I had a feeling that Trent wasn't going to be able to get past my past and the relationship I had with John—and, apparently, my fat ass.

"Don't leave me," Trent begged from between my hands.

His face was millimeters from mine. His eyes were blood shot, his cheeks wet with tears, and his lips trembled as he waited for an answer. My heart broke in half. I knew I needed to be with my family, but I also knew that I'd be leaving half of my heart with Trent. That piece of me that he took at the start of all this was never going to re-grow in my chest. *That piece will be forever his, no matter where he goes or what he's doing.*

There was no doubt in my mind that he'd be able to move on. He was a rock star after all—a sexy, sought-after rock star in a hot ass band. He'd never have a problem finding a woman.

"Lexi, I need you—I love you," he said, taking the back of my neck in his hand and pulling my forehead to meet his.

That was the first time he'd actually said it. Sure, he had a crowd scream Trent loves Lexi, but he'd never said "I love you" to me. His thumb caressed my cheek and, as it all sank in, I felt my own tears roll down my face.

Am I crazy for leaving? He tilted my head to read my reaction, but I had none, except the few tears that rolled down my cheeks. His eyes were begging me to say something, but the words wouldn't come. I knew I cared about him, maybe I loved him. *What is love?* I wasn't sure I even knew. What I did know was that I thought I loved someone before, but it didn't work. *Is that my problem?*

Am I afraid it's not going to work out, or that it's going to turn so south that I end up making excuses for staying with him because I don't want to be alone?

Of course, that was my problem. I was terrified of him leaving me, the way John use to threaten me about leaving me for other women toward the end. Hell, just the other night I flipped out when I saw him with another woman. So my way of dealing would be to run first, before I got hurt.

As I talked to myself this way and then that, I felt Trent's hands grab at the hem of his shirt, pulling it up and over my head. I knelt before him naked, possibly for the last time.

"You're so beautiful, don't go. Just stay with me," he begged as his hands made their way up my sides and then back down my hips.

No one in their right mind would say no to a man like Trent. He reached behind him and pulled off his own shirt. His pants weren't even buttoned and it was painfully clear he had gone commando. His hands came up to my breasts. Swallowing hard, I tried to keep my focus but the only thing I could focus on was his hands massaging me and bringing my body to bend to his every whim.

I thought that standing would break the spell he was casting over me, but it only made things worse. He pulled me closer his arms wrapping around my bottom and pulling me flush to him. His soft lips left kisses along my torso. I held his head, my fingers running over the stubble of his hair. His scruffy beard tickled my flesh as he continued to kiss every inch of me. *Would it really hurt to do this one last time?* I chewed on the inside of my cheek as his lips kissed under my breasts. *No, it won't hurt. It'll feel fucking amazing. I'll worry about the rest later.*

I climbed on him, my legs wrapping around his waist. I settled on his lap, making sure not to say anything. I kissed him with a hurried manner, taking his lips, then neck, then his lips again. I held onto him tightly. He fell back, clearly still drunk and unable to balance himself yet alone both of us.

He held my shoulders back for a second and smiled up at me. That sexy smirk of a smile that I fell in love with shone brightly up at me, and I could do nothing but smile back at him. I sat back and tugged his already un-buttoned jeans down. I took him in my hand as I sat back on his jean clad legs, stroking him softly. His eyes closed and his hands gripped the sheets tightly beneath him.

He sat up abruptly, grabbing me, and tossed me on the bed. He shoved his pants down to his feet, grabbed my ankles, and pulled me to the edge of the bed then flipped me over so I was on my stomach. Taking my hips between his hands, he pulled me up on all fours. I sat up on my knees, my back to his front. He moved the hair from my neck, wrapping it around his hand to tilt my head to his liking as he whispered roughly in my ear. "I need to fuck you."

His breath swirled around my ear as heat pooled be-tween my legs. He'd never talked to me like that before. It was always sweet and heart-poundingly romantic with Trent. He always took care of me and never let me leave without finishing, but this, the roughness and the de-mands were a whole new experience together, and I liked it.

Sure, sex before could get a little rough, but this was a whole new level. It was fucking at its rawest. No kiss-ing, no touching. It was him getting what he needed and me getting what I needed. There was no concern for the other person. I touched myself. He smacked my ass and held my hair tightly around his hand. It was what we both needed, in that raw, intense moment.

When he was finished, he took a step back from me,

stumbling, then fell onto the bed next to me, his pants still around his ankles. He passed out cold. I lay there, staring at the ceiling for a few minutes. It got cold, so I reached for a blanket and when I did, Trent moved beside me, draping his huge arm around me and pulling me closer to his damp body. I knew I should have moved away from him, knowing all that had happened between us, but I welcomed the comfort. I needed to be held. My world had flipped upside down in less than twelve hours, and all I wanted was a hug and someone to tell *me* it was going to be all right.

Chapter 24

Trent

*W*hy is the room spinning? I covered my face with a pillow to block the bright sunlight from coming through and blinding me. I was naked and neatly tucked under the covers. It was painful to open my eyes. The burning and heaviness of them kept weighing them down. I rubbed them vigorously then slapped my face a few times to wake up. *Damn, how much did I drink last night?*

I turned on my side, stretched my arm out and hit nothing but cold sheets. I sat up abruptly, and saw a single piece of paper lying on the pillow where Lexi's head should have been. I took the paper from the pillow and read.

> *Trent,*
> *I think this will be the easiest way to do this.*
> *By now I'll be on a plane back home, so don't even think about trying to come after me.*

I know you don't understand why I'm leaving, but I need you to trust me. I know what I'm doing. I can't just give up on my family because I've found a new one in you and the rest of the guys.

The label knows that I've left, and since I've planned things out for the next month, they will hire a replacement for me before the month is up. Tell Reece it'll probably be the girl who interviewed before me. I'm sure he'll be happy about that.

Last night, you told me what you really thought about me, and about me leaving, and maybe you're right. Maybe in some deep dark part of my heart I do still love John like that. But I want you to know, I'm leaving now because he's my oldest friend, my stepbrother, my family, and he needs me. My mom needs me.

I understand that you're mad at me, and it's fine if you move on. I want you to move on. You're a great man and any woman would be lucky to have you. I just don't think that woman is me. Let's face it, I'm not even your type. I'll see ya around, muscles

Lexi

I sat on the bed staring at the written words. They came into focus then out of focus as I stared blankly. Suddenly last night's argument with Lexi made a clear presence in the forefront of my mind. *Shit! What have I done?*

လ၇ၑ

Bang.

Bang. Bang.

It registered in my head that someone was banging

on the door, but I couldn't move. I was glued to the bed.

Bang. "Trent—Lexi!" Bang. "Trent, man, you in there?" It was Reece calling from the other side of the door. "Jesus fucking Christ, man, if you guys are in there, give me something!" he yelled. Bang. "Fuck!" Bang, bang, bang. "Trent—That's it, I gotta call security, they're not answering," I heard him say to someone else.

I assumed that it was whoever he brought back with him the night before, or even one of the other guys. Somehow, I pealed myself from the bed, pulled my pants up, and trudged to the door. I opened it to see Reece standing in the doorway with his phone to his ear.

"Never mind," he said into the phone. "He's alive." He hung up, not saying bye, and just shoved it in his back pocket. "Dude, what the fuck's going on? We've been calling you and looking all over the place for you," he asked as he pushed his way inside the room.

He stopped a few steps in and surveyed. It was a mess, covers where everywhere, bloody towel and shirts were on the floor. He peeked into the bathroom and saw the blood on the floor and the cracked mirror. I knew he was scanning the place for Lexi but he wouldn't find her.

"What happened in here? Where the fuck is Lexi?" he asked, turning toward me as I slammed the door and headed back to the bed. I reached into the bed and grabbed the single piece of paper that would explain everything to him. I held it out for him to take.

"What's this?" he asked, taking the paper from me.

"Just read it, it'll explain everything," I said, sitting on the edge of the bed.

Reece stood for a moment then sat in the chair that was across the room from the bed. His slender figure reclined in the high-backed chair as he read the words that put the final dagger in my chest.

"Is this a joke?" he said, holding the paper in one

hand and leaning forward in the chair with a brow raised almost to his hair line. His red Mohawk wasn't spiked up so he had to keep moving it from his face. If it wasn't spiked up, he usually had it gelled back off his face, but he clearly skipped that particular grooming step that morning.

"I wish to fuck it was," I replied.

"Why the fuck did you let her leave? Are you out of your mind!"

"You think I wanted this to happen? If I could have stopped her, I would have, but I passed out last night. She must have snuck out," I said, shrugging my shoulders.

"So now you're what, just sitting here like a fucking looser?"

"What do you want me to do, man? She doesn't want me. Did you read the fucking letter?" I snapped back.

"Yeah, it says she's going home to help her family out."

"Did you miss the part where she wants me to move on?"

"And you're going to listen to her?" he challenged me.

"What other option do I have? Please enlighten me," I said, sitting back on the bed, waiting for his bat shit crazy response.

"I don't fucking know, but, dude, you can't just let her go. You two are good for each other. I haven't seen you as happy as you are with her in a long fucking time."

"So what do I do? Leave you guys and go after her? Hell no, we all worked our asses off to get this far, and I'm not quitting on you guys to chase after someone who doesn't even know if she loves me."

"I have an idea. Why don't you call her like a normal person?"

There were a lot of things that got to me, but Reece

being right about something had to be the worst.

"Fine." I reached across the bed and grabbed my phone from the other nightstand. I flipped through my contacts found her number and hit call.

Ring—Ring—Ring—

"Hey, it's Lexi. Leave me a message." Click.

"Voicemail," I said, holding my hand over the receiver.

"Well, leave her a message," Reece said as if it was as easy as saying "hey, call me back." I didn't have time to think before it beeped and went silent. I fumbled in my brain trying to think of something to say to her.

"Lexi, it's Trent. Please call me, let me know how you are." I left it at that and hung up.

"It'll be all right, dude. I really hate to do this but we gotta get to the bus. We're already a half a day behind," Reece said, standing and clasping my shoulder.

"Yeah, all right. Give me a few minutes to get dressed, I'll be right down."

Reece nodded down at me, slapped my back, then left the room. I sat on the bed for a moment, my hands rubbing over my face as I tried to wrap my head around everything. A vibrating came from my lap along with a chirp. I picked my phone up and saw a message from Lexi.

~ *I can't talk to you. But I'm fine.*

The message was short and sweet and I wanted more. I needed to know more. I knew I said some fucked up things, but I didn't see why we couldn't work it out, unless I was right and she doesn't care about me at all and I was nothing more than a rebound for her. But I refused to believe that.

What we had was not a rebound. It was love and I had to make her see that.

~ *You're not fine. I know you. I fucked up, Lexi, I*

know I did. I hurt you and I swore I never would. I'm sorry. Please call me so we can work this out.

I was stepping on the bus as my phone went off. As I came around the corner, all the guys and Kitty were staring at me, waiting for me to say something.

"I'm going to take the back room for a while. That okay with you all?" I asked, addressing each of them.

"Yeah, man, take all the time you need," Kane said.

"Trent, if you need anything, we're all here for you. We'll do whatever you need us to do to get her back. She's making a huge mistake, I'll talk to her if you want me too," Kitty said, coming to give me a hug.

"Thanks, Kitty. I think it's best just to let the dust settle for a bit."

"Okay, we love you, Trent," she said, leaving a tender kiss on my cheek.

The moment I was in the room alone, I reached into my pocket to read the message.

~ *I said I can't talk to you.*

~ *Fine, no talking. Can I text you?*

~ *Stop being a smartass.*

~ *What? It's not talking. Just writing words. Lexi, I know you're there. I can do this all day,* I typed

Five minutes later…

~*Sun's out here*

Ten minutes later…

~ *Thinking about getting a new tattoo. What do you think?*

Five minutes later…

~ *Nah, maybe not. Read any good books lately?*

Fifteen minutes later…

~ *What about movies?*

Three minutes later…

~ *I really want to see that new super hero one.*

One minute later…

~ *You're not going to stop, are you?* she asked.

Finally a response!

~ *Nope!*

~ *Fine, we can text. But I have to go now.*

~ *Okay, I got what I wanted*

~ *I'm rolling my eyes, in case you're wondering*, she texted.

~ *I know you are*

~ *I'm leaving now*

~ *Okay*

~ *Good bye, Trent*

~*Bye, Lexi*

⌒⌒⌒

I barricaded myself in the back of the bus the whole way to our next show. I slept most of the time, waking up in jolts, thinking my phone was ringing or that Lexi had whispered in my ear. But it was all in my head, because she didn't call me or magically show up. I was alone again, and I was fucking terrified it'd be that way for the rest of my life. The only hope I had for getting her back then was through text messaging.

Chapter 25

Lexi

I walked into John's room and then right over to the windows. I took the cord to the blinds in my hands and pulled. The afternoon light came flooding in, making the darkness disappear. I stood at the window, undid the latches and lifted it half way up. The cool fall breeze made the curtains dance next to me and my shirt stick to my body. I took a deep breath of the fresh air, exhaled and turned around toward John who was still in bed with a pillow over his face. "Rise and shine," I said cheerily.

"Go away, Lex, I'm not in the mood today," John grumbled back.

"Why aren't you in the mood? Is it because it's beautiful out, and you're too chicken to get out of bed?"

He'd have days where he wouldn't get out of bed and then days where he'd do too much. This was one of the I'm-not-getting-out-of-fucking-bed days. I stood at the foot of his bed, arms crossed and brow raised. I was daring him to say something smart back. I'd been home for a month. He'd been released a week after I arrived. He hadn't had any more close calls and all his wounds were healing if not healed. His leg and arm were in casts, and he still had a large incision on his stomach but it was healing exactly the way the doctors wanted it to.

"Go back to LA, Lex, I'm fine. You don't have to babysit me anymore," he said, sitting up in bed and wincing from the soreness that still plagued him in the mornings.

"I don't think so. You're not fine. The farm will fall apart if I leave. John, it's two o'clock in the afternoon. If I wasn't here to help Mom, the poor cows would be drying up, the chickens would be up to their heads in eggs, and the pigs would have started eating each other. Until you're back to yourself, I'm not leaving."

"Cut the crap, Lex. You would rather be in LA than stuck here with me working the farm."

"Well…"

"I can hire someone till I'm better," he said, wincing again as he put his casted foot on the old farmhouse floorboards.

It's a poor-pitiful-me day too, wonderful… "No, John, it's fine, I've missed the work. It's a nice break."

He looked up at me and rolled his eyes.

I returned his look, giving him one of my own. "What?"

"Oh, nothing," he said, reaching for his crutches next to his bed.

He was in his boxers and nothing else. Since being back, I looked at him as the patient. His body had transformed. He was slender and his muscles weren't as thick as I was used to seeing them. His clothes hung on him. Honestly, he looked like he needed a hearty steak dinner. His skin was still tan from the summer, and as clean as the day he was born. No tattoos, no piercing, just clean. He looked over at me from the side of the bed, his blue eyes boring into me like they always did.

"Speak, Johnny."

He hated when I called him that. I used to call him Johnny all the time when we were little, to make fun of him.

"Lex, you hate milking the cows. I've seen you punt a few chickens for pecking at your feet, and you squeal as much as the pigs do when you get in their pen. You hate the farm."

"Not true—"

"True," he said, moving toward me on his crutches.

I was taken aback at his closeness, even though I'd been helping him bathe and get dressed for a month, something was different about that morning, or afternoon. "I love this farm. It's my home. I might not enjoy pecking chickens or sloppy pigs but I would never turn my back on it," I said, standing a little straighter.

"So you just came back to take care of the farm?" he challenged.

And there it was. I'd been waiting for this conversation since the day I arrived. "John you know why I came back," I said squarely.

"Do I? Lex, you left me after I proposed to you, and you haven't called or even visited since that day. Did I mean anything to you?" he asked.

"John, I'm not going to argue with you about this. I'm here to help you get better and keep the farm running."

"But as soon as I'm back on my feet you're leaving right?" he asked.

"Yes," I said flatly.

"Then I'm not getting better," he said, moving the crutches and sitting on the edge of the bed.

"Really, John, this is childish. You know why I said no to you, and you know why I left."

I went to walk by him and, as I did, he grabbed my arm. Suddenly my heart pounded, my throat went dry, my hands clenched into fists.

"Lex, I've changed. I haven't had a drink since you left. I know I fucked up, I guess…I guess I didn't realize what I had until it was gone."

I nodded in agreement.

"I don't want to fight with you. I miss you. I miss you so fucking much. You were my best friend, I just want to make things right again," he begged. He let my arm go to hold onto my hand. "I understand you can't go back to the way it was before you left, but I'd like to go back farther, I'd just like my friend back."

This was the John I fell in love with. This John could make me laugh and go on adventures with me. This was the John who held me as an eight-year-old girl after my father died.

Somehow, we'd managed to get back to the good, back to the fun of us. The month that I'd been home was like a flashback to our youth. He in his room and I in mine, sending secret codes through the wall, except it was now messages for me to come help him to the bathroom or to get him some food, but it was good, we were good.

"I think I can do that," I said, sitting down on the bed next to him. I laid my head on his shoulder like I used to, and we just sat there in silence as the two kids we once were came rushing back.

My phone buzzed from my pocket and broke the silence. I knew who it was and didn't want to make a big deal about it, because it wasn't a big deal anymore.

"All right, you need to get in the bathroom and attempt to wash up," I said, smiling up at him. "I'll be down stairs. Call me when you need help coming down the steps, we have work to do today!"

"Work?"

"Yeah, you might have a broken leg but you can still ride in the side-by-side and help me wrangle some cows." I stood and went to leave but stopped at the door. "John, I didn't just come back for the farm, I came back to take care of my family," I said, smiling before walking out the door. It was the truth. I didn't come back to just help with the farm, I came back to help my family and he was my family, simple as that.

~ You were right two nights and he's already slept with the new girl, Trent texted.

~ I told you! Reece is going to get an STD, fact.

~ How's patient X?

~ How's Chloe?

~ Touché.

࿇

Chloe's band was officially linked with ONS for the rest of their tour. It ended in their hometown, and I was going to surprise Trent by showing up at the bar Kitty's father owned.

It was a good three-four hour drive from me, but I'd make the trip. Even though I said it was better to be apart, I was a fucking moron for even thinking it was the "right thing" for us both.

I missed Trent so much. I was in deep with him and I prayed that he was still in deep with me.

Our texts over the last month were sweet. He kept me in the loop about the guys, and I...well, I didn't have much to report on so I told him about the farm and my mom. I never said anything about John, and, if he asked, I'd simply ask how Chloe was, and he'd shut up about it.

᪉᪉᪉

I ran from the side-by-side and stopped at the bushes. I'd been tossing up my lunch at least twice a week for the last four weeks. My body wasn't used to the hard work anymore. *Go figure. I take six months off and I've lost all my farm girl muscles.* I was sore, tired, and grumpy. I was so grumpy, I found myself yelling at my mom for no reason and don't even get me started on John. If he even looked at me the wrong way, I'd let him have it.

"Are you all right?" John asked as I dragged my feet back to the side-by-side. A week ago, he had his casts removed so his arm was good to go but his foot still had one of those plastic boots. He could walk on his own, but only for a little while. He was working at sixty percent and building up the muscle that he had lost the previous two months.

"No, John, I'm not fine, do I look fine?" I snapped at him as I jumped back in the side-by-side.

"Geeze, Lex, maybe you should take the day off," he said, leaning away from me.

"I'm not sick."

"The puke in the bush says otherwise."

"Just shut up and drive," I snipped at him.

I had one week until I was going to surprise Trent. The mental count down in my head was getting shorter and shorter with every day.

~ *Lexi, I need to call you*

~ *No, Trent*

~ *Something happened*

~ *???*

~ *Can I just call you?*

~ *What happened?*

I was still in the side-by-side with John when my phone rang. Trent's number popped up.

"Ugh…" I grumbled.

"Who's that?" John asked from the driver's side.

I decided to ignore John and his questions and answer the phone. "Why are you calling me?" I asked.

I wanted to keep pretending like I was over him, so that when I showed up at their home town bar he'd be overjoyed, we'd run toward one another, I'd jump into his arms, he'd hold me tightly, we'd kiss passionately…you get the idea. I had this whole mini movie in my head and talking to him would ruin the suspense I'd been building up for two months.

"Because, I needed to hear your voice."

I need to hear yours too.

"I did something," he said.

My heart sank. *It finally happened, he's moved on. My mini romantic movie just turned into a horror film.* "I don't want to know. Don't you fucking tell me either," I snapped.

"Damn, Lex. Who the hell you talking to like that? I thought you reserved that attitude for just me?" John asked from beside me. "I'm a little hurt."

"Who's that?" Trent asked.

Oh, fuck…I shouldn't have answered the phone. I shouldn't have answered the phone. "Stop the vehicle," I said to John.

"No, we have to get back. We don't have time to stop, unless you're going to puke again?" he asked, leaning away from me.

"Lexi, are you sick?" Trent asked, bringing my attention back to the phone call.

"Trent, I'm fine," I said, trying to calm him down because I knew him and I knew he worried.

"Trent, you never told me about a Trent," John said from beside me.

I wanna die, right now I want to crawl in a hole and die.

"That's John, isn't it?" Trent roared from the phone.

My head was spinning and I felt like I was going to faint, I did faint. John stopped the vehicle and turned to me. My head fell on his shoulder, the phone was still in my hand, and I was helpless to stop what happened next.

"Lex, Lexi! Babe—" John said, shaking my shoulders. "Babe, wake up," he said, touching my face.

"Get your fucking hands off her," I heard faintly through the phone.

I was awake but not awake. I remember things, but it was like a dream, parts were blurry and choppy.

"Who is this?" John said, taking the phone from my hand and putting it up to his ear as he addressed the person on the other end.

"Who the fuck is this?" Trent roared back.

"John."

"Well, that's fucking perfect. Don't lay a hand on her, or I'm going to make sure you won't have one when I'm through with you."

"Who the fuck do you think you are, her boyfriend? FYI, she doesn't have one and I'm pretty sure she wouldn't want one like you. Trust me, I know."

"Yeah, I bet you do, you ruined her. You ruined us! I know she thinks that you're her family but you're just a weak, punk-ass abusive asshole."

"You don't know shit about me!" John growled back.

"Actually, I do. She told me everything."

"I never hurt her."

"The fuck you didn't. The first time I—this is pointless, why am I arguing with you anyway? Where's Lexi?"

"I'll have her call you back after I take her home and

put her to bed." Click. He turned back to the steering wheel and gripped it so hard his knuckles went white. "I don't know who the hell that was, but I don't like him, Lex."

"Just take me home, John, I feel like shit, and I really don't have the energy to fight right now—not with you or with him."

Chapter 26

Trent

I stared at my phone, trying to figure out what the fuck had just happened. I ran through everything in my head. Lexi was with John, which I knew, but still I hated hearing him because it made him real. I also knew that she was feeling sick, and from the sound of it she fainted, or blacked out. The other thing I realized was that they were on good terms. She clearly wasn't still ignoring him or mad at him anymore.

From the conversation I had with John, I also realized that she hadn't told him about me, or that I even existed. But the good thing was that she seemed to have things under control, or at least she had him under control.

"Hey, man, you ready to go to sound check?" Kane asked, stepping onto the bus. He took one look at me and went into calming mode and move in front of me. "Dude, I don't know what happened but I need you to bring it down a notch."

"She's with him," I snarled.

"Well, you knew she was with him. I mean, we all know that much."

"No, Kane, she's hanging out with him. They're being cordial, friendly, I heard them joking over the phone. She's going to go back to him." I could feel the anger rising from the pit of my stomach. I knew men like John. They said that they'd changed, when really they hadn't at all. I had a sickening feeling that the moment she gave in to him and let him back in her life that he'd go right back to being a dick to her.

"You called her? I thought she didn't want to talk yet? And didn't I see you with—"

"Shut-up, Kane, I don't need you to bring that up right now."

"Maybe you need to move on, man," Kane said, clasping a hand on my shoulder.

I pushed it away as I stood before him. I had a good five inches on him and an easy fifty pounds of muscle. I'd been taking my frustrations out on my body in grueling workouts every day, sometimes twice a day if time allotted. Other than my texts with Lexi, it was the only thing keeping me sane.

"Like you moved on from Kitty?" I challenged him.

"That was completely different, and you know it. You're still in contact with Lexi. I was left in an airport, looking like a fucking fool. So of course I moved on. Things with Lexi and you are different, if she sounded happy, let her be happy. Bro, you deserve to be happy too, maybe Lexi wasn't the one—"

"That's the thing, Kane, she *is* the one, I know she is, and if she gets back together with that fucker John, she'll get wrapped up in his lies and be miserable."

"Weren't they friends first? Maybe they're just friends again?" Kane suggested, shrugging his shoulders.

I rolled my eyes and turned from him.

Reece ran on the bus a moment later, I turned to see him jolt to a stop and look around the bus. "What's going on guys?" he asked, looking between the two of us.

My fists were still clenched and I was even more pissed after Kane's "pep-talk," if you could even call it that.

"Nothing—What do you want?" I snapped at Reece.

"Calm down, dude, I just came back to get my sticks. You do know that we have sound check in fifteen, right?" he said, scooting between the two of us to grab his sticks from his bunk.

"He called Lexi," Kane said bluntly.

"He what? Wait—weren't you with Chloe last night?"

And there it was. I fucked up last night. We had played to one of the biggest crowds we had ever stood in front of last night. We were on such a high, we went out and drank, and drank, until most of us couldn't see straight. I made the mistake of watching Chloe dance. She saw me and, before I could stop it, I was holding her from behind and stumbling my way to her hotel room.

"That was a mistake," I roared.

"So you did sleep with her?" Kane asked, crossing his arms.

"You did *what*?" We all turned and saw Kitty standing behind us, hands on her hips, her wild hair pulled back, and a very displeased look on her face. She stomped over to me, pushing me with her tiny hands. "How could you do that?!" she screamed up at me.

"I didn't mean to," I said back, shaking my head and holding my hands up.

"I just got off the phone with Lexi, I talked her into talking to you but—Trent, what were you thinking sleeping with Chloe?"

Her small hands pushed me again in her anger.

"I wasn't. I was drunk. It didn't mean anything!" I yelled back.

"That's my cue—" Reece said, pointing to the exit with his stick.

"I don't think so, Bozo!" Kitty yelled. He stopped in his tracks and sat on the closest chair. "You two idiots knew about this, and you didn't stop him?" she yelled at Kane and Reece.

"It's not my fucking job to babysit him, Kitty. She doesn't want to talk to him. It's been two months, the man can move on," Kane bellowed.

"No! No he can't. She just needs time to…she needs time to realize she's making a huge mistake."

"She's not you, Kitty," Kane said on a deflated sigh.

"I know that. I—I just can't give up hope that it will work out for them like it worked out for us." She had tears behind her eyes, as she remembered the path she walked down to be with Kane.

"Baby, they're not us," he said, moving toward her.

"Why not? Why can't they make it work? You need to suck it up and get your shit together!" Kitty pointed at me. "You need to go out there and fight for her. You just let her walk away," she shouted at me.

"Kitty," Kane said, trying to calm her down. He held her shoulders as she went to hit me again.

"No she's right, I did. I just let her go."

"See—"

We all stood there as an annoying clicking sound filed the bus.

"What is that noise?" Kitty asked as we all scanned the bus for the cause of the sound.

I watched as Kane looked over Kitty's body. Her pocket was glowing and, as she and the rest of us looked down at the source, her eyes became huge. She pulled the phone from her pocket, the clicking got louder as did the thumping against my chest. Quickly she put the phone up to her ear.

"Hello?...Lexi?" she called into the receiver.

"Did you hang up the phone after you talked to her?" Kane asked, snatching the phone from her hand.

"Yes...I'm pretty sure I did."

"Pretty sure and positive are two completely different things, Kitty!" Kane snapped at her.

I fell to the couch behind me. All the wind in me had been sucked out. I watched as Kane tried to call her back, but it just kept going to voicemail. *I should have known. What was I thinking, that she'd actually forgive me or understand?*

Kane kept hitting redial, over and over again, but it was no use. She had heard everything, *If she wasn't sleeping with John now, she sure as hell would be.*

"I'm going to fix this," Kitty said, looking around Kane.

"Fix what? There's nothing left to fix, it's over," I grumbled, slumping back on the couch. I sat there holding my head in my hands. *God, I'm a jackass.*

"Man up, Trent!" Reece yelled from the other side of the bus. He stood before me, arms crossed over his lean chest. "You fucked up, big deal. We've all been tempted by that harlot of a wench! Lexi knows that. You need to get off your sorry ass and make her see it meant nothing and that she is still the only woman you want in your life."

There was something about Reece's' speech that resonated within me. That spark in me that knew I belonged with Lexi, and Lexi alone, was still there. It'd been snubbed out by alcohol and Chloe's devious actions, but the spark was still there, and the more I thought about her being stuck with John, the brighter and stronger it became.

I stood from the couch. As I did, Reece took a step back, probably thinking I was going to punch him. Instead, I grabbed him in a tight hug. "You're right," I said in his ear. Pulling back I clasped his lean shoulders, slapping my hands on them twice. "You're fucking right, Reece, I need to man up."

Reece stood there, not sure of what was going on. He nodded along with me, his brows scrunched together. When he finally realized I wasn't going to kill him, he held on to my shoulders as well. "Let's fucking get her back. I need those lips on me as much as you do," he said, grinning up at me. I froze, my face falling. "Or maybe not, maybe…" He cringed through a half smile. "I should just shut up now, shouldn't I?"

"Good idea." I lightly slapped his face, and turned to Kitty.

"I'm so sorry, I didn't mean for that to happen," she cowered up at me.

"I know. It's fine, at least she knows. Now I just have to get her back."

"I'll do whatever I can to help."

I smiled down at her. I knew Kitty wanted nothing but the best for all of us. She wanted each of us to find what she and Kane had, and I was pretty sure she'd go to any lengths to help us.

Chapter 27

Lexi

"Lex, you all right?" John asked while he stood in my doorway.

I sat on my bed, a pillow on my lap, my stomach in knots. What I knew was going to happen all along was just brought to light via a butt dial. Although, he didn't come out and say it, the lack of defense was worse than hearing Reece say that Trent had slept with Chloe. *And here I was going to surprise him, tell him I was coming back, I was going to tell him I was his and no one else's.* Then something as small and innocent as a butt dial had ruined all that.

"I'm going to go get Mom in a minute if you don't start talking," John threatened.

"I'm fine."

"Doesn't sound like it. This have anything to do with that guy Trent who was on the phone?" John asked, walking all the way into my room and sitting down on the edge of my bed.

"I'm not going to talk to you about this. It's weird and I still don't...I just don't want to talk to you about this part of my life," I said, hoping that he'd drop it.

It was bad enough that I fainted and had to be treated like a baby. I didn't need John trying to decipher my love life.

"Why? Why can't you talk to me? You don't think I've changed, do you?" he asked deadpan.

"I...well...no, I don't. John, what we had was great when we were teenagers. But it all changed in college. You changed. You might not remember, but I do. I remember every drunken fight and nasty word you said to me. You were over bearing and possessive. It would just be weird, okay? Can we leave it at that?"

I released the pillow and placed my hands on either side of me, preparing for a fight or at the least a heated conversation. But that didn't happen. I looked straight ahead waiting for the roar of his deep voice to cut the silence. Instead, his fingers brushed over mine. The feather light touch of his fingers caressing mine was like a flash back. We're thirteen, sitting in the barn the same position as we were now. It was the first time he'd touched me like that. Sure, we'd wrestled, and played tag, all the innocent kid games, but that time was different. We were older, hormones were raging, and having the cutest boy living down the hall from me finally sank in.

My eyes closed the same as they did eleven years ago, but unlike then, I opened them soon after. I watched as his fingers traced mine. His hand was ruff and calloused from working on the farm for so many years. The thirteen-year-old skin was gone, replaced with rough, worn, twenty-five-year-old skin. We'd been through so much, the two of us, and, for the most part, we were able to comfort one another. It was only when I left him, that we had ever truly been apart.

It was as if the air had been sucked out of the room, I found myself taking in gulps of it to keep from passing out again. There was an energy bouncing off of us, an energy that I thought had died long ago when he turned into someone I didn't know, someone who hurt me and threatened me at every turn.

I was screaming from the inside. *What are you doing? What are you letting* him *do?* But I did nothing I just sat there. Thoughts were rushing past me. *Trent slept with Chloe. He doesn't care about me anymore. I should have never left. Did John change? Is he back to the person I fell in love with? Was Trent really just a rebound? Why does this feel right? I should just do it. I should get back at Trent for sleeping with Chloe. Is this where I'm meant to be? Do I want to be here?*

I was staring into John's blue eyes, and he was staring into mine. I didn't know what to do, I didn't know what to feel, but I was pretty sure it was a mix of pissed off, horny, betrayed, used, and loved. I was all over the place.

Soon the hand that rested over my own was brushing the hair from my face and tucking it behind my ear. The hand that, a year ago, I was terrified of, caressed me and wrapped around the back of my neck.

"I lied, Lex," he said, licking his lips after he spoke.

I sighed into his hand. "John—"

"I don't just want to be friends."

How could we truly ever go back to just that, "just friends"? My stomach did a flip as a wave of worry came over me.

He leaned closer and, for a split second, I thought about moving away from him, I thought about what it would do to me and Trent, and then I remembered, he'd slept with Chloe and that there was no more me and Trent.

So, as his lips, lips I'd kissed a thousand times, landed on mine I stood my ground, accepting the fact that
maybe John was supposed to be with me, after all.

It started off slow, as most first kisses do. That's
what it felt like, a first kiss. He'd never kissed me like
this as a man. As a lovesick teenager, everything about
him was romantic and sensual, but as a man he was anything but.

This new, older sensual John was like kissing a new
man, all together. Just when I thought I was fine, my
stomach flipped again. A bubbling from deep within
made me break the kiss.

I held his shoulder, tipping my head as yet another
wave came over me.

"I have to—I need to." I tried to back away from him
but he held my arm, keeping me planted on the bed like
he used to do. "John, let me go," I begged.

"What is it, Lex? Tell me. Tell me you want this as
much as I do. I miss you so fucking much…" With each
word his grip got tighter and tighter on my arms.

I began to panic.

I managed to get out as another bubble came up from
my stomach. "I'm going to be sick."

He released me and I ran like a bat outta hell into the
bathroom down the hall. Slamming the door behind me, I
hugged the toilet for the rest of the day.

❧

Make that a week. I hugged the toilet for a week. I
was in bed and running to the bathroom every other hour
for a week!

I had the worst stomach bug known to man. I avoid-
ed the conversation I knew was coming with John by acting like I was sleeping or running to the bathroom. But I

wasn't going to be able to skirt him for much longer.

He was everywhere, bringing me water and crackers, which was the only thing I could keep down. He'd bring me blankets and check on me throughout the day.

"Alexis, I'm worried. Maybe I should stay home," my mother said from my bedside.

I was curled up in my covers and in the fetal position. *Cramps—on top of being sick, I was having cramps!*

"Mom, I'm fine, it's just a stomach bug. Go on your cruise. I'll be fine, my boy nurse is here, and the farm is doing great."

My mother gave one of those raised-eyebrows-I'm-not-sure-if-I-should-trust-you looks. She watched as John brought in a fresh glass of water and a few crackers on a plate and set them on my nightstand. Her untrusting look at me turned into a full-on grin as she watched John fuss over me.

"I prefer 'man' nurse," John said, smiling down at me.

"Whatever, nurse Johnny," I snickered back.

"This is good…" My mother began, crossing her arms over her chest. "Seeing the two of you together and smiling, it's nice."

"Good, so you can leave. Karen and Bob are waiting for you in the car. Your bags are packed, the tickets are paid for, you deserve this, Mom. Go have some fun," I said.

"Okay, but if she gets worse, you better be calling me and taking her to the doctors. Do you hear me, young man?" my mother said, threatening John, who was still staring down at me.

"Don't worry I'll watch out for her," he said, pulling the cover up closer to my neck.

∽ఎ∾

Two days later:

"What do you want to do?" John asked from the other side of the couch.

I moaned and pulled a cover up to my chin. "Lay here and never move again,"

"Come on, Lex, you've been moping around for a week now, time to get over it," he said.

"What are you talking about? I've been sick. I'm not moping," I snapped back. *Lies, you're moping and avoiding the elephant in the room.*

"We going to talk about what happened in your room?"

"Nope," I said, making the word pop.

"You can't keep avoiding me. It happened. We kissed."

"Nope," I said again.

"Just tell me what you're thinking."

"Nope."

"I want to make it work again."

"Nope."

"Alexis!" he roared, standing from the couch and leaning over me.

"No," I said a final time.

"Then why did you kiss me back? Stop fucking playing with my head, Lex—" He tossed his hands in the air, "I gotta get outta here, I'll be back later."

"Where are you going?" I asked from the couch.

"Oh, now you want to talk? I'm going out."

"Don't do this, John. Don't go down this path again."

I knew where he was going, the same place he went when we were together. To get a drink, numbing whatever was bothering him.

"I told you, I don't do that anymore. You really have no faith in me, do you?" he yelled.

"What do you expect me think? That in eight months you've changed and have become some sort of saint?"

"Maybe you're right, maybe I can't change. We'll find out when I come home, won't we?" he challenged me.

"Don't bother if you're going to be drunk. I'm really not in the mood to be man-handled tonight." I saw the hurt on his face as the words left my lips.

His whole demeanor changed, his shoulders slumped, and his head fell. "I'll be back," he said over his shoulder as he turned and left the family room, and me sitting on the couch, wondering if maybe he had changed and turned himself around.

Even though the first month he wasn't able to get out of bed, these past few weeks he was in good health and pretty much back to normal, and I hadn't seen him drink anything, not even a beer.

Chapter 28

Trent

It was late out, almost midnight by the clock in my truck. I tried calling Lexi again…

Damn, straight to voicemail. She either turned her phone off or got a new number.

"No answer?" Reece asked.

I tossed the phone on the dashboard, watching as it spun before hitting the window. "How much farther?" I threw over to the passenger's seat where Reece sat.

"It says it's right up here on the right, but it also said that about five miles ago—stop, stop, stop," Reece yelled, hitting my arm and pointing to the side of the road.

A lonely mailbox with the numbers 6485 on them stared back at me. *We're—I'm fucking at her house and she has no clue.*

I drove down the long gravel driveway. Turing on my high beams, I was able to see the large farmhouse in the distance, the multiple barns around it, and the fences that kept in the animals Lexi had told me about.

The closer we got, the more anxious I became.

Reece and I took off after we played at BJ's. We were back in our hometown for a week, and knowing that Lexi was only a couple hours away, I decided to go after her. Apologize till I was blue in the face and beg for fucking forgiveness. I had screwed up. In a drunken haze, I let Chloe take advantage of me, and it wasn't until I was screaming Lexi's name in pleasure that I sobered up and opened my fucking eyes to see that it was Chloe on top of me, instead of the woman I loved more than the air I needed to breathe.

Call me lovesick, a fucking pansy, I don't give a shit. I loved Lexi, and I was determined to get her back. Of course, it would have been a lot fucking easier if my dick hadn't betrayed me for a quick lay.

I stopped the truck around the front of the house where other cars and trucks were parked. I saw Lexi's old jeep Cherokee, the one that she raved about every day in LA. Her jeep was her baby, it was also her father's, and she'd told me she'd do anything and everything to keep it running and in perfect condition. Next to the Jeep, an older Chevy truck was parked crooked, the driver's side door was still open and the light in the cab was on.

As I turned off my truck, Reece and I exchanged a look. "What are you thinking?" Reece asked while he took off his seat belt.

"I think I'm going to piss my pants."

Reece smiled at me, hitting my shoulder. "Well, don't do that."

His skinny ass slid out of the truck, slamming the door behind him. I watched as he walked over to the truck with its door still open. He stuck his head in, looked back at me, shook his head in confusion, and closed the door.

It was my turn, I opened my door and stepped down

from my massive black-as-night truck and closed the door behind me. I shoved the keys into my pocket as I took in my surroundings. The lights were on in the house, the front porch was lit up, and the lights around the barn were lit up as well. For being so off the beaten track it was easy to see, not only because of the lights but because there was a full moon and not a cloud in the sky.

I had a sweatshirt on, one of ours from the tour. I pushed the sleeves up my forearms. I was still in the same jeans I wore on stage at BJ's, the bar that we considered home and the place where we got our big break a little over a year ago. I made sure to spray some cologne and splash some water on my face before Reece and I left to find Lexi.

Reece nodded in the direction of the large front porch. I nodded back, and we walked together up the few stairs that were going to lead us to the front door.

"What are you waiting for? Knock on the door," Reece said after a few minutes of standing in front of it.

"Maybe this is a bad idea," I said.

"Are you fucking kidding me? Did you see what I left behind tonight to come all the way out to bum fuck West Virginia for you?" Reece quietly yelled up at me.

He was shorter than me and about fifty pounds lighter, but he was a quick little shit with an even quicker mouth.

"No one made you come out here," I snapped back.

"Yes, you did!" he ranted.

"No, I didn't. I told you all I was coming out here after the show. You volunteered, ass. I didn't make you do anything."

"All right fine, maybe I did. Even still, you're not walking away. We're here, knock on the fucking door, so you can make up, kiss her, and then she can kiss me for dragging your ass out here," he said, as if it was his idea all along and I was forced by the scrawny, redheaded prick.

"You're twisted."

"So I've been told. Now knock on the door and grovel at her feet," he said, with a huge grin.

I wiped my brow, which was beading with sweat, and swiped the back of my hand on my jeans. I cracked my neck from side to side to loosen up. My knuckles were next, along with a few shrugs of my shoulders.

"Are you getting ready for a MMA fight, or are you groveling to your girl? I honestly can't figure out which one you're doing right now," Reece asked, studying me. I didn't have a smart remark for him. Instead, I raised a brow and cracked my neck again. "All righty then, dually noted," he said. "Let's just keep all the rage bottled up a little longer so I don't get a black fucking eye, shall we."

"Stop it"

"Did you hear that?" I asked, referring to the disembodied voice coming from the other side of the door.

"Was that—"

Reece didn't even have a chance to finish before I pounded on the door with a clenched fist.

"Lexi!" I shouted as I banged on the door again. I placed my ear to the door, trying as hard as I could to hear what was going on, on the other side. I held the knob to the door so tightly my hand was turning white. "Lexi!" I roared again into the door. I tried turning the knob again and again but it was locked and not moving an inch.

"Sss—ttt—op—" we heard again this time softer and at the end of a sob.

By now we were both shoving on the door and yelling for someone to open it.

Reece ran down to a nearby window, but turned back to me shaking his head. "Nothing. I can't see anything or anyone," he said, before walking past me to another window on the other side of the door.

"Lexi! Open the door!" I yelled again, hoping that she could hear me.

"I'll run around the back and see if there's a back door that's open," Reece said as he jumped of the porch and ran around the huge, old farm house.

I stood there, shoving on the door again and again with my shoulder. I took a step back and kicked the door once. No movement. Twice. The hinges moved and the wood creaked. Third time, I gave it all I had. I kicked with everything in me. The door crumbled against my foot, slamming against the wall and bouncing back with so much force I had to hold my hands up to stop it from hitting me in the face. I pushed past the door, calling for Lexi. I could hear her whimpering and followed the sound around the corner and down the hall to a back family room that attached to the kitchen.

I stopped in my tracks as I ran around the corner and saw Lexi, flat against the wall. A man was standing in front of her, holding her there by her neck. He was huge, towering over her. If I would have been right behind them, I'm sure I wouldn't have been able to see her around his frame. There was no doubt in my mind, this was John, the bastard who had ruined everything Lexi and I had.

He was whispering something in her ear and kissing on her neck. She had one hand on his forearm, trying to push him away and the other...the other I couldn't see.

"Get your fucking hands off her!" I yelled from the doorway into the room. I watched as Lexi's eyes met mine, I couldn't tell if she was happy to see me or not, for the shock on her face could have gone either way.

John backed away from Lexi. Letting his hand fall from her neck, he turned around to see who had interrupted him, no doubt. As he moved, I got my first full glimpse of the woman I loved. She looked at me, and that dimple I loved so much shone back at me. I knew she was happy to see me, but that all ended the moment her other hand went to her stomach and as it did my eyes followed. She was in an oversized nightshirt. I'd know it anywhere. It was one of mine. Her hands were clenched tightly around her stomach as she screamed in pain. That scream was like a million tiny glass shards, ripping through my heart.

I watched with her as droplets of blood hit the floor between her legs. She screamed again as more blood made its way down the insides of her thighs. She crouched over in pain, her legs gave out on her, and she crumpled to the floor in a pool of blood.

"Lex?" John watched as she fell to the floor. "Lex— Alexis!" cried dropping to his knees and shaking her shoulders.

She just sat there, her head swaying back and forth as John shook her trying to get her to speak. Her face had tears streaks down it. A vacant expression on her face, she was staring at nothing and everything, as she looked up at me.

The moment her eyes left mine and she looked over at John I was able to snap out of it. I rushed across the room and knelt on the other side of her. I took her face between my hands making her look at me, but her eyes wouldn't follow, she wouldn't look at me.

"Lexi, look at me…baby, you need to look at me," I said softly. I turned to the man, clenching my jaw. "What did you do to her?"

The large man next to me had tears in his eyes, and reeked of alcohol. "I didn't do anything to her," he choked back.

"The fuck you didn't! Look at her. What did you

do?" I was beyond rage and it was taking everything in me to keep my hands on Lexi's face, rather than pounding on John's. My mind went somewhere sick and disturbing, an image flashed past my eyes of him fucking her so hard and raw that she was having some kind of hemorrhage.

"Trent! What the fuck?" Reece said, with a panic to his voice that I'd never heard. The blood was thick and dark and pooling from between Lexi's legs. My head spun at the amount of blood that was on the floor. I held onto her face tighter and searched her eyes, but they were still vacant, and her usually flushed, full face was thin and as pale as death. *She's losing too much blood. I need to do something.*

I got to my feet, lifting Lexi with me. I held her in my arms. Her head fell against my chest and her hand gripped my shirt as if she was saying "Help me."

"What are you doing?" John asked, rushing to his feet as well.

"I'm taking her to the fucking hospital!"

"What's wrong with her?" he asked frantically.

"I don't know. Why don't you tell me what's wrong with her? I swear to god if you did this to her—"

"I didn't do anything, I love her," John roared, blocking my path to the front door.

I took a deep breath. "You don't want to do this, trust me,"

"I didn't. Do. Anything. This all started after she talked to you. Maybe you're the one to blame."

"Right, because I had her by the throat against a wall. Stay the fuck away from her," I growled back.

Chapter 29

Lexi

I had been up all night with cramps, wicked cramps. I lay on the couch, watching TV, hoping that the medicine I took would finally kick in. That's when I heard it. John's truck come pealing down the gravel drive. His door creaked open but never closed. I sat on the couch, listening as he slammed the front door open and then slammed it closed. I remembered hearing the distinct sound of the locks clicking over. He stumbled down the hall and around the corner. Standing in the kitchen, he took a glass out and got himself some water.

"Have fun?" I asked, standing from the couch. I faced him, my hands crossed over my chest. I knew he hadn't changed. I knew he'd eventually go back to the bottle.

"Shut up," he threw over his shoulder as he filled a cup up at the sink.

"What are you doing, John? Are you trying to prove something?" I asked, moving closer to the kitchen. I waited for a smart ass remark but got none. "Too drunk to come up with anything smart to say back?" I said with a cocky air.

The last year we were together, it was the worst. He'd go out drinking almost every night. The only time he didn't was when he knew he had a football game the next day. We rented a small apartment off campus our last year, and every night he'd come stumbling in, looking for a fight.

He leaned on the edge of the sink and spoke in it. "Shut. Up. Lex."

I was pushing his buttons. Maybe I had a tendency of doing so, and maybe that was why things always went from zero to sixty with us, but I did it anyway. "I knew you hadn't changed," I said, leaning against the wall and picking at my nails as if I was board.

His hands gripped the edge of the sink tighter. I saw the muscles in his forearms flex with the tightening of his hands. He took the glass under the faucet one last time and filled it, drinking the water so fast that some of it stilled over the rim of the glass and down his chin and neck.

"I don't know, I guess you're just…forever broken."

The glass in his hand hit the sink with a crash. I jumped at the sound and squinted as shards of glass flew up and bounced off the counter and floor. He moved swiftly across the distance that separated us. He wiped the trail of water that was still on his face as he stepped even closer to me.

"Is this more of what you expected?" he hissed at me.

He slapped his hands up on the wall, one on either side of my head. I wanted to cower from him, close my eyes, and pray that he'd go away, but I wasn't going to cower anymore to him or to anyone.

"Is this what you want?" he asked as he came even closer, his mouth next to my ear, his heavy breath in time with my own. "Is this what you've been waiting for, for me to lose it like I use to?"

I couldn't say anything back, I was frozen beneath him, yet I was still standing my ground. *How had I gotten here again?*

"What's the matter, Lex, nothing coming out of that smart ass mouth now is there?" He pulled back and looked down at me. His hand hovered near my cheek as he shook his head. "Maybe I need to touch you, make you remember what it was like to be with me."

"Don't touch me," I warned, slapping his hand away with the back of mine.

"Oh, right, you're dating some guy…what was his name again…Trent?" John's hand wrapped around my neck and hung there loosely as he spoke.

"Yeah and he's a hell of a lot better man than you, in every way possible," I snapped.

Brows drew together as John looked around the room and then back down at me, smiling an evil smile. "Well, he can't be that much better." He leaned in and whispered in my ear, "He's not even here. But I am. I've always been here for you, Lex."

I moved my head to put some space between us. "Yeah, sure, you've been here for me. You were here for me as you beat me down into someone I didn't even recognize."

"I never laid a hand on you, and you know that. I love you, Lex, I'd never hurt you," he said, as if the last few years of our relationship were invisible to him.

My hair caught on a sliver of warped wallpaper as I laughed right in his face. I laughed so much my stomach began to hurt. Because it was ridiculous, it was fucking outrageous and absurd, and I didn't know what else to do but laugh in his face for being a fucking fool.

"What are you laughing at?" he asked.

I kept laughing, I couldn't stop.

"Stop it!" he yelled again.

I tossed my head back a second time, still laughing so much so, that tears began to stream down my face.

"Stop laughing!" he said, determined to get me to shut up.

The hand that was around my neck shifted so that it was pressing against my collarbone. He shoved me once against the wall growling "Stop."

No use. I kept laughing. The second time he pushed harder, his hand pressed firmly into my skin. That time, I did stop laughing as my chest felt the pressure of his weight coming down on me.

I looked him straight in the eyes, as he did the same back. "Get off of me."

"Why are you doing this to us? We belong together, we always have," he pleaded, still pressing on my chest.

"Stop," I said softly as I felt it getting harder to take air in.

I placed my hands on his forearms to push him back, but he wasn't budging. He got closer, and his nose drew up my neck as he took in my scent.

Plastered against that wall, I had thoughts flashing before me, the man in front of me had transformed into a monster from my darkest dreams. I had loved John with all I had when we were teenagers, but when we grew up, he changed, I changed, and I learned that there was more to me than just him. He never saw it that way, though. He still believed we could go back to years past and forget about the bad ones, but it was clear we weren't going to be able to go back.

I didn't want to go back, because every time I

thought about it, thought about giving into him again, I'd see Trent. I'd see the man who built me back up, the man who treated me right, the man I'd given up on, for this. I realized then that I'd do anything to have him back.

"Why can't you love me?" John asked as his whisky drenched breath drifted under my nose.

He held me tight against the wall and, just as I was about to shove him back, a sharp pain in my stomach stopped me. I clutched at it with one hand while the other kept trying to push John away. It felt as if he had shoved a knife in my stomach over and over again.

"Sss—tt—op," I whimpered out best I could.

I couldn't talk around the pain, I felt my body growing weaker, my legs were becoming rubbery and if it wasn't for the fact that John had his hand on me, holding me against the wall, I think I would have fallen to the ground in pain.

The world around me got quiet. I could hear nothing but the beating of my heart against my chest and a soft ringing in my ears until…

"Get your fucking hands off her!"

I managed to look up and see Trent standing in the doorway. *He's here, he's really here*?

John backed away from me when he heard Trent's booming demand. His hand fell from my chest as he stepped back to see who was in his house. Once out of the way, I had full sight of Trent. He was as handsome as I'd ever seen him. The light above him gave the illusion of a glow around this strong, thick body.

My knight in shining armor, heroic glow and all. As I drank in the sight of him, another stabbing pain gripped me. I clutched my stomach with both hands and cried out as the stabbing pain danced around my stomach.

I felt a little relief but, as I did, I also felt a warm, wet sensation escape me. My head already facing the floor, I knew what was about to happen before it did. Dressed in only a large shirt the one I wore every night. I watched as droplets of blood hit the floor between my legs. I screamed again as another sharp pain took me prisoner, and more blood made its way down the insides of my thighs. I'd never seen so much blood leave a body before, especially mine. I had to look away, but, as my eyes drifted up, they connected with Trent's. Fear was etched on his face as he watched the blood go down my legs. I crouched over, holding my hands as tightly as I could around my stomach—foolishly thinking that, if I held myself hard enough, I could make not only the pain but the bleeding stop. My legs gave out on me, and I crumbled to the floor in a pool of my own blood.

"Lex?" John watched as I fell to the floor. "Lex—Alexis!" he cried, dropping to his knees and shaking my shoulders.

I had no strength. I simply sat there, my head swaying back and forth as John shook me. I tilted my head to look at John. He was upset, tears behind his eyes as he shook me.

With everything in me, I was able to turn away from John to find Trent. I wanted to scream for him, tell him I didn't care about what happened in the past that I just wanted him to come and take me away. I wanted to feel his arms around me one last time, because that's what I was thinking. I knew I was bleeding and losing too much blood, and all I wanted was to be held by him before I died.

One moment, he was across the room, the next he was at my side, holding my face between his hands. I wanted to look at him but my eyes were so heavy, and I was so tired, and then everything went black.

මංඋම

I opened one eye, but it fell closed. I tried again. This time I was able to open both, if only slightly. *Where am I?* The beeping beside me got louder and faster the more aware I became. I looked down, noticing all the IVs and wires that were attached to me. The room was dark but for a light to the left of me over a sink. *I'm in a hospital...I'm in a hospital...there was so much blood.* I looked down at my hands, dried blood was caked around my nails and in-between my fingers. My clothes were replaced with a blue/green hospital gown. My hand went to my face where a tube pumped oxygen into my nose. I took a deep breath of cool, crisp air.

The beeping slowed as I came to the realization that I was alive. I tried to sit up to get a better view of the room but the soreness in my stomach prevented it. I winced as dull pain constricted my stomach.

"Lexi..."

I heard my name being called to the right of me. The voice was familiar but I couldn't place it. I turned in the direction of the sweet voice and was shocked to see a skinny, redheaded, mohawked man standing over me, reaching for my hand.

"Reece?" I forced the words out over the scratchiness of my throat.

My hand went to it because my voice didn't sound like mine. It was raspy, and I sounded like I hadn't talked in weeks.

"Shh, it's okay don't talk," he said sweetly, while holding my hand in his.

Have aliens body snatched Reece? Is the world coming to an end?

"You're going to be fine. We're at the hospital and you're going to be good as new."

I looked around the room again, searching for the only man I wanted to see, but Trent wasn't there.

Without me even saying anything Reece answered my question. "He's here, but not here," Reece said, confusing the hell out of me even more.

"What's going on, Reece, what happened?" I asked.

He slid his hand over the shaved part of his head and spoke to the wall. "He's been arrested."

"Arrested!" I screeched, sitting up straight. "How the hell did he get arrested?" I asked.

Quickly addressing me, Reece shrugged. "Well…you know Trent. He can get riled up pretty easy."

"What did he do, Reece?" I questioned him harder.

"Before or after he beat John to a pulp?"

"He did *what*?" I was getting so worked up, the beeping from the monitors started racing in time with the rising heart rate.

"Calm down, the prick had it coming. Come on, even you know that," Reece said, slipping back into his distinctively sly, smart tone.

"Calm down? My boyfriend beat my ex-boyfriend/ stepbrother, most likely to an unrecognizable state. Oh my God. My mom's going to kill me." More beeping went off as I thought of what my mother was going to say when she saw John bruised and broken again.

"Lexi, come on. You need to stay calm. They said it wasn't good for the—" He stopped right there, quickly looked down at the bed, and cursed under his breath.

I whipped my head so fast to look at him I thought I was going to need a neck brace. "What, did you just say?"

"Just that you should stay calm," He said through a fake ass grin.

"After that."

"It's not good for you—"

"No, you said it wasn't good for the…What's after the 'the,' Reece?" I demanded.

I felt my stomach do a flip as my head put all the pieces together before he could answer me. *I had been sick for weeks, my stomach was cramping, and the blood between my legs—was I? Could I be? Oh my God—*

Reece must have seen the look on my face because he took my hand again and stood over me as I fell back onto the hospital bed. I turned to him, feeling the tears behind my eyes. I blinked them away. He nodded down at me, a sorrowful look on his face. I was pregnant. I *was* pregnant.

"Does he know?" I asked. Reece shook his head no. I sighed. "But they told you?"

"I might have told a white lie about you being my fiancée. They told me everything, including that we're going to have a baby in roughly six months."

I was in shock, because I thought that I just heard him say that I was still going to have a baby in six months.

"That's right, Lexi baby, I'm going to be an uncle," he said, grinning like the Cheshire cat.

"How is that possible—all that blood?" I protectively laid a hand over my stomach. I had gone from finding out I was pregnant to assuming I had lost it to once again realizing that I was legit knocked up.

"Supposedly, you were knocked up with twins, but you lost one—"

I felt my face fall at the notion of losing a baby.

"—but the other one is perfect, the heartbeat is strong and, so far, you haven't had any other problems."

Twins? My mom is going to flip when she finds out. Knocked up and not married, hell I'm not even sure if I'm dating the father anymore. All my mother's fears for me are coming true, and, go figure, he's a rock star with tattoos, to boot. I ran my hands through my hair, as a million scenarios came rushing forward. I was going to have a kid, I didn't have a job, I was living at home. Was I ready to be a parent? *Is anyone really ready to be a parent?*

Chapter 30

Trent

I sat in one of the three jail cells that lined the small town police department. I'd sit for a minute then get up and pace back and forth. Somewhere miles away, the woman I loved was laying in hospital bed. *Fuck, I hope it's a hospital bed and not the morgue.*

Thoughts like that only pissed me off more. My hand was raw from punching flesh, and my nose hurt like a bitch from taking a few. Thank God, Reece was with me. He was smart enough to call nine-one-one and, surprisingly, it only took a few minutes for them to arrive.

"Walker?" The tubby cop sitting at the desk called me by my last name. '

I shot to my feet and walked over to the bars. "That's me."

"You ready to make your one call?" he asked.

I nodded and took a step back from the door as he came over to unlock it and let me out. I went to walk past him but was shoved in the chest backward.

He held up handcuffs, dangling them in my face. "I don't think so, Rocky."

"You don't need to put those on me."

"From the look of the guy in cell one, they're getting put on. Hands up, big boy."

I held my hands up between us. *Jerk.*

He walked me over to a chair, where an old phone sat on an empty desk. Picking up the receiver he listened to make sure there was a dial tone then handed me the phone. I took it with one hand, the other close by because the bastard didn't undo the cuffs. I went to hit the numbers to call Lexi but then thought otherwise. She wasn't going to be able to answer her phone, which I was almost certain was still at her house.

My next thought was to call Reece's cell. Another bad idea, if he was with Lexi, he wasn't going to be able to answer either. I thought about calling my parents who were a good four hours away, but no. I had promised my mother that I'd stay out of jail and a call from jail might just get me disowned.

The only people left were Kane and the other guys. I dialed Kane's cell and waited as it rang and rang. *Come on, dude, answer your phone. He's probably fucking Kitty and won't answer. It's almost four in the morning.*

"Hello?"

Thank fucking god! "Kane! It's Trent."

"Trent? What the fuck, man? It's four in the morning. Shouldn't you be knee deep in Lexi by now? Why the hell you calling me?"

I could hear Kitty in the background. She was pestering Kane for answers. "Did they make up? Are they back together?"

"Listen, some serious shit went down. I'm in jail."

"What?" Kitty yelled from the background.

"Sorry, dude, she made me put it on speaker," Kane explained.

"I went to Lexi's and got into it with John. She started screaming in pain and started bleeding and passed out."

Kane sighed. "Ah, man, I'm sorry, is she okay?"

"I don't know. Reece is with her at the hospital now. I don't know which one. They won't tell me. Can you come out here and bail me out?"

"Yeah, give me the address. How did you end up in jail, though?"

"I might have taken out my frustration on an EMS guy, a fire fighter, and I think I hit a cop."

"Trent Walker, you hit a cop!" Kitty shouted.

"Not on purpose. They wouldn't let me hold Lexi. They dragged me away and I tried fighting my way back to her."

"Why was she bleeding?" Kane asked.

"I don't know. I walked in and saw John with his hand around her neck and her in only a nightshirt. I don't know if he fucked her raw or if something else is going on. All I know is that she was in a lot of pain." I gave Kane the name of the police station and told him to hurry his ass up.

"Okay, we're going to head your way now."

"Thanks."

"Time's up, Rocky," the cop said, snatching the phone from me and hanging up before I could say bye. He walked me back to my cell, undid the cuffs, and locked me inside. I sat on the bench, hands over my face, as I tried to wrap my head around the night.

I should have called Reece, found out how Lexi was. *No, if it's bad, I can't deal with that on top of being locked in a jail cell.*

"I didn't hurt her," a voice said from the cell next to

mine. "I've never hurt her," John said, as if he was saying it more for himself.

I sat back on the aluminum bench and looked over at John. "I'm not doing this with you."

"You don't have a fucking choice. We're both stuck in here, and you're going to listen to me."

I turned from him shaking my head and, for a second, I thought about ramming it against the cinderblock wall so I wouldn't have to hear the prick next to me, feed me bullshit.

"I know that I fucked up in the past. I could be rough and nasty to her but I never hit her." He paused, maybe waiting for me to say something back, but I kept quiet. "Lex is my best friend, I couldn't—when she left me to go to LA, it was my wake-up call. I know you don't believe me. Hell, she doesn't even believe me. I guess—"

I couldn't sit quietly anymore. "You guess? Do you know that, when I met her, she would cower away from me, because you put that fear in her?" There was silence on his side. "You're lucky she was strong enough to get the hell away from you when she did."

"I know that now. She is strong and one hell of a woman. Listen, if you really love her that much, I'll back off. I just want her to be happy. The only times I saw her truly happy was when she would read your texts. I don't know what happened between the two of you but—"

"What happened between the two of us, was you! You're the reason she left me, you're the reason she's where she is, and we're where we are." I couldn't sit there and listen to his bullshit any longer.

"I didn't ask her to come back here, that was her mother. She could have left long ago, but she stayed. So what the fuck did you do to her? She's been sulking around the house, sick to her stomach, for a week after she talked to you on the phone that day. You're not innocent in all this either."

I stood from the bench, mad at myself because he was right. I wasn't innocent. I fucked up big time. I'd slept with Chloe, and maybe I was responsible for what was happening to Lexi. That ate at my heart. Piece by piece, it was wearing me down. How could I have done that to the woman I loved? Maybe I wasn't anything other than the jackass she originally accused me of being.

"So you did do something. I guess we both fucked up our chances with an amazing woman."

That was the last thing he said to me. It was silent from then on between us. When the cop asked if he wanted to make a call, he declined, saying he didn't have anyone to call.

The morning sun had made an appearance when Kane and everyone else arrived. I walked out of the police station with Kane, and we all immediately made our way to the hospital.

"Did you talk to Reece?" I asked as we got in Kane's truck.

Kitty was in the back and JJ, Piper, and Aiden followed us in JJ's car.

"Just briefly. He gave us directions. It should only take about an hour to get there," Kane answered.

"He didn't say anything about Lexi?"

"She's fine, Trent, just sleeping a lot," Kitty replied from the back seat, squeezing my shoulder.

I felt comforted knowing that she was okay and sleeping, but a part of me was still freaking out. I tried to hide it, but I'm sure it was written all over my face. I made small talk to keep my mind focused.

"So Piper's in town?" I asked trying to sound even keeled.

"Yeah, she and JJ are going at it again. I swear they

fight more than me and Kane," Kitty said, sitting back and huffing in frustration over the possibility of another failed relationship for her guys. Kitty had been playing matchmaker since she and Kane got back together.

"I'm sure they'll be fine, babe," Kane said, trying to reassure his wife.

"What are they fighting about now?" I asked.

It had been back and forth with those two since we went on the road.

What it all boiled down to was distance with them. Piper was in New York, and we were…well, everywhere at the moment. JJ wanted her to give up her career like Kitty did for Kane but Piper was still young, only twenty years old. She wanted to live on her own, experience things that normal twenty-year-olds did.

"Do you have to ask?" Kitty said sarcastically from the back.

"Not really," I replied.

"That cousin of mine better shape up or he's going to lose that girl," Kitty continued ranting on and on in the back of the truck.

It was a nice distraction. It kept me from thinking about Lexi laid up in a hospital bed, battling whatever happened to her.

We pulled up to the hospital, and my heart sank to the pit of my stomach. Kane parked and we all got out. Everyone stood around a moment, waiting for me to make the first move. JJ, Aiden and Piper joined us in the parking lot moments later.

"She's going to be fine, man," Aiden said as we clasped hands and hugged.

"Yeah, I know," I said, trying to sound strong. I was anything but. My knees wanted to buckle, my mouth was dry, my eyes hurt from the lack of sleep.

"I can't believe you left Reece alone with her," JJ

said, trying to lighten the mood a bit as we said our hellos.

"Didn't really have a choice, JJ. I was handcuffed in the back of a police car."

He smiled back. "Touché."

"You want us to come with you or wait down here for a bit?" Kane asked.

"I think I should go up alone. I'll call you guys up in a few."

"All right, we'll be right here for you if you need us," Kane finished.

Kitty bolted over to me, and her arms wrapped around me tightly.

"Kitty, I'm all right," I said through a fake smile as I hugged her back.

"I know you, Trent, you're not okay. You might be able to fool those buffoons, but not me."

She did know me. She knew how much I loved Lexi, and how bad I felt about Chloe. It was Kitty who I stayed up with at night talking and running things by her on how I could get Lexi back. She was invested in my relationship with Lexi as much as I was.

"I'll be fine. I just need to get up there with her." I kissed the top of her head and backed away from her. I watched as she moved back under Kane's arm. "I'll tell Reece you guys are out here. See you in a few.

They all nodded and started mingling amongst themselves as I walked toward the rotating doors of the hospital entrance.

Chapter 31

Lexi

"Ms. Ford, it's good to see you awake," a tall, older man in a white doctor's coat said as he entered my room.

Reece and I both looked up at him. I adjusted myself in bed so I could sit up a little more. Reece stood from the chair in the corner and came to stand by the bedside.

"I'm Dr. Lisker," the man said, looking at my chart and then the machine that was beeping next to me. "Has anyone talked to you yet?" he asked politely.

I shook my head no.

"She's been sleeping most of the time," Reece answered for me.

I glanced up at him, amazed at how respectful and proper he was being. I'd never heard Reece be anything other than a dick to…well, everyone. He smiled down at me, and I almost didn't recognize him, if it wasn't for the bright, red hair.

I reached over and grabbed his hand, taking him off

guard. He adjusted and held it tightly, his thumb running over the back of my non-IV hand. He nodded as if saying, "It's going to be all right, I'm here for you."

I took comfort in that. Had I known eight and half months ago the person that'd be standing next to me through all this would have been Reece, I'd have laughed in your face.

"All right here's the gist of it, you've had a miscarriage."

I nodded yes, to let him know that I was following him.

"I'm sure your fiancé here has at least filled you in that you are indeed still pregnant. It's my guess that you were caring twins, and one of them wasn't able to hold on, but the other is moving and has a great heartbeat." The doctor had a smile on his face as he told me, but quickly adjusted it when he saw that mine was still in shock.

"So she's going to be fine?" Reece asked.

"Yes, I'd like her to stay at least two, maybe three, more days just to make sure her strength is back up and that there won't be any other issues with the pregnancy." He turned back to me. "As you know, you lost a lot of blood and that can take a lot out of a person, so we're going to pump you with fluids and meds and just keep an eye on you and the baby."

"She's pregnant?"

The three of us in the room turned as the door swung open, and Trent stood there staring at us. I squeezed Reece's hand tightly as my eyes went to saucers.

"Excuse me, you are…" the doctor asked.

"I'm her boyfriend. You said she's pregnant?" he asked, squaring his body toward the doctor and ignoring Reece and me.

"Umm, I'm not sure I understand? Isn't this her…"

The doctor caught on, and clearly didn't want to get in the middle of a love triangle with the likes of Trent.

He had changed his clothes from the night before and the cut on his face told me someone had gotten in a few hits.

"I think I'll step outside," the doctor said, "but I'm warning you, if anything happens in here, security will be called." He scooted around Trent and closed the door behind him.

The room was silent. I kept a tight grip on Reece's hand. I didn't want his scrawny ass going anywhere.

"Trent—" Reece began but was cut off.

"You knew about this, that she was knocked up, and you didn't think to tell me?" Trent spoke softly, which made it worse.

"Don't talk to him like that," I yelled, speaking up for Reece, since he just stood there. "You don't get to say that to him."

Trent took a step then swiveled on his foot and faced the closed door. His hands went to his hair, hair that was longer than I'd ever seen it. The mass that was his back, opened as he held his hands above his head. He was mad that was clear, but I wasn't going to let him take it out on someone who had nothing to do with it.

When he turned back around, there was hurt in his eyes. His lips pulled tight together as he searched for words that just wouldn't come to him. "How could you do this? I came out here to get you, and I find you knocked up by the one person I thought you'd never let touch you again."

He wouldn't step any closer to the bed and I was glad he didn't because I would have hit him upside the head.

"You have no room to talk!" I snapped back.

"Guys, why don't we all calm down—"

"Shut up, Reece," Trent and I barked in unison. He held is one hand up, the hand that I wasn't squeezing.

"You guys seem like you need some space. I'm going to go get a coffee. I'll be back," Reece said, clasping the top of my hand that was clutching onto his. He kissed my forehead and headed toward the door, stopping next to Trent. They stood shoulder to shoulder. Reece turned his head and said something to him but I couldn't make it out.

The door closed behind Reece, and the two of us just stared at each other.

"You two seem especially chummy."

"What do you want, Trent? Yes, we're chummy. He's been here with me the whole time, unlike you, who was…where were you again?…oh right, in jail," I answered for him.

"They tried to take you from me. Nobody takes you from me," he said deadpan.

I wanted to roll my eyes at that stupid remark, but the hopeless romantic that was buried deep within me kept me from doing it.

"So you're pregnant with John's baby," he said evenly.

That time, I did roll my eyes. "Is that what you think?" I asked.

"It's what makes sense. There's no way it could be mine. I haven't seen you in months."

"Two and a half months, Trent. I'm two and a half months pregnant." I stared him down and watched as it sank into his thick skull. His brows rose, his mouth fell open, and the hands that were firmly planted on his hips fell to his sides.

"It's not John's?" he asked, shaking his head back and forth.

"No, Trent. It's not John's."

Chapter 32

Trent

ll right here's the gist of it," I heard a man say from the other side of the door.

I stood there instead of continuing inside. If it was bad, I didn't want Lexi to see me break down, I wanted to be strong for her.

"You've had a miscarriage."

What?

"I'm sure your fiancé here has at least filled you in that you are indeed still pregnant. It's my guess that you were caring twins, and one of them wasn't able to hold on, but the other is moving and has a great heartbeat."

I knew Reece was with her, but to hear him say "fiancé" to someone other than me hit me like a Mac truck. I had to snap out of it to keep listening. My heart was racing and shattering all at once.

"So she's going to be fine?" Reece asked.

"Yes, I'd like her to stay at least two, maybe three, more days, just to make sure her strength is back up and that there won't be any other issues with the pregnancy. As you know you lost a lot of blood and that can take a lot out of a person, so we're going to pump you with fluids and keep any eye on you and the baby."

He had said it again, that she was pregnant, referred to her and the baby. This wasn't a dream. She was carrying someone else's baby. We'd been apart for months. *How could it be mine?* I was furious. I'd done everything in my power to come get her, I saved her from John, and this was how she repaid me. She let him manipulate her and eventually get her knocked up. I couldn't stand behind the door and take blow after blow any longer.

"She's pregnant?" I said, swinging the door open.

The doctor stood at the foot of the bed that Lexi was lying in. Reece was by her side, holding her hand and looking like he'd magically matured in the last twenty-four hours. I expected to take them all by surprise but it fucking killed me to see the terror in Lexi's eyes as they fell on me.

"Excuse me, you are…" the doctor asked.

"I'm her boyfriend. You said she's pregnant?" I asked, squaring my body toward the doctor and ignoring Reece and Lexi for the moment.

"Umm, I'm not sure I understand? Isn't this her—" The doctor caught on, and clearly didn't want to get in the middle of a love triangle with the likes of me. "I think I'll step outside, but I'm warning you, if anything happens in here security will be called," he stated before scooting around me and closing the door behind him.

The room was silent as I stared at Lexi and Reece. She had his hand in a vice grip, holding onto him like a life jacket.

"Trent—" Reece began but I quickly cut him off.

"You knew about this, that she was knocked up, and you didn't think to tell me?" I tried to keep my temper reeled in when I addressed him, because, even though, I was pissed he didn't tell me, he was the one reason Lexi even made it to the hospital in the first place.

"Don't talk to him like that," Lexi yelled from the bed. "You don't get to say that to him."

I could essentially feel the anger boiling in my veins. I had to look away from her, I was so mad. I was mad but more than that, I was sad, disappointed, deflated. I wanted to blame her, I wanted to be mad at her, but I wasn't any better. I'd slept with Chloe, and I was the one who let Lexi leave in the first place. I could have run after her, ignored her stupid note, and proved to her I wasn't going to let anything come between us, but I chickened out, took the easy way.

"How could you do this? I came out here to get you, and I find you knocked up by the one person I thought you'd never let touch you again," I said, turning back to face them both.

"You have no room to talk," she snapped back at me.

And maybe I deserved that but she fucking got knocked up! I just had one drunken night.

"Guys, why don't we all calm down—"

"Shut up, Reece," we both barked in unison.

Reece held one hand up in defeat, the hand that Lexi wasn't squeezing.

"You guys seem like you need some space, I'm going to go get a coffee. I'll be back," he said, clasping the top of their hands. He kissed her forehead and headed toward the door. Stopping next to me, he whispered, "Don't fuck this up. I care about her, too." He walked out the door and closed it behind him.

"You two seem especially chummy," I stated as I stared across at her.

"What do you want, Trent? Yes, we're chummy. He's been here with me the whole time, unlike you who was…where were you again?…oh right, in jail."

"They tried to take you from me. Nobody takes you from me," I said as if it should have been common knowledge.

As I spoke, I took a few steps toward her. She adjusted in the bed at each one of my advances. *We're back to the beginning? Her backing away from me, cowering from me?*

"So you're pregnant with John's baby," I said evenly.

She rolled her eyes at me and, for a moment, I was glad to see her attitude back. "Is that what you think?" she asked.

"It's what makes sense. There's no way it could be mine, I haven't seen you in months," I stated, knowing that I was right, and that there was no way it could possibly be mine.

"Two and a half months, Trent. I'm two and a half months pregnant." She stared me down, daring me to challenge her.

It hit me then, it could be mine. I felt the color drain from my face, my mouth fell open, and my hands slipped from their perch and fell to my sides. "It's not John's?" I asked, shaking my head in disbelief.

"No, Trent. It's not John's."

My hands went to my head. I held them there as everything sank in. Lexi, the woman I loved was pregnant with my child. *I'm going to be a dad. Holy fuck, I'm going to be a dad!*

"I can do this on my own. You don't have to be involved," she said, messing with the IV tube that was stuck in her hand.

My hands fell as I whipped my head up from watching her fiddle with her IV. She glanced up and, when she caught me watching her, she looked down again and fixed the covers at her waist. Beneath the covers and ugly hospital gown, resting peacefully within her, our baby was alive and growing every second. *How could she even think that I wouldn't want to be involved?*

"Are you out of your mind?" I snapped back.

"No, I'm not out of my mind. I don't need your help," she said, making eye contact again.

"I'll be goddamned if anyone but its father raises my child!" I didn't understand her reasons for not wanting me around. She knew how much family meant to me.

"Ha, that's funny," she snickered under her breath.

"What's the matter with you?" I asked, getting fuck-ing pissed that she wasn't taking me serious.

She continued to chuckle. Rubbing her eyes a few times, she pulled her hair back off her face and twisted it so that it all fell over one shoulder. "What's the matter with me?" she repeated in a monotone voice, glaring at me. "Where do you want me to start?"

I wanted to put out there that it was she who left first, but I held my tongue.

"Why don't we start with the fact that you slept with Chloe?" she said, raising a brow.

"Fine, I slept with her. I was drunk and missing you, and she took advantage of the situation. You know her, you know she gets off doing that shit," I said, hoping that it might help my case a little.

"I was going to come back to you."

"What?" I took another step toward her. I was at the foot of her bed, holding onto the plastic foot rail.

"I had planned on surprising you at BJ's—tonight, actually. I was going to beg you to take me back." She was looking up to the ceiling, shaking her head as if what she had said was ridiculous. "Then I found out you slept with Chloe, and I realized then that it was going to be a mistake if I showed up. I was right all along. You're a rock star, a growing-more-famous-by-the-day rock star, and I can't compete with all the beautiful women who are, and will be, throwing themselves at you. I wasn't your type when we met, and I'm a stupid, silly girl for ever thinking that that would change," she finished and returned to messing with the tubes and wires coming from her body.

"How can you say that? I love you, Lexi, I never stopped. Just because you were gone didn't mean that I stopped. Sure, I was pissed you left me for John but I had faith in you, in us."

"Well, it doesn't matter now. You proved what I thought all along—you're an asshole and can't keep it in your pants, even if I'm the one you're in love with. All it took was one drunken night and me not being there for you to go back to your sleeping-around ways."

I wanted to yell at the top of my lungs. I wanted to punch a hole in the wall. I wanted to strangle Chloe for taking advantage of me when I wasn't thinking clearly. But even all of that wouldn't help the situation.

"I don't believe you," I said, realizing that I didn't.

The way she looked at me the night I came for her wasn't the look of her giving up or moving on. She looked into my eyes, and I saw her fucking sole begging me to come and take her away. She was putting on a good front, trying to be strong, but the scatterbrained, smart-mouthed woman who stole my heart was begging me to set her free.

"What don't you believe, Trent? I can't do this with you."

"Yes, you can."

She refused to look at me. I was determined to make her see me, see the seriousness in me. I moved from the foot of her bed and sat down beside her in the chair Reece had been occupying. I took her hand, the one that was resting over her stomach. I laced my fingers with hers and brought them to my lips. She was shaking her head no, but didn't fight me holding her hand. "Don't make me do this," she begged. Tears were welling up behind her eyes but not spilling over. "Don't hurt me, you promised me that you weren't going to hurt me."

I went to speak, to tell her I'd never hurt her and that I was sorry if I had but she wouldn't let me.

"You can go about your life, be the rock star you've always dreamed about. I won't bother you for money or anything. I just want you to let me be."

I smiled up at her. "Not going to happen, baby."

"You told me you'd never have a baby mama and now you do, just walk away and—"

"Baby mama?" I questioned her.

"Don't you remember?"

"Oh, I remember, but you're not just my baby mama, you're the love of my life, and you can pretend all you want but, I'm the love of yours."

She sat back, shaking her head at me. "You're insane. This is going to ruin you. Ruin your chances of fame, not to mention the guys', nothing says rock star less then babies crying."

"I don't care," I said simply, because I didn't.

Sure, I wanted to be famous, tour the world with the guys, and make incredible music, but that was only temporary, what I wanted more than that, what I had *always* wanted more than that was a family of my own. I wanted to love a woman more than air, and I had that with Lexi, and now that I was going to be father, nothing else could trump that.

"Yes, you will, you'll care when all the guys are out at a bar and you can't be because you have to change dirty diapers and do the three a.m. feeding because I'm too exhausted—" She stopped there.

"See? You do see us doing it together!"

"No." She tried to save herself "I don't. I'm just try-ing to show you—"

"Show me what? How wonderful it could be?"

"No, how horrible it could be," she cried on a sob.

"I don't see it that way. I see me being there for you, I see us traveling together, I see us raising our child to-gether. I see us happy, but most importantly I see us to-gether."

She kept shaking her head no. With every turn of her head, another tear rolled down her beautiful face. I scoot-ed the chair as close as it would go and brushed the tears with my thumb.

"You see us together?" she asked.

I nodded yes and kissed her hand.

"And what happens when we fight and you get drunk and there's a willing participant who isn't mad at you for whatever reason and would do anything to sleep with you?"

"That's not going to happen," I said matter-of-factly.

"Why? What's going to change next time?" she chal-lenged.

"Because next time I won't be thousands of miles away from you. I'll be on the other side of the bed, prob-ably pissed, but I'll be next to you."

"But what if you're gone, and I'm not with you?"

"Lexi!" I said, getting frustrated that she wasn't catching on. "I'm in love with you, I'm not leaving you, you're not raising this kid on your own, you are coming back with me, and you're going to marry me!" I said, get-ting carried away.

Chapter 33

Lexi

What did he just say? I looked over at him. He had sat back in the chair next to my bed as he ranted on and on. His hands on his thighs, he sat there looking as shocked as I was.

"What did you say?" Brow raised, I watched as he realized what he had said.

"You know what? Fuck it!" he said, standing from the chair.

It screeched on the tile floor as he pushed it back with his legs. He let my hand go for a moment as he turned to the nurses' table next to the bed. He was moving things around and opening drawers. He closed the last drawer and came back over to me. He took my hand and knelt on the floor by the side of the bed. My eyes widened and the beeping on the machines next to me started getting louder. *What the hell is he doing?* Of course, I knew what he was doing. He was down on one knee, my hand in his, and his warm brown eyes were set on mine.

"Lexi—"

"Trent, get up," I said, tugging on his hand as best I could to get him to stand up.

"Lexi," he continued.

I averted my eyes, looking anywhere but at him. The beeping was getting faster with every second. I watched the screen that showed my blood pressure, heart rate, and oxygen fluctuate all over the place.

"Eyes on me, beautiful," he said in that deep seductive voice that could get me to do anything.

In his other hand he held a pen, he took my IV free hand and began drawing on my ring finger. "I know this isn't typical but," He dragged the pen around my finger, carefully making a perfect circle. "I want to do this right."

He stopped right before the circle was complete. He held my hand in his. The warmth that radiated from our palms soothed all my nerves, and all I could see was him. I couldn't help the smile on my face or the fluttering of my stomach.

He hadn't even asked, when I beat him to the punch. "I want to marry you." I covered my mouth with my free hand.

"Hump." Trent snickered. "All right then. I'll marry you."

He let go of my hand a little to finish drawing on the ring. He wasn't an artist, by any means, but he drew the most beautiful and interesting two-dimensional diamond ring a mound of muscles could.

ভেচ্চ

Three Days later:

"Are you all right?" Trent asked.

I turned to look at him from the passenger's seat of his truck. My eyes narrowed, I stared him down.

"What's that look for?" he asked, smiling back.

"I'm fine. I was fine a minute ago, and two minutes before that, and five before that, and I'm not a fortune teller, but I think I'm going to be fine when you ask me again in two minutes," I said, grinning up at him.

"Ha, very funny. I'm just making sure you're okay."

"It's very sweet, and I know it's hard for you to turn the knight-in-shining-armor thing off, but you do need to turn it off, at least until you get me home."

He settled for holding my hand the whole ride home, instead of pestering me every other minute.

As we drove down the driveway, I squeezed his hand a little tighter. I saw John and my mother sitting on the front porch. I had forgotten she arrived home late last night from her vacation. She stood on the front steps, leaning against the poles that held the porch up. Her arms were crossed over her chest, and she looked pissed.

John was standing next to her, leaning on the other side of the pole. They both watched as Trent pulled up and parked next to the other vehicles.

Putting the car in park, Trent held my hand tighter, "Lexi—"

"I'm fine, Trent." I cut him off, answering his questions before he could even ask it.

"And, by fine, you mean that you're freaking out and wishing that I would just start the truck back up, turn around, leave, and never look back."

He had hit the nail on the head.

"Listen, I didn't want—I'm sorry I dragged you into all of this," I said, gesturing to myself, the farm, and my family.

"You didn't drag me into anything. I came after you, and I'd do it again and again and again…"

I smiled over at him, my sexy part-time rock star/ knight in shining armor. I had hit the jackpot with Trent. There wasn't a man out there that was better made for me. He challenged me, respected me, and most importantly, he loved me.

I squeezed his large hand one last time before letting go to get out of the truck, slid down from the seat, and closed the door behind me. Thanks to Kitty, I had a new shirt and sweat pants on. I was grateful she went out and got them for me, since my nightshirt looked like it was dipped in blood. My mother stepped down off the porch and headed my way.

"You better start explaining why I had to bail your brother out of jail this morning, why there was a pool of blood on my floor, and why you're with this...this..."

She eyed Trent up and down. He was wearing jeans, a T-shirt, and his beanie hat. I knew she was judging him for the tattoos on his arms, the piercings in his ear, and the pure size of him.

"It's nice to meet you, Mrs. Ford," Trent said, coming to stand by my side.

"Alexis, what is going on. John won't tell me anything. He's gone mute for some reason," she said, turning back and glaring at him. "Ben won't answer his phone and you—what is *that*?" she said, pointing to the shiny, simple, beautiful diamond ring that was on my left ring finger.

Once I had blurted out that I'd marry Trent before he even asked, he left the hospital in search of a real ring to put over the one he'd drawn on my finger. With Kitty to help him, the two had found the perfect one, and some new clothes for me to wear when I got released. I had taken pictures of the ring Trent drew. I never wanted to forget what it looked like, and I didn't tell him, but when he was out shopping for a real one, I was planning on getting an exact replica of the one he drew, tattooed on my finger. He was right it wasn't typical, but it was mine and no one would ever have one like it.

I wiggled my fingers and crossed my arms over my chest. All while the blood was draining from my face and the world started to spin a little faster. I didn't know where to begin, where to start my story. My mother was never going to let me live it down. I'd be the black sheep of the family. Hell, who was I kidding? I'd be the black sheep of the whole fucking town with her mouth. Knocked up before marriage, engaged to a thug, as she would most likely call him, I would of course be blamed for getting John arrested, and I was sure she'd find a way to blame Ben for not answering his phone on me too. To put it simple, I was afraid of my fast-talking, disapproving, and severely Southern-cultured mother.

I needed to get it over with and fast. I held my head up, tried to stand a little taller, and address my five-foot-five mother as a woman instead of the small child she was making me feel like.

"It's an engagement ring," I said definitively.

"An engagement ring?"

Still standing strong, I nodded. "Yes."

She turned back to John who had moved to sit on the front steps. He shook his head no at her, and she quickly turned back to me with the devil in her eye.

I was going to explain everything to her, but I never got a chance. Trent took me under his arm, holding me against his body. I let my hands fall. The left one he took in his as he admired the beautiful ring he had given me, and the one that he drew which was fading under the real one.

"I know it's not the way I pictured doing things, but, Mrs. Ford, I love your daughter, I've loved her from the day I sat next to her on a plane ride across the county. I'd like to ask for your blessing to marry her. But if you don't give us your blessing, know that I'm going to marry her anyway, because she has everything I've always wanted resting peacefully in the depths of her stomach."

I'm going to smack him upside the head! How could he spill something like that now of all times? My mother stood there, shell-shocked. For a moment, I thought we might have to call nine-one-one.

She clutched at her chest and shook her head at me. "I don't know what to say. How could you do this, to me, to John?"

I felt Trent tense up next to me. "Mom—"

"I don't even know you anymore." Her accent was thick and, as she spoke, tears filled her eyes.

"I'm in love with him," I said, putting my foot down to all the dramatics.

"How can you be in love with someone like that," she said, looking at Trent, "when John here is the one you're supposed to be with? I don't understand. You two are perfect for each other…"

She kept on going until finally John yelled. "No!"

We all turned to him. Still sitting on the steps, he looked up at all of us, mainly my mom. "No, we're not perfect for each other."

"What are you talking about? You've been together since you were kids, of course you're perfect together," my mother stated.

"I'm not good for her, I know that now."

My mother shrugged his words off. "John, don't be silly."

"Carole, drop it!" John yelled.

I'd never heard him raise his voice when my mother was near. It took her completely off guard.

"Just listen to her, listen to what your daughter is telling you," he begged.

My mother turned from John and studied Trent and me. "You love him?" she asked me.

I turned to Trent, smiled up at him, and nodded. "I love him," I said, holding on tightly to his hand.

I was afraid my mother was going to kick me out of her life for being a failure in her eyes. As much as my mother was old school and a pain in the ass, she was my mother and, besides Ben, she was the only family I had left, and I didn't want to lose her.

"Well, does he at least have a job, a way to support you?" she asked.

Trent and I both chuckled at that.

"I have a job, a pretty good one that pays well, but if it falls through I'm one hell of a plumber and there's always jobs in that field."

"Well, what do you do now? How are you going to take care of my daughter—" She swallowed the lump in her throat before continuing. "—and my grandchild."

She waited for an answer as Trent looked at me for a clue as to what to tell her. I shrugged my shoulders and gave a what-do-I-have-to-lose look.

"I'm in a band," he said, after taking a deep breath.

My five-foot-five spitfire of a mother looked like she was going to cry, or pass out. It could have gone either way. "You're in a band?" she demanded, narrowing her eyes and losing her temper.

"I worked for him and his label when I was in LA, Mom."

"We're touring right now, and getting ready to release our first album. It's slated to do really well by the record label," Trent added.

My mother was smiling, laughing. Me, I was terrified.

"Your father is rolling over in his grave right now, young lady." She had to bring him into it.

If there was anything that was going to make me feel bad about my situation, it was going to be her saying that my father was disappointed in me. I felt the tears behind my eyes as I thought of my father not being here to give me away or see his grandchild.

"I think he'd be elated," John said, stepping up next to me and Trent.

I can't believe it. For the second time, in a matter of minutes, John was sticking up for me and for Trent. I smiled over at him, showing my appreciation for everything he was doing. *Maybe he has changed?*

"Carole, look at her, she's happy. Be happy with her or you're going to make her run away like I did, and, trust me, there is nothing worse than someone running away from you."

Chapter 34

Trent

I stood next to Lexi, holding her close to me. I never knew one woman could be so harsh to her own daughter. I felt for Lexi. She clearly wanted the approval from her mother but Carole Ford was not giving it up so easily.

So when John, stepped up and came to our defense, I was relieved to have him on our side. Only a few nights before, I had him in a head lock, ready to put him out of his misery. I could see why Lexi cared about him. If this, the man, who was sticking up for us, was the one she fell for all those years ago.

It was still going to take some time for me to get over the way he treated her in the past, but like she had told me before, he was everywhere. He was in her past, still in her present, and he was going to continue to be in her—our future. I needed to put it behind me. I moved from Lexi's side and turned to John. I held out my hand. With Lexi standing between us, he clasped his hand against mine and an unspoken thank you, sorry, and understanding was made between the two of us.

We moved back to our places next to Lexi, and the three of us stared at her mother, waiting to see what crazy thing she was going to say next. She didn't. She didn't say anything, just stared at her daughter. There was silence between all of us, nothing but the mooing of cows off in the distance and the faint sound of a car driving by at the end of the driveway.

"I presume you're getting married in a church?" her mother finally said.

I felt my lips turn up at the question.

"Will it make you shut up about everything if we do?" Lexi asked back.

Her mother crossed her arms and thought for a second. "It will certainly help."

"Fine, Mom, we'll get married in a church," Lexi said as if it was a chore.

"And we'll have the reception here at the farm—"

"Mom!" Lexi said, interrupting her.

"No arguing about it, Lexi. Your father would have wanted that. He would have wanted to have his family, and this new family that we are joining, to be together on his farm, on his family's land." Lexi nodded in agreement. "That is, if your family is willing to come and isn't part of some biker gang," Carole said to me before turning back to Lexi. "I'm not sure your father would like a biker gang messing up the fields."

"My family is pretty normal, Mrs. Ford. No biker gangs in our family that I know of," I stated.

The relief on her mother's face was priceless. "Well then, let's get inside and start planning this wedding. Can't have you showing on your wedding day."

"Mom, we can wait till after, no need to rush," Lexi said, following her mother into the house.

"I'm going to have to get on your mother's side for this one," I said, walking beside Lexi up the front stairs.

"Are you kidding me?" she shrieked, stopping at the front door.

"Not at all." I took both her hands in mine. Interlocking our fingers, I stared into her beautiful honey silver eyes.

"Trent, we don't have to rush."

"Yes, we actually do, Lexi," I said softly, pulling her closer to me. "I want the world to know that you're mine."

"I am yours." She smiled up at me, the dimple on her left cheek present.

I leaned over and kissed her lips. "I don't want to wait," I whispered against her lips. "If I could, I'd marry you tomorrow, today, right now."

She pulled back from me, her brows scrunched up, her lips curled up in a grin. She was beautiful. Confused and all, she was the most beautiful woman I'd ever known, and she wasn't even my type.

Chapter 35

JJ

Again, I was stuck living under a fucking newly-wed couple—literally! They couldn't go on a honeymoon to the tropics or hell anywhere? Nope, they decided to skip the honeymoon and head back to LA with us. So there I was lying in bed listing to the blissful couple try to make another baby. Don't they know it won't work? She's already knocked up!

About the Author

M. E. Gordon, was born and raised in Maryland, where she still resides with her husband. She is a stay at home mom to four children, three boys and one very, spoiled, little girl. Growing up, Gordon was an avid journal writer. She wrote her first romance novel at the age of fourteen, and it was pretty bad, but over the years and through all the kids, she honed her craft. When Gordon doesn't have her mom hat on, you can find her reading, working on her next story, or watching guilty pleasure television.

www.ingramcontent.com/pod-product-compliance
Lightning Source LLC
Chambersburg PA
CBHW061131200626
46817CB00016B/744